THROUGH THE BARRICADES

FRIENDS ARE WITH YOU FOR A LIFETIME

D C MAHER

CONTENTS

First Edition published independently June 2020

ISBN 979 8 6432301 3 7 Paperback Edition

Second Edition published September 2021

ISBN 978 1 7399598 2 1 Hardback Edition

ISBN 978 1 7399598 0 7 Paperback Edition

ISBN 978 1 7399598 1 4 Ebook Edition

Revised Second Edition reissued June 2026

ISBN 978 1 7399598 2 1 Hardback Edition

ISBN 978 1 7399598 0 7 Paperback Edition

ISBN 978 1 7399598 1 4 Ebook Edition

INTRODUCTION

"The Eighties did not begin on January 1 1980, they began on May 4 1979 with the arrival of Margaret Thatcher in Downing Street. Queen Elizabeth may have reigned but it was Thatcher who ruled the Eighties."

Sarfraz Manzoor

A NOTE ON CHAPTER TITLES

The chapter titles in this novel are taken from songs connected with the 1980s. Sometimes the whole song reflects the spirit of the chapter; sometimes it is a single line, mood, or association that felt right for the moment.

They are not meant to be definitive markers of release date or chronology. Their purpose is to help capture the atmosphere, emotion, and soundtrack of the story.

I would like to acknowledge, with thanks, the artists and songwriters whose song titles are referenced here. Readers may enjoy putting together a playlist from the chapter titles as a companion to the novel.

CHAPTER

ONE

ANOTHER BRICK IN THE WALL, APRIL 1979

As they crawl under the hedge and through the hole in the wire fencing around the school, they both start laughing, nervous and breathless. They check behind for any teacher on patrol, see the coast is clear, and set off on the twenty-minute walk to the local outdoor pool.

Bunking off is a regular enough occurrence, but today is more complicated than most. Keagan should be meeting his form teacher after lunch to explain the packet of ten Rothmans she found in his jacket pocket.

'What are you going to say to her?' Peter asks.

'I'll just say I forgot,' Keagan says, lighting up from a non-confiscated packet.

'That's original. I'm sure she'll be perfectly happy with that.'

'I'm probably in for a week of lunchtime detentions,' Keagan says. 'But look on the bright side — there are worse ways to spend your lunch hour than sitting opposite Miss Roslyn.'

Miss Roslyn, their form teacher, is the current obsession of more or less every boy in the year. Newly qualified, she also takes French, which is why four years of barely managing bonjour has, in recent months, been replaced with something approaching genuine enthusiasm.

Keagan is sixteen and already passes for older — five foot ten, dark wedge haircut, the easy confidence of someone who learned early that charm will get you further than a row. He plays on every school sports team worth playing for, and his teachers know it, which is why expulsion from said teams is about the only threat that actually works on him. Out of uniform he passes for eighteen without trying, which has proved useful in pubs and clubs. Being the youngest of five helped; his brothers taught him their tricks, and he's been borrowing them ever since.

Peter, walking alongside him, is a few inches shorter, fair-haired, with a slightly pale look that Keagan has always put down to his mum keeping him wrapped up. He's quieter, more cautious, less likely to jump first. They both got into the grammar school on merit and have been coasting along since — bright students who could try harder, according to every report either of them has ever brought home.

As they pass through the subway at Gants Hill underground station, the usual smell of urine hits them both. Peter slows near the ticket office, coughing into his handkerchief — a rough, catching sound he muffles quickly and tries to ignore.

'Another cold?' Keagan says. 'Your mum'll have you off for a week.'

'You're just jealous.'

'Too right. I'd be told to get my lazy arse out of bed and get to school.'

They come out the other side and carry on up towards the High Street.

'Who's going to be there?' Peter asks.

'Danny and Eddie. Not sure about Mark. They've been every day this week — I honestly don't know how they manage it.'

'If you were a teacher,' Peter says, 'would you want Danny in your class? I reckon they actively encourage him to take the day off.'

'I bet half his teachers don't even know who he is,' Keagan says.

It is a bright, sunny day in late April, which makes the whole business easier to justify. Valentines Park Lido is a 1920s outdoor pool that has seen better days, but it is the only outdoor pool for miles and on days like this it fills up fast. The changing rooms are cramped and tired, the fixtures going on sixty years old, the mirrors on the walls still advertising Vimto in that stubborn way old things stay when nobody bothers to remove them. Past the changing rooms, the pool opens out in the sunshine — long, blue, carrying the noise of a dozen conversations and the smell of chlorine that somehow always seems like summer.

Their friends have already claimed the sun-beds at the deep end. Danny Wade — known as Shoulders, for obvious reasons, the product of five days a week in the gym and whatever else he flatly denies taking — is stretched out with his arms behind his head. Eddie and Mark are alongside him.

Everyone exchanges the afternoon's escape stories. Danny had a fight this morning, which is nothing new, and he gives Keagan the full account with the enthusiasm of a man who finds this sort of thing genuinely enjoyable. Peter, with equal enthusiasm for not being involved in that kind of conversation, drifts over to Eddie and Mark, who are deep in plans for the Ian Dury and the Blockheads concert at the Gants Hill Odeon the following week. Eddie's mate works at the cinema and is apparently getting them all in through the back doors.

'Who's up for a swim, then?' Keagan says, when Danny finishes.

All five get up. At the edge, Keagan grabs Danny's legs and tips him straight in.

'You're a dead man, Devlin.' Danny surfaces, shaking his hair back.

Keagan takes a run-up and bombs in after him, landing with a crash that sends water in all directions.

'No bombing!' the attendant shouts from his high chair.

The afternoon goes by the way those afternoons do — mostly in the water, inventing games that reliably end with someone getting hurt. They're sixteen, technically nearly men, but today that fact doesn't seem to interest anyone, and nobody mentions it. The sun stays warm and the pool is theirs.

As it starts to move towards the end of a normal school day, the five of them are lying on the beds again when Danny suggests one last race. They line up at the deep end — Keagan and Danny given a bit of extra space because they always make a competition of it — and dive in together. Danny touches the wall first. Keagan is just behind. He hauls himself up and looks back across the pool.

Peter is still in the middle.

His arms are flailing, not swimming, and Keagan is back in the water before the thought has properly formed. He cuts back across as hard as he can. Peter's head is going under and coming back up and going under again, each time a little slower.

Mark, at the edge, looks towards the lifeguard's chair. Empty.

'Over here!' He climbs out and shouts across the water, trying to get anyone's attention.

Keagan reaches Peter and gets hold of him. 'I've got you — take my arm, come on.' But Peter is past hearing him. In blind panic he grabs for Keagan and drags them both under. Keagan kicks hard, pulls them back to the surface, gets an arm around Peter's chest from behind and starts pulling for the side. Peter is still fighting him, which makes everything harder and more dangerous, the pair of them barely making ground.

Mark has sprinted around the pool edge and found the lifeguard coming out of the changing rooms with an armful of towels.

'Our friend's in trouble out there.'

'If this is more messing about—'

'Get in the pool. He's drowning.'

The lifeguard looks, and what he sees makes him move. He drops everything, sprints for the edge, and goes in with barely a pause, covering the distance in a few fast strokes. By the time he arrives, Keagan has somehow got Peter into a hold and is inching them towards the wall. Peter has stopped struggling. He's barely moving at all now, and that frightens Keagan a great deal more than the grabbing and pulling did.

The lifeguard takes hold of Peter and manoeuvres him to the side in seconds. Danny and Eddie are already at the edge reaching down, and between the three of them they haul Peter out onto the tiles. The lifeguard is out behind him, checking his breathing, clearing his mouth, shouting instructions as a second attendant arrives, who is sent running for the phone.

Keagan gets himself out and pushes through to where Peter is lying. His lips are going blue, his skin the colour of paper. Keagan crouches beside him and says nothing.

Peter coughs — sudden and violent — and brings water up with force. The coughing becomes breathing, rough and struggling, but breathing.

The lifeguard rolls him carefully onto his side. 'He'll be all right. Get me those towels — keep him warm.'

They pile towels over him. From not very far away, the ambulance siren starts.

Danny stands back, still breathing hard. 'Bloody hell. That was close. What happened?'

'I don't know,' Mark says. 'I didn't realise until I saw Keagan going back.'

'He must've swallowed water and panicked,' Eddie says.

'No shit, Sherlock,' Danny says.

Two ambulance men come through to the poolside and take over, checking Peter, wrapping him in the big red blankets, getting him onto a stretcher. Keagan stands up and straightens.

'Danny — go round to Peter's mum. Tell her we'll be at King George's.'

'Yeah, no problem. I'll take his stuff. Want me to take yours?'

'It's all right, our bags are together. I'll take them.'

'I'll grab them,' Eddie says, already heading off.

Danny looks at him. 'So what do I actually tell her?'

'We were supposed to be at school,' Keagan says.

'I know that.' Danny pauses. 'I'm telling her it was your idea.'

'Brilliant. Cheers.' Keagan takes the bags from Eddie and follows the stretcher out.

The ambulance moves off with the siren running, and the sound of it makes everything feel suddenly serious in a way that the afternoon hasn't been. Peter is on the stretcher-bed with the oxygen mask on, still pale, watching the ceiling. The ambulance man runs through his checks. Keagan sits on the opposite bench, pulling his school jumper on over his swimming trunks, already rehearsing what he's going to say to Mrs Chubb.

She has always fussed over Peter in that quiet, comprehensive way that never quite explains itself. She wraps him in cotton wool — that much has always been obvious — but it has always seemed like ordinary mothering, the sort that Peter is embarrassed by. Keagan has never thought much about it beyond that. He's thinking about it now.

And then there's his own mum. Quite possibly worse.

'How are you doing?' he asks, leaning forward.

Peter raises a hand and gives him a thumbs-up.

'I'll tell her it was my idea. All right? The whole afternoon.'

Peter looks at him with an expression that says everything. Good luck with that.

Keagan manages a small smile. She'll know already. She always knows.

At King George Hospital, the crew wheels Peter straight through the double doors and into admissions. Keagan is pointed to the reception desk, gives Peter's details to a woman who writes them down without looking at him, and is told to wait. He takes a seat. The waiting area is packed in the usual A&E way — a bloke with a cloth held to his head, a young mother with a toddler who won't stop crying, somebody at the far end of the room having a genuinely miserable afternoon. Keagan sits with his bags at his feet and watches the room.

Mrs Chubb comes through the main doors about ten minutes later. He waves from across the room, and he can see it in her face as she spots him — a flash of relief, and then the worry coming straight back.

She is in her fifties, greying hair, solidly built, with the bearing of a woman who has spent a long time keeping things together through force of will. She and Keagan have always got on well enough, largely because she is fond of him despite the regular evidence against it. He is braced for all of that to have changed.

'What happened? Your friend said he nearly drowned. What were you doing at the pool? Where is Peter?'

She does not wait for answers, which is fortunate. He points her towards the emergency area and she goes. Keagan exhales slowly and gets to his feet, starts making his way along the row of chairs.

He catches the stool with his foot before he sees it — nearly goes over, grabs the back of a chair to steady himself. The stool has a leg resting on it. The leg belongs to the girl at the end of the row, her ankle packed in ice, elevated off the floor. She is wearing her P.E. kit with her school blazer over the top, a badge he doesn't recognise.

'Thanks,' she says. 'That's exactly what I needed.'

'Sorry — I didn't see you. Are you all right?'

'I was, until you kicked me.'

But she's smiling when she says it, and the smile makes coherent thought slightly more difficult. It's not only the smile — it's her eyes, a shade of green he can't quite place, clear and bright, the kind you find yourself looking at twice and then feel awkward about. Her hair is long and dark-blonde, lighter where the sun has caught it, falling loose around her blazer collar. Everything about her suggests she finds things funnier than she probably should.

She looks him over thoughtfully. 'Why are you walking around in your pants?'

'Swimming trunks,' he says. 'There's a difference.'

'There really isn't.'

He starts to explain — the pool, the race, Peter going under, the ambulance — and she is actually listening, not just waiting politely for him to stop. He's halfway through the story when he hears Mrs Chubb's voice behind him.

'Keagan — can we sit down somewhere? I need to talk to you.'

Something in the tone of it stops him. He says a quick goodbye to the girl, frustrated he hasn't even got her name, and follows Mrs Chubb to a corner of the waiting area.

'Keagan.' She says his name first, and he has learned that this means brace yourself. He waits.

'I want to thank you for what you did today.'

He had prepared a different kind of speech entirely. He doesn't say anything.

'We've spoken to Peter about telling you this more than once. He's always said he'd do it when the time felt right.' She pauses, steadies herself. 'Because of today, he's agreed that now is the right time.' Her voice, when the words come, is quiet and careful. 'Peter has an illness. It's called cystic fibrosis.'

Her voice falters on the last two words. Keagan reaches across and she takes his hand in both of hers, holding it in her lap.

'It doesn't affect him every day, but he has had a poor week, and that's most likely what got him into trouble in the pool. He has an infection on his lungs and they need to keep him in for a few days to treat it. He'll be all right — he's been through this before, he's used to it — but it'll be a few days before he's home.'

All of it is going through Keagan's mind at once: what is cystic fibrosis, what does it mean, is he going to get worse? He holds onto the questions and says nothing. Now is not the moment.

The long absences. The colds that were never quite ordinary colds. The way Peter would reappear at school after a week or two and say nothing about where he'd been, and Keagan, without knowing why, had never quite pushed it. It all makes a different kind of sense now.

'He's never wanted to tell you because he didn't want to be treated differently,' Mrs Chubb says. 'He's never wanted pity. He just wants to be ordinary — to be treated as normal.' She tightens her grip on his hand. 'You can be a bit of a sod, Keagan. I'm not going to pretend otherwise. But he values your friendship, and I know you'd never let anything bad happen to him.'

'I'm sorry, Mrs Chubb,' Keagan says. 'Today was my fault. He was in that pool because of me.'

'You got him out of it.' She looks at him steadily. 'Don't treat him differently now you know. That's the one thing he'd hate. Just be his friend — the same as you've always been.'

'I will.'

A short silence settles. Then: 'Could I ask you a favour?'

She gives him a careful look.

'When you speak to my mum — if you could maybe let her know I was just there helping Peter?'

She shakes her head slowly, but she is smiling, and the smile explains a great deal about why her son keeps his company. 'You're a good lad,' she says. 'Sometimes.' She squeezes his hand once more and stands up, leaning down to kiss him on the cheek. 'Go home. Your mum will be worried. And for heaven's sake, put your trousers on.'

He watches her go back through the double doors.

It is gone six. He is already over an hour late.

He looks back across the waiting area. The girl's seat is empty. The stool, the ice pack, all of it gone. Somewhere between Mrs Chubb and now, she must have been called through.

He stands there for a moment longer than he needs to. He would have liked to ask her name.

He picks up his bags, finds the toilets, changes back into his school uniform, and heads for the exit. Outside, the evening is still warm and pale and unhurried. He starts the walk home.

WE ARE FAMILY, APRIL 1979

Keagan walks through the open back door and into the kitchen. His mum is at the large Formica table with a cup of tea by her side and a cigarette resting in the ashtray, peeling potatoes for tonight's dinner.

Lizzie Devlin looks up from the potatoes and gives him the sort of smile that says she is pleased to see him and already suspicious. She is five foot two in her slippers, grey-haired now, broader than she used to be, with the worn patience of a woman who has raised five children and heard every excuse going. Her apron is dusted with peelings. From the back room, beyond the kitchen, her industrial sewing machine sits quiet for once — a rare mercy when an urgent order from the rag trade can keep her at it past ten. She has long since developed the essential maternal skill of separating truth from invention, and while she doesn't always pursue it, every one of her children knows that when it matters, they haven't got a chance.

'Hello, Mum. Sorry I'm late.'

'Where've you been? It's past six.'

'Sorry, I forgot to mention we were going swimming after school.

Peter got in trouble and we ended up at the hospital.' He says it casually, which doesn't fool her for a second.

She stops peeling and picks up her cigarette. 'Is he all right?'

'Yeah. A lifeguard got him out. He's all right, but they're keeping him in for a few days. His mum's with him now, that's why I'm late — I had to wait for her at the hospital.'

'I hope you weren't doing anything stupid.'

'Of course not. We were just swimming. What time's dinner?'

'About seven, when your dad gets in.'

That's unusual. Most Friday nights his dad goes straight to the pub after work and isn't back before nine at the earliest. It must have something to do with the argument Keagan heard this morning about the bills.

'Why's dad home early?'

'Haven't got a clue.' She draws on her cigarette and returns to the potatoes.

'Right. Is Maureen home yet?'

'Not yet. She said she'd be home about six.'

'Oh, all right.' He pauses. 'Mum — do you know about cystic fibrosis?'

She stubs the cigarette out in the nearly full ashtray and looks at him. 'His mum told you then.'

'What — you knew?'

'Of course I knew. She told me years ago, but she said to leave it until Peter was ready to tell you himself.' She lights another cigarette and draws the first puff. 'Is this why he's in hospital?'

'Sort of, yeah. He'll be in a few days, she said.' He leans against the kitchen doorframe. 'I'm not sure I understand it properly. I know it's to do with his lungs. But will he — is it going to—'

'It's serious,' she says, before he has to finish the question. 'But they've got treatments that help. It's about infections on his lungs — he gets them a lot and they're hard for him to clear. When they're bad, in he goes. They can't cure it, but they can treat the infections and keep him going.' She pauses. 'There were times, when he was little, when they weren't sure how far he'd get. But look at him — sixteen, and no worse than he was as a little lad. Who knows.'

'Yeah.' Keagan looks at the floor. 'But I don't know how.'

'You can't do anything about the illness. But you can look after him a bit. He'll need a friend around.'

'I just don't know what to say. Or whether I should say anything at all.'

'He'll talk when he's ready. Just be there to listen.' She picks up another potato. 'It's all you can do, son.'

'Yeah. You're right. Thanks, Mum.' He pushes himself off the doorframe. 'I'll go up. Can you call me when it's ready?'

'What am I, your flipping servant?' She says it with a smile.

KEAGAN WAKES to the Big Ben repeater alarm clock showing half past eight. It's a bright Sunday morning but his mood, already low since Friday, hadn't been much improved by watching West Ham draw with Wrexham yesterday — a dismal ninety minutes followed by too many beers that he'll be feeling until at least lunchtime.

Hearing his sister stir, he's out of his room and into the bathroom before she gets there. He's learned that lesson the hard way.

Downstairs, his mum is at the gas cooker doing the Sunday breakfast. It's the one morning of the week they eat properly — white pudding, fried eggs, bacon, and baked beans fried in the bacon fat, which is Keagan's favourite part, served with tea and a pile of fresh crusty bread. The tradition is so fixed that a story about his eldest brother Niall still gets told at the table: the time Niall came home from his Saturday job at the local delicatessen without the bacon. When their mum went for him, he pointed out that it was a kosher delicatessen and didn't sell bacon. He received a clip around the ear anyway.

From the back room, Mario Lanza is singing 'If I Loved You' at considerable volume. His mum's favourite album is as much a part of Sunday morning as the bacon. It'll stay on until his dad comes downstairs in about ten minutes and changes it over, which Keagan can already anticipate from the sounds of movement above.

'Morning, Mum.' He plants a kiss on her cheek and reaches for a half slice of bread from the basket by the cooker. The spatula catches him across the knuckles before he gets there.

'Good morning. Can you set the table — it's nearly ready. Is your sister up?'

'Yeah, I heard her go into the bathroom.'

'You going to Mass?'

'Is it optional?' he says, with a smirk.

'Don't be a cheeky git. Get the table laid.'

'Sorry. Just checking.'

Mass at ten-thirty on Sunday has been compulsory since he could walk, for every member of the family under eighteen. His mum is Church of England — the other man's church, as his dad puts it — so she's exempt. Once you turn eighteen you make your own choices. His sister Maureen exercised that right from the morning of her eighteenth birthday, which happened to fall on a Sunday, much to the joy of Maureen and the considerable displeasure of her father.

Keagan is less certain he'd drop it even if he could. There's a part of him that feels close to the church — something he wouldn't admit to easily. He says his prayers every night, but Mass feels different, more like a conversation that might actually be heard. His ambition in primary school had been to become a priest. Passing the eleven-plus and moving out of the Catholic school system had been the start of the change, and now sixteen, he has accepted that the priesthood and his interest in girls are not likely to sit comfortably together.

'Morning, Dad,' he says as his father comes into the kitchen.

'Morning, son. Morning, Liz.' Patrick Devlin winces in the direction of the back room. 'I'll sort that out now.'

'Here comes the diddly-dee music,' Keagan murmurs to his mum.

'Quiet, he'll hear you.' She raises the spatula.

Paddy Devlin is five feet nine with the solid build of a man who has spent decades on road construction, and he's been going bald since his twenties. He makes a point of reminding Keagan of this at regular intervals, which Keagan finds quietly alarming. His one consolation is his brother Niall, twenty-four and still with a full head of hair, which may or may not mean anything.

The Clancy Brothers replace Mario Lanza.

Maureen comes down last, as usual, still half-dressed and humming something under her breath. She is twenty now, officially too old for compulsory Mass and unofficially too busy being a singer in waiting. The record shop in Ilford pays her wages, but she treats it as a temporary stop on the road to somewhere with a stage.

Mrs Devlin serves up the plates. Keagan catches Maureen's eye and starts a silent air fiddle performance as their dad concentrates on his breakfast. Maureen dissolves into laughter. His mum gives him a look that could stop traffic.

~

St Theresa's Church in Newbury Park was the first new Catholic church built in England after the war. It's an imposing red-brick structure — a hub for the local community — with stained glass windows that catch the light on a clear morning. Attached to it is a much more modest timber-built social hall that has hosted more wedding receptions, first communions and parish fundraisers than Keagan can count. It also hosted the Irish dancing lessons of his early years, a memory he makes a point of not dwelling on.

As the only member of the family under eighteen, he goes alone. Before he was thirteen, he and Maureen used to alternate, one attending while the other disappeared with friends for the hour. They could never take a Sunday off entirely — their dad had an uncanny ability to recall the readings for the day in precise detail despite apparently never setting foot inside the church himself. It kept them honest.

Keagan takes his usual seat in the last pew, having cut two minutes off the journey by crossing the Eastern Avenue at a sprint between the lorries. The service starts around him and he falls into the familiar rhythm of it — standing, sitting, responding — while his mind moves somewhere else entirely.

He's been carrying the weight of Friday since he left the hospital. Not loudly, not in a way anyone would notice, but it's there. He sits with it now in the quiet of the church, and instead of the usual wandering thoughts about West Ham or what they're doing tonight, there's just Peter.

As the priest prepares the altar for communion, Keagan has his usual private conversation with God — the thanking, the apologising, the small honest inventory of where he's fallen short. Today there's only one thing he wants to say, and the words don't come easily.

He looks across the church at the statue of St Theresa of Lisieux, the patron saint of the parish. She died at twenty-four, he knows that much from years of being told it. A short life given over to prayer and the care of others. He looks at her and something tightens in his throat.

He prays for Peter. Not for a miracle — he knows enough to understand that isn't on offer. He prays that Peter can beat it for as long as possible, and that he finds some happiness in whatever time there is. It's the most honest prayer he's ever offered. He keeps it simple because he doesn't have the words for anything more.

As the priest reads the parish notices, Keagan slips quietly out. In the foyer he dips his fingers in the holy water, crosses himself, and makes his promise.

PETER HAS BEEN HOME from King George Hospital since yesterday. He's on the sofa downstairs now, exhausted still, while his parents and his brother Michael talk. The television has been full of the election all morning, and Michael, who takes politics more seriously than anyone Peter knows, nods towards the newspaper folded on the arm of the chair.

'So then,' he says, 'are we all meant to be terrified of Mrs Thatcher, or is she going to save the country?'

Michael is five years older than Peter, six feet tall with an athletic frame and the kind of clean, sharp features that always look composed. He works for the Foreign and Commonwealth Office in London and has a career stretching out ahead of him without limit. He married his childhood sweetheart last year.

Peter looks at his brother and feels the familiar small ache of it. He loves Michael completely and wouldn't wish his own situation on anyone in the world, least of all him. But why did it have to be Peter? Why was he the one with the rogue gene?

He pushes it away.

'Probably,' he says. 'But Mum and Dad won't be too happy about that, will you — a Conservative government.'

'For once I might think it's a good idea,' his dad says, with the slight gravity of a man confessing something. 'I might even bring myself to vote Tory. First time in my life. But somebody has to sort this country out, and Callaghan's made a right mess of it.'

'We need a woman,' his mum says firmly. 'It's about time there was one worth voting for. She gets my vote.'

'Blimey,' Peter says. 'You'll both be out canvassing next.'

Michael laughs. His parents look tolerant.

'How are you doing?' Michael asks. 'Anything I can get you?'

'I'm all right. Unless you've got a spare set of lungs going spare.'

'I phoned Keagan's mum,' his mother says, moving smoothly past that. 'She said he's at Mass, but he might come round later.'

'Not today, Mum. I don't think I'm up for it.'

'He's worried about you, Peter. It might do you good to talk to him.'

'Yeah. When I'm ready.' He shifts on the sofa. 'I just don't know what to say yet.'

He's nervous about it, if he's honest. Everything has shifted now that Keagan knows. He's tried to think about how Keagan will react — whether it'll be awkward, whether he'll start treating Peter like he's made of something fragile. He knows in his bones that Keagan would never deliberately make it worse, but knowing and feeling are two different things. He doesn't want sympathy. He doesn't want to become the sick friend. He just wants it to be the same as it was, which he's old enough to understand it can't be, not completely.

'OK, son. But you can't put it off forever.'

'I know. I'll see him at school. We can talk then.'

'All right. I'll call his mum.'

She looks across at her husband. He gives her the smallest nod. She gets up and goes to make the phone call, leaving the three of them in the quiet of the living room, the Sunday afternoon settling around them.

CHAPTER

THREE

ROCK WITH YOU, APRIL 1979

Monday nights at the Town Hall in Ilford belong to Froggy. The DJ has been running his weekly disco there for years, pulling teenagers in from across the borough — jazz-funk and soul keeping the floors packed well past nine. Peter has been out of hospital for several days and tonight he and Keagan catch the 169 from the stop outside the Horns, riding it the ten minutes into town in the first real warmth of spring.

They take the back seats upstairs, where the windows are already fogged and the smoke hangs in the warm air. Keagan pulls out his Rothmans and pauses with one unlit between his fingers.

'You all right if I have a smoke?'

'You've never asked before,' Peter says, then lowers his voice. 'Listen — while I've got you. I don't want anything to change. I don't need looking after and I'd sooner it wasn't the only thing we talked about. Can we just carry on as normal?'

'Christ, I only asked about the fag.'

'I know. I had this whole speech ready and then it came out wrong.' Peter exhales. 'Forget it.'

Keagan lights up and blows the smoke towards the window. They cross Eastern Avenue, the streetlights throwing orange bars across the seats.

'Look,' he says after a moment, 'I just thought I should ask, with your chest and all. I'm not going to make a big deal out of it. But I'm here if you want to talk.' He picks at the fabric of the armrest. 'And I haven't said anything to the others.'

'I'd rather you didn't, if that's all right. I just want to be normal. Not some sick bloke everyone feels sorry for.'

He explains what he can, keeping it brief — diagnosed when he was five, though it wasn't until his tenth birthday that his mum and dad sat him down and told him the full picture.

'That's the hardest part,' Peter says, staring out at the street. 'Being told you've got a life-threatening illness and you're unlikely to see your twenties. Well, I'm sixteen now and I'm not going to let it run my life. I'm going to enjoy every bit of it.' He glances across. 'And honestly — the way you smoke those things, get drunk every weekend and go fighting with Danny, I might still bloody outlive you.'

'Cheers, mate.' Keagan laughs.

'No point saving that virginity either,' Peter adds. 'Not when neither of us might live long enough to use it.'

'With your track record,' Keagan says, 'we'll both die wondering.'

'That was my line.' Peter grins. 'Come on then. Let's see what we can do about it tonight.'

GETTING off at the Red Cow, it's a short walk over Havelock Bridge to the High Street. The queue for the Town Hall's side entrance stretches back to the railings but moves quickly enough — it always does on a Monday. Inside, the hall is heaving, the bass coming up through the floor and the air thick with cigarette smoke, hairspray and cheap perfume. Froggy is in full swing. Keagan could name every track from the opening bar.

Their group are at the back, deep in an argument about West Ham's latest draw and whether the promotion push is finished. It probably is.

Keagan went to the game and doesn't need much encouragement to say so. Mark, being a Spurs man, finds this easier to bear than most. Peter, not being a football man, takes the opportunity to go with Mark to join the drinks queue.

Keagan, mid-sentence about Mervyn Day's positioning, glances over towards the bar.

He sees her straight away.

The girl from the hospital is standing in the queue, talking to her friend, already looking across with a small, recognising smile. He excuses himself from the group — probably mid-sentence — and walks over.

'Hello again. How's the leg?'

'Fine, thank you. Just a sprain.' She holds his gaze. 'I'm glad to see you're wearing trousers this time.'

'They do insist on it at the door.'

They both laugh. Her friend watches with an expression of careful neutrality.

'I'm Keagan, by the way.'

'Emily. This is my cousin Jennifer.'

Jennifer is tall, with long dark hair and sharp, assessing eyes. Pretty — the same quality of looks as Emily but expressed differently, more guarded. She says hello with an impeccable politeness that closes off any possible follow-up. Keagan catches the look — not hostility exactly, more a deliberate withholding. He wonders whether the bar is very high.

'Your friend's just ahead of you in the queue,' he says, nodding towards Peter. 'If you like, I can ask him to get your drinks in while he's there.'

'That would be lovely. Two Cokes, please.' Emily reaches for her purse.

Keagan shakes his head. 'Don't worry about it.'

Jennifer's expression shifts marginally — not warm, but noting something.

'We'll be over by the stage,' Emily says. 'Near the side door.'

Back at the bar, Peter and Mark are still laughing about something between themselves.

'What?'

'Your admirer,' Peter says. 'The tall one. She looks like she wants to kill you.'

'I only said hello.'

'The famous Devlin charm,' Mark says cheerfully.

'Yes, wonderful, the pair of you. One of you is coming back with me. Mark, you've got a girlfriend, so you're cleared. Peter — I need you.'

'And if I'd rather not?'

'The girl's name is Emily and her cousin is very attractive and you have about three minutes to decide you're interested.'

Peter considers this for one second. 'Fine. What are we drinking?'

They carry the drinks across the busy floor and find Emily and Jennifer by the stage as promised. Peter says hello and Emily asks after him — how he's recovered, whether he's all right. He tells her he's fine and has made a private decision never to go swimming with Keagan again as he values his life too much. The girls laugh. Keagan, seeing an opening, begins to embellish the original rescue story in his own favour until Emily, pleasantly but without mercy, reminds him that his rescue operation put her in casualty.

After a few minutes, Keagan steers Emily half a step away from the others. 'Can I ask — your cousin. Have I done something?'

'It's not you specifically,' Emily says. 'It's that group you were standing with. They've got a bit of a reputation around here.'

'They're our friends. They're fine, honestly.'

'I believe you. She's just protective. Don't take it personally.' She glances across to where Peter and Jennifer have fallen into conversation, heads bent together over something. 'It looks like he's doing all right, though.'

'He always does,' Keagan says, with only mild resentment. 'Why don't you both come and meet the others? Then she can make her own mind up.'

The introductions go better than Keagan has any right to expect. The boys are on their best behaviour — Danny keeping his language to something approaching acceptable and managing to sustain it for almost ten minutes before the mask slips. But the conversations find their level quickly and Jennifer, to her credit, recalibrates visibly. She's fair-minded underneath the protectiveness.

Peter, in the middle of winding Keagan up about being only half a proper Londoner, is interrupted when Jennifer mentions that her own father is from Ireland and came over as a child. Keagan explains, as he always does, that he is in fact a proper Cockney on his mother's side — his mum was born within earshot of Bow Bells — which Peter disputes with great enthusiasm while knowing perfectly well it's true.

'By the way,' Jennifer says during a gap in the argument, looking at Keagan directly for the first time with something approaching ease. 'Only my parents call me Jennifer. My friends call me Jenny.'

'Does that mean we're friends now?'

'On probation,' she says, and almost smiles.

It's nearly ten o'clock when Keagan suggests they head off and beat the rush for the bus. The girls live in Barkingside, only a couple of stops past Newbury Park on the 169. Emily says give them five minutes.

The farewells are in the usual spirit. Danny, shouting across the hall as they move towards the exit, wants it noted that he is available for double dates. Thursday night, the Horns, eight o'clock. Keagan confirms he'll be there. Peter says he doubts it — his brother's coming over that evening.

They wait by the doors in the cool air.

'You're getting on well,' Keagan says.

'Jenny's lovely.' Peter is quiet for a moment. 'It wasn't really about you, for what it's worth. She just doesn't know you yet.'

'Comforting.'

'I thought so.'

~

On the bus, Peter leans in with a suggestion. When they reach Emily's stop, he'll stay on with Jenny and see her home, and Keagan can walk Emily. When they put it to the girls, they agree easily enough. Keagan takes this as a good sign.

He offers his hand to Emily as she steps down from the bus — more reflex than intention. She takes his arm as they cross the road and it feels, he thinks, entirely natural.

It's a clear spring night, the moon nearly full, bright enough to see her face when she turns to speak. He is walking slowly without noticing.

They talk about what comes next — the future that is already arriving. Emily has an interview with NatWest Bank; her dad works there and she's heading into the City after her O-levels. Keagan would like to stay on for sixth form, maybe university eventually, though he can't see how his parents would manage the money. His family are all in the building trade. That's probably where he'll end up.

'What would you study? If you could?'

'Maths, maybe. Science.' He hesitates. 'You'll laugh.'

'I won't.'

'I'd love to be a pilot. RAF. I spoke to the recruiting people during careers week.'

'Why would I laugh at that?'

He shrugs, and something passes across his face — not quite regret, more an awareness of the distance between wanting and having. It's there for a moment and then gone.

'You should try,' Emily says. 'Talk to your mum and dad. You never know.'

'Yeah. See how the exams go first.'

They walk on. He is quietly glad she didn't just leave it there.

'This is me,' she says.

They've stopped outside a pebble-dashed terraced house, a Vauxhall Viva on the driveway.

'That was quick. You weren't lying.'

She smiles. 'Thank you for walking me home.'

Neither of them moves to end the evening. He takes the pause for what it is and, before he can think better of it, asks whether she'd like to go out sometime.

She doesn't answer immediately. The silence stretches long enough to make him wish he'd said nothing, and then she says, 'I'd like that. Call me later in the week.'

'Yeah. Wednesday?'

'Wednesday's good.' She takes a pen from her bag and writes her number on a scrap of paper, presses it into his hand. He pockets it without looking at it.

'Goodnight, Keagan.'

He leans in and kisses her cheek. She squeezes his hand briefly, opens the gate and walks to her front door, turning once as she finds her key. He waves and heads off down the quiet road for the twenty-minute walk home, not minding the distance in the least.

AT SCHOOL THE FOLLOWING MORNING, they compare notes at their lockers during morning break. Peter thought the night with Jenny went well and says he'll call her once Keagan has spoken to Emily — maybe they could all go out together, make it a four. Keagan agrees. He is trying to sound casual about Wednesday and failing.

'Are you going to music at lunch?' Peter asks.

'Yeah. Mr Mills wants me to go in for grade six in the summer. I need to sort out my theory.'

Keagan has had lunchtime lessons with Mr Mills since the first year, when the head of music spotted ability as well as enthusiasm and offered to take him through the grades for free. The price was the school choir, which Keagan pretends to resent more than he does.

'You could carry on with it if you stayed on,' Peter says. 'You're actually not bad.'

'What, be the next Elton John?'

'I was going to say Rick Wakeman. But all right.'

Keagan closes his locker. 'What did you think of Emily?'

'Very pretty. Though I think Jenny's prettier.'

'Of course you do.'

'I had to do some explaining on your behalf, by the way. Convince her you couldn't help it — coming from where you do, the way you were raised. She took it remarkably well.'

'You're a real friend, you know that?'

They head towards the double doors at the end of the corridor. Keagan remembers a textbook and goes back, telling Peter to wait.

Peter leans against the wall by the top of the staircase. The corridor has emptied out — most of the school in the yard or the canteen, the usual low-level noise coming up from outside. He hears the footstep a moment before Martin Davis comes around the corner.

Martin Davis is the tallest boy in the fifth year by some distance, broad and solid from years as prop-forward for the school rugby team, his face already mapping its history in small scars. Most of the school give him room without needing to be told why. He has left Peter alone since their first year — less out of goodwill than out of a calculation, kept in place by the memory of what happened when he tried things with Keagan. The broken nose, the story goes, had needed resetting. Peter has never asked for details.

He moves to step past.

'Careful, shrimp.'

Peter keeps his voice flat. 'Sorry.'

Martin looks along the empty corridor, taking his time. 'On your own? No bum-chum today?'

Peter turns for the double doors.

'Oy.' The hand comes down on his shoulder. 'I'm talking to you.'

The doors open. Keagan comes through and reads the scene in a single glance — crosses the corridor in a few strides, takes Martin's arm and bends it cleanly back, walking him into the wall. When he speaks, his voice is quiet, his mouth close to Martin's ear.

'Unless you'd like to find out what your nose looks like facing the other way, I'd go now.'

He releases the arm and gives him a short, deliberate push towards the stairs.

Martin turns. He and Keagan hold the gaze for a long moment, long enough for everyone watching to remember it. Then Martin looks past him towards the group of boys waiting at the bottom of the staircase, shakes his head and goes. His friends move aside and close in around him.

Peter watches him go.

'I was handling it,' he says.

'I know,' Keagan says, and picks up his bag.

They head to class. Neither of them mentions it again.

Emily's house is a three-bedroom terraced in a quiet road off Horns Road in Barkingside — the same house her parents bought after they married, the same one Emily was born in, and Anna two years after her. On Tuesday evenings, with George out at football training and Valerie at her mother's around the corner, the house belongs to the sisters. Jenny comes over every week without needing to be asked. There are always sandwiches.

Anna is fourteen and looks so much like Emily that strangers regularly mistake them for twins — something she considers a compliment in direct proportion to how much it irritates her sister. She is already on the sofa when Jenny carries the plates through from the kitchen, and she looks up with the alert expression of someone who has heard a name mentioned in passing and intends to hear more.

'So,' Jenny says, settling down. 'Tell me about Keagan.'

'Who's Keagan?' Anna says immediately.

Emily explains — the ankle, casualty, she hadn't expected to see him again, but there he was at the Town Hall with his friend Peter.

'Isn't that the group with the reputation for fighting?' Anna asks.

'That's what I thought,' Jenny says. 'They were all right in the end, though. His friend Peter's very nice.'

'She's barely mentioned Peter,' Emily observes.

'He's just a friend.'

'For now.'

Jenny ignores this with dignity. 'Was he a gentleman?' she asks Emily.

'He walked me to the gate.'

'To the gate,' Anna says solemnly. 'Em. Don't rush into anything.'

Emily throws a cushion. 'He seemed quieter than I expected, actually.'

'He wasn't quiet,' Jenny says. 'He was being careful. There's a difference.'

'And you can tell that after one evening?'

'I can tell quite a lot after one evening.'

Anna looks at Emily. Emily looks at the ceiling.

'He's going to call tomorrow,' Emily says. 'I said Wednesday.'

'Your dad will hate him,' Anna announces, with the serene confidence of someone delivering useful information. 'He supports West Ham.'

'Anna—'

'Dad will never stand for it. You know what he says about West Ham supporters. You might as well bring home a cat burglar.' She considers. 'Though dad's not selective in his hatred. A cat burglar of any persuasion would do it.'

They eat their sandwiches and the subject drifts through other things — dance exams, Anna's plans to audition for professional dance school after her CSEs, which Emily admires and expects their father to resist. Jenny listens and asks questions, understanding less of the technical detail than she lets on. Her own plans are pointing towards medicine. She keeps that thought close for now.

The front door opens.

'Only me!'

'Mum!' Anna is already halfway to the stairs. 'Emily's got a boyfriend and he supports West Ham!'

Emily closes her eyes briefly.

Her mother appears in the doorway, takes in her daughter's expression, and raises one eyebrow.

Emily shakes her head, and smiles despite herself.

CHAPTER

FOUR

GIVE ME THE NIGHT, APRIL 1979

The Chase is what the locals call it — an overgrown footpath running over the Central Line railway, connecting Newbury Park to Barkingside in about five minutes if you walk with purpose. It used to be called Lover's Lane, which tells you everything about what it once was and nothing about what it is now: poorly lit, a bit neglected, and perfectly serviceable if you know where you're going and don't mind the dark.

Keagan minds it rather less than usual tonight.

He walks quickly through the undergrowth, hands in the pockets of his quilted jacket, and tries not to think too hard about meeting Emily's parents. He is wearing his best jeans, brown winkle-picker shoes and a shirt that he'd considered bold when he put it on and now suspects might simply be loud. The jacket is covering most of it. He is also, he notices, sweating, which he is telling himself is the speed of walking.

He has never been the type to worry about what people think. He has spent most of his school years being the council-estate kid at a grammar school, the Irish boy in a largely English crowd, the one who doesn't quite fit the mould the teachers had in mind when they offered

27

him a place. He's learned to carry himself confidently enough that most people don't notice. But this is different. He wants to be liked. Not just tolerated — liked.

The terraced house looks exactly as he remembered it from last week: pebble-dashed, well-kept, the Vauxhall Viva on the driveway. What he didn't notice last time, because he only got as far as the gate, is the sticker in the back window of the car.

I FOLLOW THE SPURS

He rings the bell and waits, hearing movement inside — voices somewhere towards the back of the house, then a pause, then footsteps coming to the door.

It opens. Relief: it's Emily.

She's wearing a floral lace cardigan over a pink top, faded jeans, her hair down. The slight colour in her cheeks when she sees him makes the walk through the dark entirely worth it.

'Hi, Keagan. Come in.'

He steps into the hallway. 'You look lovely.'

'Thank you.' The colour deepens slightly. She steps aside and lowers her voice. 'Mum and Dad are just in the living room. Do you mind saying hello for a minute?'

The look tells him this is less of a question than a kind warning.

The living room is at the back of the house, opening onto the kitchen through a half-door. George Callison is standing at the threshold between the two rooms with a tea towel over his shoulder and a football shirt that Keagan doesn't immediately recognise — local side, he thinks, not First Division. He's a compact, straight-backed man in his late thirties with the kind of handshake that expresses an opinion without needing words.

'Hello, Keagan.'

'Evening, Mr Callison.'

Valerie Callison is on the sofa and smiles a genuine and easy smile. Keagan can see immediately where Emily gets it from — the same eyes, the same warmth in the expression. She gestures to the armchair beside George's.

'Sit down a minute, Keagan. You've got a little time before the film.'

He sits. Emily takes the seat next to her mother.

'Emily tells me you're at the grammar school,' Valerie says. 'Are you ready for your exams?'

'I think so. My mocks went all right. It'll be hard but I'm hoping I've put the work in.'

'He wants to be a pilot,' Emily says.

Keagan glances at her. She raises an eyebrow very slightly, as if to say, well, you do.

'RAF?' Valerie asks.

'That's the idea, yeah. I spoke to the recruiting people at careers week. It's a long road but—' He leaves the rest of it unfinished. George hasn't said anything yet, which Keagan clocks.

'Do you play any sport?' George asks, settling into his chair with the easy authority of a man who considers it a reasonable opening question.

'Football, mainly. Rugby at school, cricket in the summer. Football's my favourite.'

'I've heard that.' George pauses just long enough. 'West Ham supporter, I'm told.'

'Yeah, but I'm generous about it. I told Emily I'd let her wear her Spurs scarf at Upton Park if she wanted.'

George's expression doesn't quite become a smile, but it moves in that direction. 'Who said I like football?' Emily says.

'You didn't need to,' Keagan says. 'Your dad does, that's enough.'

George does smile at that — briefly, but sincerely. He asks a few more questions, the usual getting-to-know-you circuit: family, school, the journey over from Newbury Park, what Keagan's father does. Keagan answers honestly and without dressing anything up. He's from a council estate, his dad's in the building trade, his mum works part-time. It's not complicated.

When George stands and picks up the tea towel again, it has the feeling of a verdict delivered through gesture rather than word.

'Eleven o'clock, Emily.' He looks at Keagan. 'Good to meet you. Make sure she gets home safely.'

'I will, Mr Callison. Cinema and straight back.'

They say their goodbyes at the door, and Keagan follows Emily down the path and out through the front gate. The night air is cool and clear, the street quiet.

'Well done,' she says quietly, once they're far enough down the road.

'Did I pass?'

'The football joke was good. He appreciated that.'

'I live to serve.'

She takes his arm without making anything of it, and they walk.

～

THE ABC CINEMA is a fifteen-minute walk through the town centre, its Art Deco frontage lit up against the dark. A small crowd mills about outside — people waiting for friends, couples arriving. Keagan and Emily join the ticket queue and are asked their ages by a young woman behind the glass who clearly finds the question procedural rather than pressing.

They take seats near the back. Maltesers, two Cokes — Emily insisting on paying for one of them — and then the lights begin to dim as the Pearl and Dean reel starts.

'You know Peter and Jenny are going out tonight,' Emily says, leaning close so she doesn't have to raise her voice.

Keagan turns to look at her. 'You're joking. He never said a word. All week I've been talking about tonight and not a word.'

'All week, you said?'

'You've got me.'

'Lucky I said yes, then.'

'Never in doubt,' he says.

'Confident.'

'How could you possibly resist?'

'Deluded,' she says, but she's smiling.

The Bee Gees soundtrack starts and Keagan reaches across in the dark and takes her hand. She doesn't pull away.

～

GRANGE HILL STATION sits on the Central Line's eastern end, the platform half-open to the sky. Peter comes up the steps from the underground into the cool evening air and follows Manor Road south. The houses out here are something else entirely — post-war but extended, brick-built and set well back from the road, with mature trees lining the verges and proper driveways. He slows his pace slightly without meaning to.

He finds the right road and double-checks the number, then rings the bell.

The door opens and Jenny is standing in a white dressing gown, her hair damp.

'Hi,' she says. 'Come in. I was in the pool — I don't normally answer the door like this, I should say.'

'You have a pool?'

'Come and see.'

She leads him through the house and out onto a wide patio. The steam rises off the water in the evening chill, catching the light from the windows. It is a proper pool — not enormous, but heated and clearly well-used, the surrounding tiles clean and pale.

'Would you like a swim?'

'I'd love to, but I didn't bring anything.'

'We've got trunks. I'll get you something — no Speedos, I promise.'

She leads him to the changing room beside the pool, finds him a pair that will do, and leaves him to it. Peter changes, and when he comes back out she is already in the water.

'I should say,' Jenny says as he comes down the steps, 'I completely forgot about what happened at the pool. Are you all right with this?'

'Completely. The problem the other week was a chest infection, not a water phobia. This is lovely.' He drops under and comes back up. 'You're in here a lot?'

'Every day in the summer. My dad gets the barbecue going on Saturdays. You'll have to come.' She says it easily, without much ceremony. 'How's your volleyball?'

'Terrible. But enthusiastic.'

'That'll do.'

They talk in the pool and they talk after it, sitting in the kitchen with mugs of tea while the windows cloud with warmth. The house is quieter without her parents — they're out for the evening — and the conversation finds its level without effort. Peter tells her about his plans for the butcher's shop in Hainault; his dad has spent his life in the market trade and has agreed to help set him up. It'll take a couple of years to get right.

'Will Keagan be involved?' Jenny asks.

Peter considers this with visible amusement. 'Absolutely not.'

'Too bossy?'

'He's my best friend. He also has a very strong sense of how things should be done. If he worked for me I'd end up working for him inside a week.' He wraps both hands around his mug. 'He has his own ideas about the future anyway. He'd like to fly, if the path's there.'

Jenny is quiet for a moment. 'Emily was worried, when she first told me she liked him. About his reputation, the crowd he goes around with.'

'I know. But she couldn't be in safer hands, Jenny, honestly. He takes care of people. He's not always polished about it, but he means it.'

She nods, turning her mug slowly on the table. 'I can see that. I just needed to be sure.'

~

ON SCREEN, John Travolta is alone on the dance floor in his white suit, the lights cutting shapes around him. The film has drawn Keagan in despite himself. He'd expected to enjoy the music. He hadn't expected to care about the story.

'Do you like dancing?' Emily murmurs, her head tilted slightly towards him.

'Love it. I'm at the Greengate most Saturdays. You should come.'

She considers this. 'My dad would never let me near a nightclub. Is it as bad as people say?'

'Depends on the night. Danny helps keep things interesting.'

'Danny — the one with the enormous shoulders?'

'That's the one.'

'I could see he might attract trouble.'

'Oy,' Keagan says. 'What does that make me?'

'It makes you someone who looks after his friends,' she says. 'Which is different.'

He looks at her in the dark for a moment. That is more perceptive than he was expecting. 'Yeah,' he says. 'That's more or less it.'

The music builds. Keagan nods towards Travolta in the white suit. 'That's me, by the way. Minus the suit. I'd never wear that in public.'

'Not with me, you wouldn't.'

'You'd make it a condition, would you?'

'I'd make it a condition,' she says firmly, and steals a Malteser.

~

THEY COME out of the cinema into the high street, blinking in the brightness of the shopfronts. Emily is still humming something from the soundtrack without seeming aware of it.

'Well?' Keagan asks.

'I didn't expect to like it as much as I did,' she says. 'I thought it would just be disco music and a plot.'

'It's better than that.'

'It is, actually.' She glances at him sideways. 'I never thought I'd say this, but the Bee Gees were all right.'

'Don't let anyone hear you say that in Newbury Park. The shame would destroy you.'

She laughs. 'Can we go to Rossi's? I know it's late but if they're still open—'

'Course they are. Come on.'

The ice-cream parlour on the high street is busy with post-cinema stragglers, the display cabinet lit up inside. They decide on takeaway — Keagan a 99, Emily a tub of vanilla and raspberry ripple, and they find a low wall on the way back and sit with the warm night around them.

It's quiet here, away from the main street. They eat without rushing, the way you do when you don't particularly want the evening to be over. Keagan watches a car pass, then looks at the ice cream, then at Emily.

'Thank you,' he says. 'For tonight.'

'You're thanking me?'

'Yeah. I was nervous coming to meet your parents, I won't pretend I wasn't. And tonight's been — it's been really good, Emily.'

She is quiet for a moment. Then: 'You didn't need to be nervous.

They liked you. Well—' she tilts her head, 'my mum liked you straight-away. My dad's going to take a little longer, that's just how he is. The football joke bought you some time.'

'How long does he usually take?'

'The last boy I brought home lasted until dessert before he said something my dad didn't like. You've already exceeded that.'

'What did he say?'

'He said he didn't really follow football.' She shakes her head with the solemn expression of someone describing a genuine calamity.

Keagan finishes the last of his 99. 'Right. Tactical error. I'll bear that in mind.'

She leans across and kisses him — not long, just certain, the way you kiss someone when you've decided you mean it. He doesn't move for a moment after, and then he takes her hand and they walk the rest of the way back to her house in the dark without needing to fill it with conversation.

The gate clicks shut behind her at two minutes to eleven. She waves from the step.

That had to count for something, Keagan thinks, and turns for home with his hands in his pockets and the music still going in his head.

CHAPTER

FIVE

HERSHAM BOYS, APRIL 1979

The Horns is already three-quarters full when they arrive, the Friday evening crowd packed around the bar and overflowing into the narrow corridor between the saloon and the public. Keagan gets the first round in while Danny finds them a corner, and Peter settles at the end of the bench with the careful arrangement of someone who has learned to position himself nearest the exit without making a thing of it. It's not something he talks about. Keagan noticed it years ago and never said a word.

They drink their way through two rounds, then three, the noise rising with the number of pints, and somewhere around half nine Danny starts on about the Greengate.

'I'm not bothered,' Peter says.

'Come on,' Keagan says. 'When's the last time you came out properly?'

'Properly meaning a nightclub and a probable fight?'

'Meaning a dance, a laugh, a couple more pints. Danny'll behave himself.'

'I always behave myself,' Danny says.

Peter looks at him with the particular expression he reserves for statements he finds not worth arguing with. 'I'll come for an hour,' he says. 'One hour.'

'Sound.' Keagan drains his pint. 'Let's go.'

THE GREENGATE SITS JUST along from The Horns, a converted public house that someone with an eye for opportunity and a decent set of speakers had transformed into one of the area's more reliably busy discos. The late seventies had thrown up venues like this all over East London — somewhere between a pub and a club, relaxed about exactly what it was, relaxed about quite a few other things besides. Thursday nights were better known for it, when the door staff applied the age restrictions with something less than precision, but Friday was lively enough. The queue moves steadily and they're inside within ten minutes, the bass thudding up through the floor as soon as the doors open.

It is, as always, loud and hot and packed. The bar has three deep of people trying to catch the eye of the two staff running the length of it. The dance floor takes up most of the middle, the DJ's booth raised at the far end, coloured lights cutting through the artificial fog. Keagan loves it in here. He always has. It's the energy of the thing — the music, the movement, the fact that for a few hours nothing much outside it matters.

Danny shoulders through towards the bar with the focused determination of a man with a mission.

'I'll go,' he says, not as a question.

'Cheers, mate,' Keagan says.

Danny disappears into the crowd. Keagan and Peter find a small standing table near the edge of the floor, far enough from the speakers to have something approaching a conversation.

'You all right?' Keagan asks.

'Yeah,' Peter says. 'It's just loud.'

'That's the point.'

'I know what the point is, Keagan.'

Peter is surveying the room with the mild interest of someone who is pleased enough to be out but is not going to pretend it's his natural habitat. Which, to be fair, it isn't. That's never stopped him coming. He shows up when Keagan asks because he's Peter, and that's what Peter does.

Danny returns with a tray and a face like a man who has been mildly wronged.

'Twenty bloody minutes,' he says, setting down the glasses with enough force that a small amount of lager goes over the side of each. 'Twenty minutes. Someone else is going up next time, I'm telling you that now.' Danny puts Peter's pint down in front of him first, without comment, then shoves the tray at Keagan.

'Should've got your round in at the pub,' Keagan says. 'You tight-fisted git.'

'It's nearly a pound a pint in here. Do you know that? Nearly a pound.'

'It's seventy-pence, which is about the same as the two rounds you didn't buy at the Horns.'

Danny points at him. 'One day, Devlin, I'm going to kick your arse.'

'Yeah, you keep saying.'

Keagan grins at Peter, who is looking at his pint with the expression of a man choosing not to get involved. Danny takes his drink and moves off towards the dance floor with the particular swagger of someone who has decided the conversation is beneath him, which is Danny's standard response to losing an argument.

'So,' Keagan says, leaning on the table, 'how's it going with Jenny?'

Peter looks up. 'All right. Good, actually. I met her parents the other week.'

'And?'

'Fine. Nice enough people. Her dad's a bit quiet but not unfriendly.'

'Nice house though,' Keagan says. 'Very nice house. I can't get over the pool, you lucky sod.'

'It is a good pool.'

'I've got a tin bath in the kitchen.'

'That's not true.'

'It might as well be.' Keagan drinks. 'I'm just saying, if you're going to be up there every week you might want to put a bit of work in. Danny could get you sorted down the gym, build you up a bit, stop embarrassing yourself in your trunks.'

Peter gives him a look of complete composure. 'I'll have you know Jenny seems very happy with what she sees.'

'God help her.'

'Thank you, Keagan, as always, for your support.'

'You're welcome.' Keagan straightens. 'She's nice, Jenny. You did well.'

'She is,' Peter says, and leaves it at that. But the way he says it is enough.

They stand for a while in the comfortable silence that comes from knowing someone well enough not to need to fill every gap. The music shifts — the DJ dropping into something with a proper groove, the floor filling quickly. Keagan feels the familiar pull of it.

'I'm going for a dance,' he says.

'There's a surprise.'

'Don't sulk.'

'I'm not sulking, I'm standing here perfectly happily.'

'Right.' Keagan finishes his pint and sets the glass down. 'Don't talk to any strange men.'

'It's you I'm worried about,' Peter says.

~

THE DANCE FLOOR IS PACKED, which is how it should be. Keagan works his way towards the middle, spotting Danny and Eddie near the DJ booth and making his way over. He dances without much self-consciousness — he always has, it's one of the things he likes about himself — and within a few minutes he's pulled a girl in a red dress into the space beside him and they're doing what the floor is designed for, which is moving to the music without either of them needing to talk about it. A month ago he might have stayed with the girl in the red dress longer. Tonight he smiled, danced, and kept just enough distance to know he was behaving himself.

He's mid-spin when Danny appears at his shoulder.

'Mate.' One word, said in a particular way. Keagan knows the tone.

He turns, scanning the room in the direction of Danny's eyes. A group of five or six lads are standing at the edge of the floor, too close to the action to be watching it, not close enough to be part of it. The one at the front — stocky, dark jacket, the kind of expression that has been practising confrontation all evening — is saying something to the others and laughing.

'What happened?'

'They keep pushing Eddie, deliberately. Every time he moves near them, they're at it.'

'Where is he?'

'Gone for the others.'

Keagan exhales. He looks at the group again, at the ring-leader doing his calculations. He's seen a hundred versions of this. Lads who come out looking for something to happen, who pick a target, who can't see past Saturday night.

'All right,' Keagan says. 'Let me talk to them. They're just scroats, I'll sort it.'

'If they don't listen—'

'If they don't listen, you'll know about it. But let me try first.'

'Tell them if they don't stop I'll kick their fucking heads in.'

'Yeah, I'll put it exactly like that.'

He rolls his eyes and crosses the floor.

The ring-leader clocks him coming and straightens up with the studied ease of someone who wants to be seen straightening up. Keagan stops close enough to be heard over the music but not so close it reads as aggression. He keeps his voice level.

'Look, mate. I don't know what the problem is, but do yourself a favour. Move away from our lot, have your night, let us have ours. Nobody needs any of this, all right?'

The lad's eyes are slightly unfocused. He's been drinking since before he got here. 'He called me a cunt,' he says.

'Who did?'

He jerks his head towards Eddie's general direction.

'Right,' Keagan says. 'Well, he's not going to win any prizes for vocabulary. But the way to deal with that is to ignore him and have a good night, not to stand here winding yourself up.' He pauses. 'Now do yourself a favour and move away.'

'You trying to be funny?'

'Mate, I'm genuinely not. I'm trying to save everyone a lot of aggravation. So be sensible. Yeah?'

He feels Danny step up behind him, close enough that the lad can see him. Keagan turns to say something — and Danny's arm is already moving, a wide right hook that connects with the lad's nose before Keagan can get a word out. The sound is immediate and conclusive. The lad drops back and the group comes forward all at once.

It goes the way these things go, which is quickly and badly. Fists coming from three directions, Keagan taking a shot to the side of the head that makes his ears ring, responding by swinging into the nearest face without stopping to think about it. There is lager under his shoes and someone's elbow in his ribs and, for half a second, he has no idea whose hand is on his collar.

The floor clears around them in seconds — it always does, the crowd sensing trouble the way a flock senses weather — and there is screaming from somewhere near the bar and the DJ has killed the music and then the doormen are there, four or five of them, wading in from the edges. Three of the group are on the floor by that point. The rest are being dragged. Keagan finds himself moving backward by one arm, which is fine, he's not fighting the doormen, there's no percentage in that.

They go out through the exit doors with a degree of ceremony. One or two of the doormen land their own contributions on the way, which is standard. The night air hits cold after the heat of inside.

～

THE MEXICAN IS WAITING. That's what everyone calls him — no one knows where the nickname came from and no one has ever asked to his face. He runs the door with an air of permanent mild disappointment in humanity, which, given his line of work, seems fair. He looks at Keagan and Danny the way a man looks at something that keeps coming back even after he's explained the situation.

'You two,' he says. 'What have I told you before?'

'Come and see you if there's trouble,' Keagan says.

'Exactly. So why didn't you?'

'They jumped us. We didn't get a chance.'

The Mexican looks at him with the expression of a man who has heard better. He looks at Danny, then back at Keagan. Several of the other lads are being dealt with further along the pavement, the doormen efficient and unsentimental about it.

'How many times is this?' he asks.

Keagan considers giving an honest answer and decides against it.

'This is the last time,' the Mexican says. 'You understand? Once more and you're barred. Both of you. That clear?'

'Yes, boss,' Keagan says.

'Now get out of here. You're not going back in tonight.'

'But I've only just got a pint.'

'Don't push it, son.'

Keagan nods, pauses, makes the face of a man who has just thought of something. 'Can you do me a favour?'

The Mexican looks at him. 'What?'

'My mate Peter — he's still inside, short bloke, quiet, you'll have seen him around. It's his birthday tonight, first time he's come out in ages. He'll be wondering where I am, he's not used to all this, he'll be worried. Could you just let him know I'm out here and I'll wait a few minutes if he wants to come out? I'd hate for him to think something's happened to me. He worries, you know how it is—'

The Mexican holds up a hand. 'Stop.'

Keagan stops.

'It's not his birthday,' the Mexican says.

'Well—'

'You've got one chance. One. You step on anybody's toe, look at anybody funny, breathe on anybody the wrong way, I'm putting you both out myself. Understood?'

'Completely,' Keagan says. 'Absolutely. Thank you.'

The Mexican shakes his head at something, probably his own judgment, and turns back to the door. Keagan and Danny follow him in.

THE MUSIC IS BACK UP, the floor already filling again. The group are around the table — Eddie back with reinforcements who arrived at least two minutes too late to be useful, which Keagan doesn't bother to mention. There is a brief and energetic reconstruction of events, everyone's version slightly more heroic than the last, Danny's version best of all.

Keagan comes to stand beside Peter.

Peter looks at him. The particular look — measured, unsurprised, taking in the general state of Keagan's evening. There is a small cut above his eyebrow that Keagan is going to have to explain to Emily tomorrow, and the side of his face is going to colour up by morning.

'What?' Keagan says.

Peter picks up his pint. 'How long did the talking take?'

'It would have worked if Danny had waited.'

'You thought that was going to work?'

'I always think it's going to work,' Keagan says. 'That's not the same thing as it working.'

Peter looks at the cut on his eyebrow with the clinical interest of someone assessing damage. 'Emily's going to love that.'

'I'll tell her I walked into something.'

'She's known you five minutes and she already knows you better than that.'

He thinks of George Callison in the doorway with the tea towel over his shoulder, saying make sure she gets home safely, and of Emily on the low wall outside Rossi's looking at him as if he was better than the stories around him. The cut above his eye began to sting more sharply. Keagan picks up his pint. The music has found its level again, the floor filling, the lights going, the whole machine of the evening restarting as if nothing interrupted it. That's the thing about a place like this — it absorbs everything and carries on. He can feel the side of his head beginning to settle into a proper ache.

'I need another drink,' he says.

'Your round,' Peter says.

'It's always my round.'

'Yes,' Peter says. 'It is, rather.'

Keagan looks at him — the dry expression, the slight satisfaction of the man who has made a fair point and knows it — and despite the aching head and the certain knowledge that Emily is going to have thoughts about this tomorrow, he starts to laugh.

'All right,' he says. 'Same again?'

'Please,' Peter says. 'And perhaps this time, no drama at the bar.'

He laughs because Peter is funny, and because Danny was already telling the story wrong, and because the music had started again and everyone around them seemed willing to pretend nothing had happened.

But when he touched the cut above his eyebrow, he thought of Emily's front gate clicking shut at two minutes to eleven, and the laugh thinned a little in his throat.

CHAPTER
SIX

I DON'T LIKE MONDAYS, MAY 1979

The O-level exams start next week and the mood off the bus reflects it — boys who normally larked about all the way from the stop are quiet, pale, shuffling through the gates with the hunted look of people who haven't done nearly enough revision. Keagan and Peter join the parade, neither of them immune to it entirely, though Keagan is rather better at pretending.

'Tonight though,' Keagan says, falling into step beside Peter. 'We need a plan for tonight.'

'I know the plan. We're going for a meal. Italian restaurant. Jenny's birthday.'

'I know that. I mean what are we doing after? Are we going back to hers? Going out after? Because if we're going out, I need to know now so I can tell Emily.'

'You could just ask Emily.'

'I'm asking you.'

'Then I don't know,' Peter says. 'I hadn't thought past the restaurant.'

'That's the difference between us. I think ahead.'

44

Peter gives him the look that particular statement deserves.

'You all right?' Keagan asks, because Peter has been quiet since the bus stop — not his usual quiet, which is thoughtful and dry, but somewhere else entirely.

'Yeah. I'm good.'

'You're doing the thing.'

'What thing?'

'The thing where you say you're fine and you're not.'

Peter is quiet for a moment. They pass through the school gates, joining the current of bodies moving towards the main entrance. 'Just thinking,' he says eventually.

'About Jenny?'

'She's not all I think about, you know.'

'Yes, she is.'

'Piss off.'

Keagan grins and slaps him across the back. 'Chippy at lunch, my treat.'

'It's about time you got them.'

'Bollocks, it's always my turn.' He holds the door open for Peter. 'Geography first. Mr Patterson's going to talk about sedimentary rock formations again, I can feel it in my bones.'

'Better than sitting in the library revising trigonometry,' Peter says.

'I'd take maths over Patterson and his bloody rocks any day.' Keagan shakes his head. 'Right, registration. Let's see what Miss Roslyn's wearing today.'

~

'BENNET.'

'Here, Miss.'

'Brown.'

'Here.'

'Chubb.'

'Here, Miss Roslyn.'

'Devlin.'

'Here, beautiful.'

She looks up over the top of her glasses. 'What have I told you, Devlin?'

'Sorry, Miss. It just slipped out.'

'Be careful before my ruler slips across your knuckles.' She shakes her head and looks back down at the register. 'Everett.'

'Here, Miss.'

'Fisk.'

~

THEY PART WAYS in the corridor — Peter towards the library, Keagan towards the new block and a double lesson of rocks. The morning moves at the pace mornings before exams always do, which is slowly and not without a low-level sense of dread. Keagan settles into the back row and does his best with Mr Patterson, who is indeed talking about sedimentary rock formations, and who has the particular gift of making interesting things seem less so.

~

IN THE LIBRARY, Peter can't concentrate.

He has his Maths textbook open in front of him but the numbers aren't landing. He reads the same line three times, puts the book down, picks it up again.

The problem isn't Maths. The problem is Jenny.

Not Jenny herself — Jenny is the best thing that's happened to him in a long time, maybe ever. Her house, her parents, the way she laughs. The pool in the garden that Keagan will never shut up about. The way she looks at him, which is the particular way he has wanted someone to look at him for longer than he can properly remember.

That's the problem.

He knows what he has to tell her. He knows his mother is right — that Jenny deserves to know the truth, that the longer he leaves it the worse it will be, that he is being unfair to her and to himself. He knows all of that. He's been arguing with his mum about it for the past week, coming home from Jenny's late and finding her waiting in the kitchen, not angry exactly, just concerned in the way that's harder to deal with than anger.

'Tell her, Peter. She needs to know.'

'I will, Mum.'

'When?'

He didn't have an answer for that. He still doesn't.

The thing is, it's all so good at the moment. Better than good. Once he tells her properly — not the careful half-truths, not the jokes, but all of it — everything changes. Maybe permanently. He doesn't want her pity and he's frightened of losing her care, and he knows those two things are not the same but they're tangled up together in a way he can't separate at quarter to nine in a school library.

He just wants a normal life. Not rich, not famous, nothing spectacular. Just normal. The ordinary future that everyone else seems to take for granted without even thinking about it. Marriage. A family. Planning ahead without a shadow across every plan.

It's not a lot to want.

From across the library comes the sound of laughter — the sharp, aimless laughter of people who aren't doing any revision either but are considerably less troubled by the fact. Martin Davis and his group have colonised the far corner, a loose arrangement of chairs and bags, rulers being deployed as catapults against anyone unfortunate enough to be within range.

Peter puts his head down and tries the Maths again.

'Oi, shrimp.'

He doesn't look up.

'Oi — catch this.'

He hears it before he sees it — a blue rubber, propelled with some force from a ruler, narrowly missing his head and hitting the shelf behind him with a crack.

Martin Davis is grinning across the room at him. The library assistant at the desk looks up, starts to say something, and thinks better of it.

'Send it back,' Martin calls.

'Get it yourself,' Peter says, and turns back to the page.

Martin crosses the room to retrieve it. Peter keeps his eyes on the textbook. He hears Martin stop beside him, can feel the proximity of him, and doesn't look up because looking up is what Martin wants and Peter has been in enough of these situations to know that much.

The blow comes without warning — a hard right hand across the back of his head, open-palmed but heavy enough that Peter goes off the chair and onto the floor, the chair scraping sideways, his books scattering. From across the room, the laughter starts.

Peter gets to his feet. His ears are ringing. His eyes are stinging and he forces that back, forces it down, because he is not going to cry in front of Martin Davis.

'You fucking bastard,' he says quietly.

'Where d'you think you're going, shrimp?' Martin says as Peter starts to gather his books.

'Leave me alone.'

'You're lucky I don't shove this up your arse, you bloody little queer boy.' Martin holds the rubber up in his face, close enough that Peter can smell the stale cigarette smoke on his jacket.

Peter picks up his textbook. He's not going to engage. He's going to leave and find somewhere else to revise, and then he is going to tell Keagan later and Keagan is going to — actually, Peter doesn't want Keagan to find out because he knows what will happen and he doesn't need that today of all days.

Martin's hand comes down on his shoulder, heavy, turning him.

GRAHAM DAVIES HAS BEEN WATCHING from near the door for the last two minutes, deciding what to do. He makes his decision.

He is across the corridor and through the connecting passage to the new block in under a minute, taking the stairs two at a time. Through the glass panel in the geography room door, he can see Keagan in the back row, who is — as ever — looking out of the window rather than at the board. Graham starts waving. It takes three attempts to get his attention. He points, makes the shape of it with his face, and watches Keagan stand up.

'Sir — can I just pop to the toilet?'

'Yes, Devlin. Be quick about it.'

The door opens. 'What's up?' Keagan says.

'It's Peter. Martin's started on him in the library. I thought you should know.'

Keagan is already moving.

~

He comes through the library doors at a run, taking in the room in one look — the cleared space, the crowd of boys bunched around the far corner, the shelf that's been pulled at an angle, the books on the floor. He goes through them the fast way, leapfrogging a table, shouldering through the last two boys who fall back without argument.

Martin has Peter by the collar, half-pinned across the table, his other hand around Peter's throat.

The sight of it — Peter's face, the fear there, the fact of it — trips something in Keagan that bypasses calculation entirely.

He grabs Martin by the back of his jacket and hauls him backwards. Martin stumbles, tries to spin, and Keagan's right hook is already moving — it connects with the side of his head and Martin goes sideways into the bookshelf.

'You all right?' Keagan says to Peter, who is standing now, steadying himself on the table.

Peter nods, shakily. He's not crying. He won't.

Keagan turns back. Martin has straightened up, his face already beginning to colour, something changed in his expression — less certainty in it now. He throws himself forward and Keagan steps to meet him, absorbing two punches to the body before getting Martin against the remaining shelves. Martin shoves back. They go down together, rolling, and Martin gets two or three punches into the side of Keagan's head, connecting solidly.

Keagan gets clear, back on his feet. He picks up the nearest metal library chair.

He doesn't think about it. He swings.

The chair catches Martin full across the side of the head. The sound of it is wrong — too loud, too hard. Martin goes backwards into the shelving unit and the whole thing comes down with him, the shelves collapsing, books cascading across the floor. Martin is down and trying to get up and not getting there.

Blood is running from his nose and there is a cut across his cheekbone, swelling already, and Keagan drags him upright by the tie and hits him again. And again. Martin's head is going back and forth with each punch and his legs have given out and it's only the tie keeping him vertical.

'Keagan.' Peter's voice. 'Keagan, stop.'

He hits him again.

'Keagan, stop. Stop!'

Martin's friends are shouting. The watching boys have gone quiet. Keagan pulls back his arm.

The crowd clears as if a single thought has passed through all of them at once, and Mr Watts comes through it the way he comes through rugby scrums — solid, fast, with absolute authority. His arms wrap around Keagan from behind, pinning his arms, lifting him off his feet, walking him backwards with the calm efficiency of a man who has done this before.

Martin collapses.

Keagan stops fighting it. The anger is draining out of him rapidly now, the way it always does, leaving him cold and slightly sick. Mr Watts sets him down on a chair and keeps one hand firmly on his shoulder.

'Out,' he says to the room. 'All of you. Now.'

The room empties. Keagan catches Peter's eye. He shakes his head once — *go, don't stay, get out of here* — and Peter goes.

Mr Watts crouches down beside Martin. He is unconscious but breathing. He checks him over with the methodical care of someone with first-aid training and calls for the school nurse, who arrives within two minutes and takes over with the quiet efficiency of a woman who has seen most things.

'Right,' Mr Watts says, standing. He takes Keagan by the arm — not rough, but not negotiating either. 'Come on, my boy.'

They move through the school hall, Keagan looking straight ahead.

'What the hell was that about?' Mr Watts says.

Keagan says nothing.

'I'm asking you. What happened in there?'

Silence.

Mr Watts shakes his head. He places Keagan in the chair outside the Headmaster's office with the practised positioning of a man who has delivered boys to this particular chair more times than he'd like. 'Don't move,' he says, and goes inside.

Keagan sits. Through the opaque glass panel in the door he can see the shapes of figures talking, Mr Watts gesturing. He looks at the wall opposite. There is a display about the school's sporting achievements, a mounted photograph of a rugby team from five years ago, a printed reminder about the examination schedule.

He knows what's coming. He's always known what's coming with things like this. He just didn't think it would be quite this bad.

THAT WAS FORTY-EIGHT HOURS AGO.

He's spent two days in the house, which is its own specific punishment — not because his mother shouts, but because she doesn't. Lizzie Devlin can do cold disappointment better than anyone Keagan has ever met, and she has been deploying it with precision since he got home that afternoon. She is not a woman who throws plates. She is a woman who puts your dinner in front of you without a word and goes back to the kitchen, and somehow that is worse.

He had missed Jenny's birthday meal. Peter had gone because Jenny deserved not to have the evening ruined as well, though from what Peter said on the phone it had been ruined anyway, quietly, under the table and behind every smile.

Emily had rung once. His mother had answered and told her Keagan was unavailable. Unavailable. As if he were a tradesman who had missed an appointment rather than a boy sitting in the front room with his knuckles split and his future folding in on itself.

Graham had sent word through Danny that he was sorry, though Keagan wasn't sure what for.

He spoke to Peter on the phone last night. Peter told him that Martin had been taken to hospital — nothing permanent, it seemed, but enough. The police had been at the school the following morning. Several of the boys from the library had been questioned, Peter among them.

'Don't worry about it,' Keagan had said.

'I'm worrying about it,' Peter said.

'It'll be all right.'

'Will it?'

'Yes,' Keagan said, with more confidence than he felt. 'His dad probably doesn't want the aggravation.'

'I shouldn't have let Graham come for you.'

'You didn't let him do anything.'

'I knew what would happen.'

'No you didn't.'

But neither of them knew whether that was true.

Peter hadn't said much after that. Neither had Keagan. The silence on the line was not comfortable.

HE IS SITTING in the same chair outside the Headmaster's office. His mother is beside him, not looking at him. She received the call from the school yesterday afternoon — a meeting requested, and no indication of the outcome. She has barely spoken to him since. She is wearing her good coat, which tells Keagan something about how seriously she is taking this, because Lizzie Devlin does not put on her good coat for just anything.

The door opens and Mr Wilson stands in it, gesturing them through. He takes his seat behind the large oak desk and offers them the two chairs opposite, which he does not say have been positioned there for this precise purpose but which clearly have been.

He does not waste time with preamble. Martin has been discharged from hospital. He is not yet back at school but is expected to return in time for the examinations. The police were involved in the immediate aftermath, but the boy's father has indicated that they do not wish to pursue the matter.

'That's something at least,' Lizzie says, quietly.

Mr Wilson continues. He explains the internal investigation — the boys spoken to, the accounts gathered. He acknowledges that the situation was not straightforwardly one-sided. He acknowledges that there were circumstances.

'However,' he says, and that word falls into the room and sits there. 'This type of behaviour cannot be tolerated. We have thought very carefully about the implications, and I want to be clear that this decision has not been taken lightly. But we have concluded that Keagan's expulsion must be permanent. He will not be permitted to sit his examinations next week. With immediate effect, he is no longer a pupil of this school.'

Lizzie sits very still for a moment. Then: 'You've made this decision without once asking Keagan for his account of what happened. How is that a fair process?'

'Mrs Devlin, I have personally spoken to every boy who was present in that library. I understand that Martin Davis's behaviour was not without fault. I understand there were mitigating factors.'

'Then—'

'There is nothing that could be said,' Mr Wilson continues, carefully, 'that would justify the harm Keagan caused to that boy. He hit him with a chair. He continued hitting him when he was unable to defend himself. If Mr Watts had arrived thirty seconds later, we might be having a very different conversation.' He pauses. 'I'm sorry. I know what this means. But there is nothing further that can be done. The governors have already confirmed the decision.'

Lizzie makes two more attempts. Keagan can hear her trying to find the angle that works, the argument that will land differently, and he watches Mr Wilson's expression and knows she won't find it. He is a fair man, Mr Wilson. That's the worst part, in a way. If he were unreasonable, there would be something to push against.

Keagan sits in silence and looks at the desk.

He knew it would be bad. He told himself suspension, told himself a few weeks, told himself it would be dealt with and they'd move on. He didn't think it would be this. The exams he hasn't revised for nearly enough but had believed he'd scrape through. Sixth form. The idea of staying on — vague, half-formed, more aspiration than plan, but there.

The kind of future that doesn't advertise itself until you're looking at it being taken away.

His mother glances at him. She is still angry — he can see it in the set of her shoulders, in the particular way she holds her jaw. But she feels it too, what this is. He knows she does.

Mr Wilson is talking about next steps, about contacting the local education authority, about other options. His voice has gone procedural, the kindness behind it doing its best within the formal structure of what has to be said.

Keagan stares at the oak desk and says nothing.

Outside, through the high window of the office, he can hear the sound of the school going about its morning — distant footsteps in a corridor, a bell, someone calling across a yard. The ordinary sounds of a place he is no longer part of. It is remarkable how quickly that can become past tense. Forty-eight hours ago he was in the back row of geography, thinking about chips at lunch and Jenny's birthday and what to do after the restaurant.

He thinks about Peter in that library. The look on his face.

He'd do it again. That's the honest truth of it, and he's not certain what that means about him.

He thinks he'd do it again.

CHAPTER

SEVEN

I GOT YOU BABE, JULY 1980

The holiday is booked for a Saturday check-in at Pontin's Little Canada on the Isle of Wight, though they are leaving on the Friday night because it is the only ferry crossing they could get at the height of the school holidays. This means an uncomfortable night's sleep is in store — in Keagan's car, a beige Mark II Cortina with the compulsory brown vinyl roof — and nobody is under any illusion about how glamorous it is going to be.

They set off with Keagan driving and Emily in the front as designated DJ. The excitement is genuine despite everything, because this will be their first holiday together. Emily and Jenny have prepared an itinerary, which runs to two sides of A4 and includes sensible allowances for rest periods between sightseeing visits, which Keagan has studied with the expression of a man confronting evidence of his own inadequacy.

They have been together for over a year now, all four of them so tangled up in each other's lives that Keagan's friends have started making pointed comments about it. He still has the occasional boys' night out with Danny, but mostly he is at Emily's in the evenings, her parents

55

having reached the pragmatic arrangement of allowing him to stay over on the sofa if he is working early the next day. Peter barely joins the nights out at all any more, preferring to spend every available minute with Jenny, which Keagan takes every available opportunity to mock him about while doing exactly the same thing with Emily.

Planning the holiday had not been entirely friction-free. Danny and a few of the lads were going to Ibiza that same week, and whilst Keagan had made clear he would not be going, Danny had kept at it. Then Keagan had made the additional mistake of mentioning to Emily — once, briefly, with what he would later describe as catastrophically poor timing — that they might consider moving their week so he could do both. He had recognised the error the moment the words left his mouth. Emily had received them with the particular silence that is considerably worse than any argument.

～

THEY BOARD the Red Funnel ferry at Southampton and park the car on the lower deck. Going up to the upper deck to see the lights, Peter announces he needs the toilets and heads off with Jenny to the rear of the boat, leaving Keagan and Emily at the front rail.

The night is clear enough now after the earlier rain, and the lights of Southampton shimmer across the wet estuary. Keagan puts his arm around Emily, feels her shiver, and takes his jacket off without comment, draping it across her shoulders. She takes his hand and turns back to the water.

'Looking forward to it?' he asks, reaching to tuck a strand of hair behind her ear that the wind immediately retrieves.

'Very much. I wasn't sure for a while if you actually wanted to come. You'd gone quiet about it, and with the Ibiza business I thought you might be regretting the choice.'

'It wasn't really a choice, was it.' He says it without resentment. 'I just didn't want Danny to think I'd abandoned him. He wanted me there to back him up, mainly. Stop him doing something stupid.' He pauses. 'Or possibly join him in doing something stupid, I'm still not entirely sure.'

'Yes, and the two of you would've ended up in a Spanish prison.' She is not laughing when she says it.

'We don't go looking for trouble.'

'I know. It finds you.'

'Yeah,' Keagan says. 'That's going to change, though. I mean it.' He turns to look at her. 'I want to do better, Em. For you, for us. I want you to be proud of me.'

'You idiot,' she says, pulling him in, standing up on her toes. 'I am proud of you. Just work on the temper and you're perfect.'

They stand there for a moment in the dark with the wind coming off the water.

'Peter worries about you, you know,' she says.

'I know. You'd think he had enough on his plate.' He shakes his head, but without irritation. 'He's the most thoughtful person I know, honestly. Don't ever tell him I said that.'

'I wouldn't dare.'

Peter and Jenny reappear from behind them, slightly wind-battered, and the conversation turns to the practical question of where to sleep for the night once they are off the ferry. The girls are emphatic on this point: somewhere well-lit, somewhere with people about, not a country lane and certainly not a woodland car park.

'There's a twenty-four-hour petrol garage about a mile from the terminal,' Keagan offers. 'Nice and bright. Lots of foot traffic.'

Jenny clips him round the back of the head.

Peter watches this with quiet satisfaction.

AFTER A NIGHT of almost no sleep — the storm that descends on the island in the small hours turns out to be the worst the place has seen in years, and the inside of a Cortina is not designed to accommodate four adults and four bags with any dignity — they pull through the entrance to the holiday camp as a pale, exhausted, slightly damp unit.

The reception building is tired yellow brick with a large circular grass area in front of it, dominated by a twenty-foot totem pole that announces the Canadian theme with some commitment. The car park is around the side. The check-in woman behind the desk has the careful brightness of someone who has processed a great many arrivals and knows that the first hour matters.

Peter and Jenny receive the keys to Ottawa. Keagan and Emily are in the adjoining chalet, Winnipeg. They collect the bags from the car and wait for the tractor-pulled train, which circuits the camp every twenty minutes and is the primary mode of transport between the main complex and the chalets. It is open-sided. The rain, which had paused briefly for their arrival, resumes.

They sit huddled in the middle of the carriage, bags on laps, watching the rain come in through the sides.

'Ibiza wasn't necessarily a terrible idea,' Keagan says.

Emily clips him round the ear. That is two in under twenty-four hours.

'God, does everyone think it's fine to hit me around the head?' he says.

'We're trying to stimulate the brain cell,' Jenny says. 'It doesn't seem to function independently.'

THE CHALETS ARE small but clean and smell of damp wood and someone else's suntan lotion. Once they have unpacked — a process Keagan completes in approximately four minutes by the method of leaving everything in the bag and pushing it under the bed — they make their way to the main complex for an early lunch and to look at what the week has in store.

The complex is built around a large main hall: tables at one end, a stage at the other, a dance floor in between. The restaurant to the side does all the included meals and doubles as a snack bar during the day, with a separate ice-cream counter for the children, which is clearly already the most popular attraction on the site.

They get sandwiches and sit down.

'So,' Peter says, looking at the activities board. 'What are we thinking?'

'I'm not getting on that stage,' Keagan says. 'And I'm not dressing up.'

Emily looks at Jenny. 'He's never minded before.'

'That rules out most of the evening entertainment, then,' Peter says. 'Sports?'

'I'm up for the football, but I'll be on my own for that one, so probably not worth it. Honestly, I'd quite like to just take it easy. Sit by the pool when the rain stops.'

'We could go to The Needles one day,' Jenny says. 'There's a cable car. I've always wanted to do it.'

'Agreed,' Emily says, before anyone can object.

They finish their lunch and agree on a quiet first afternoon — a walk around the camp, early dinner, a drink at the bar. They are moving back through the hall towards the exit when Keagan slows.

At a round table near the stage, a family are watching two young girls perform. The girls are about eight and nine, flushed with effort and very much in earnest, doing a full song-and-dance routine for an audience of two beaming parents who are providing enthusiastic applause at every available moment. The elder of the two notices them watching, leans in to whisper to her sister, and then both of them come running over.

'Hello,' says the elder girl, with the direct confidence of someone who has been going to stage school long enough to treat every room as a venue. 'My name's Gracie. Would you come and watch us? We'd like to know what you think.'

The four of them look at each other.

'Course we would,' Emily says.

The parents — Nick and Kathy, from Leeds, on their second week — make room at the table and introductions are done. Kathy explains, with the fond exasperation of a woman well accustomed to this situation, that the girls had missed the talent show in the first week because the family were out for the day and didn't get back in time.

'They'll never forgive us if we don't let them enter this time,' she says. 'I'm sorry they dragged you over. As parents, our opinion on the matter stopped counting some time ago.'

'Not at all,' Emily says. 'We'd love to see it.'

The girls launch into their rendition of It's a Hard Knock Life from Annie, complete with choreography. They are genuinely good — precise, committed, entirely serious about it.

'They go to a stage school at home,' Nick says, watching them with poorly concealed pride. 'They love it. We get a lot of shows at home, to be honest. Our opinion doesn't count either.' He grins. 'Nice to have outside witnesses.'

The performance ends. Everyone claps properly. The younger girl — Josephine — makes a beeline for Keagan and climbs directly onto his lap.

'What do you think?' she asks him. 'Can we win?'

'Without a doubt,' Keagan says, and his tone is so straightforward about it that Josephine looks briefly satisfied in the way that only the very young and the very certain can manage. She and Gracie then embark on a joint explanation of all the other songs they had considered for the show, a list that goes on for some time and includes several titles Keagan has never heard of, delivered with the assumption that he will find this as fascinating as they do.

He sits there listening to them with his full attention.

Kathy watches this and turns to Emily. 'He's a natural with them.'

'He's got nieces and nephews at home,' Emily says.

'What about you?'

Emily smiles. 'Hopes,' she says.

Kathy holds her gaze for a moment with the warmth of a woman who understands exactly what that word is doing in that sentence. 'Well. You seem like a lovely couple.'

'Keagan,' Peter says across the table, in the tone of someone who has been waiting for the right moment. 'You should enter the show.'

'I told you, I'm not dressing up.'

'That's not what I mean. There's a piano over there. Why don't you have a go?'

Keagan shakes his head. He is trying to deflect it, playing it down, but Gracie and Josephine have caught the word piano and they are not letting it go. Both of them are now looking at him with an attention that cannot simply be declined.

'I've never heard you play,' Emily says. She keeps her voice light, but she means it.

He looks at the piano at the side of the stage. He looks at Emily. He looks at Josephine on his lap, who is watching him with complete confidence in the outcome.

'One tune,' he says. 'And I choose what.'

Gracie and Josephine immediately begin shouting requests. He stands up with Josephine under one arm and carries her over to the piano, fetching a second stool for both girls to perch on beside him. He sits down, finds the keys, runs a quiet scale. Settles himself.

He glances back at Emily across the room.

Then he turns to the piano and plays.

The opening bars of the Moonlight Sonata move across the hall with an ease and control that makes the sound feel inevitable, as though the piano has been waiting for it. It is not showy. He plays at a measured pace, patient with the music, letting it breathe.

The handful of people scattered around the hall go quiet. A woman near the bar turns to look. Kathy puts her hand on Nick's arm without seeming to notice she has done it.

Emily does not move.

She has known about the piano in the abstract — Peter mentioned it once, said he was good, but Keagan never spoke of it himself and she had filed it away as one of those things she would ask him about eventually, when the moment was right. This moment was not planned. There was nothing strategic about it. He is just sitting there at the piano in a Pontin's holiday camp on the Isle of Wight, completely absorbed, playing Beethoven for two girls from Leeds and a handful of strangers, and it is the most completely himself she has ever seen him look.

Jenny touches her arm. 'I didn't know he could actually play,' she says quietly. 'I mean really play.'

Emily nods. She doesn't trust herself to say much more than that.

Across the table, Peter sits back in his chair. He is not surprised — he has always known this about Keagan, or known that there was something like this in him, some whole different dimension that Keagan keeps to himself, that he protects the same way he protects everything he cares about, which is by pretending it does not exist. The music gives a small glimpse of it. Not the loudness and the temper and the jokes, not the jacket thrown across someone's shoulders in the dark — but this. The part of Keagan that is still and careful and knows exactly what he is doing.

Peter glances over at Emily and sees what is on her face and looks away again, giving her the moment privately.

Josephine is sitting very still beside Keagan on the stool, watching his hands on the keys with total concentration. Gracie, on the other side, has her arms folded on the top of the piano and her chin resting on them, looking at him as though she is filing all of this away for future reference.

The music fills the hall. Rain taps at the windows of the complex and somewhere outside the tractor-train is making its circuit of the camp, but in here it is just this.

Keagan finishes the piece quietly, letting the final chord settle before lifting his hands. There is a pause — the kind that means something — and then the room applauds. Not a huge crowd, just a dozen people at most, but they are clapping properly, and Nick from Leeds puts two fingers to his teeth and lets out a whistle that echoes off the ceiling.

Josephine looks up at Keagan. 'That was beautiful,' she announces.

'Cheers,' Keagan says.

He lifts Josephine off the stool, sets her down on the floor, and walks back over to where Emily is sitting. He drops back into his chair and picks up his coffee cup with the carefully casual air of a man who has not just revealed something.

Emily looks at him.

'You never told me,' she says.

'You never asked.'

'I didn't know there was anything to ask.'

He shrugs, turns the cup in his hands. But he is almost smiling, and she can see it.

She reaches across the table and puts her hand over his. He doesn't pull away. He turns his hand over and holds hers.

Peter watches the two of them for a moment and says nothing.

Outside, the rain begins to ease.

CHAPTER

EIGHT

WOMAN, JULY 1980

Leaving the girls to get ready, Keagan and Peter walk down to the main complex for an early drink. The entertainment area has that particular holiday camp quality of having been cheerful once and never quite recovered — light wood panelling, aged plastic fittings, carpets that have absorbed the memories of several thousand families. They order two pints of Foster's and settle on bar stools at the end of the bar.

It is early enough that the place is still half-empty. Two men who look as though they have spent the entire rainy day on their stools are working hard for the attention of the barmaid, who is young, quite attractive, and visibly unimpressed. Around the tables, families are dressed up for early dinner — tired parents in clean shirts, children in holiday clothes already comprehensively stained, running between the tables with the energy of people who have been cooped up all day and intend to make the most of the evening.

Keagan lights a cigarette and reaches across for the ashtray.

'What do you think of it?' Peter asks.

'Looks all right. Needs a bit of paint.' He takes a long pull on his pint. 'How are you doing anyway?'

'Yeah, I'm good. Had a rough couple of weeks but got through it.'

'You weren't in hospital?'

'Just for physio. To clear the lungs.' He glances across and notices Keagan's glass is nearly empty already. 'Blimey, mate. You in a race?'

'Lots of practice,' Keagan says, grinning.

'My shout, but I'm only getting one for you. I'll be on the floor if I try to keep up.'

Peter attracts the barmaid's attention and orders another pint. As she pours, she leans forward slightly and looks at Keagan.

'Arrived today, 'ave you?' West Country accent, warm with it.

'Last night, on the ferry,' Keagan says. 'Hoping the weather's going to improve.'

'They say middle of the week. Where you from?'

'Essex.'

She sets the glass down and rests her elbows on the bar. 'I've heard all about you Essex boys. Think I'll have to keep an eye on you.'

'Don't believe everything you hear.'

'That's not what I've heard.'

'How much is that?' Peter says.

'Sixty pence, darling.' She is still looking at Keagan. 'Anything else?'

'No thanks,' Peter says, and picks up the pint and steers them both towards a nearby table.

'I don't think chatting up the barmaid is going to go down brilliantly,' he says as they sit.

'I wasn't. She was coming on to me.'

'Yeah, probably. I'm just saying. You're not in Ibiza with Danny.'

'Christ, Peter. What are you, my mum?'

Peter just shakes his head.

They sit for a moment. The Barry Manilow coming out of the speakers is not improving things.

'Listen,' Keagan says. 'I've got something to tell you before the girls get here.'

'All right.'

'I've signed up.'

Peter looks at him. 'Signed up. The RAF?'

'The Army. Parachute Regiment.'

There is a pause.

'Shit, mate,' Peter says. 'You never talked about the army. Why?'

'I want to get sorted. I don't want to be on building sites my whole life. It's fine now but I need more than that. This gives me a career, good training, options for the future.'

'You could sit your O-levels. Get into the RAF like you always wanted.'

'What school would take me? I messed it up, remember.'

'I'm sure one would,' Peter says. 'You could do an extra year in sixth form. Others have done it.'

'Nah. I want to do this.'

'You want to get shot at?'

'It's peacetime, Peter. It's training and skills and a career path. That's all.'

'It's not peaceful in Northern Ireland. Sixteen soldiers died there last month. Paras.'

Keagan says nothing.

'I've joined,' he says after a moment. 'I wanted to tell you first. I'm going to tell Emily tonight, and I was hoping you might back me up a bit. The odd "sounds like a good idea" would help. I know I'll be away at first, but eventually — when we're more settled, maybe married — we'd have a proper home, a future.'

'Of course I'll back you up,' Peter says. 'I'm just not convinced it's the right thing. Discipline and following orders have never exactly been your strong points, and I believe they're quite keen on those in the army.' He raises an eyebrow. 'But whatever you decide, I'm with you. You know that.'

'Cheers.' Keagan stands. 'And they really need to sort out the music. Another pint?'

'Yeah, go on then.'

Keagan walks over to the bar and catches the eye of the barman this time, ordering two pints. As he waits, the door opens and Emily and Jenny come in. They look around, spot him at the bar.

'What are you having?' he calls across the room.

'So much for a quiet entrance,' Jenny says to Emily.

'White wine spritzers,' Emily calls back, 'lots of ice.' They make their way over to Peter's table.

Keagan returns with four drinks on a tray, sits down next to Emily, pulls his chair in close and tells her she looks beautiful tonight.

'And you, Jenny,' he adds.

'What have you two been talking about?' Jenny asks.

Peter glances at Keagan.

'Right,' Keagan says. 'No time like the present.' And with Peter providing measured support beside him, he breaks the news. He explains, as clearly and reasonably as he can manage, that the army is not dangerous in peacetime, that the training and skills he will gain will stand him in good stead, that this is about building a future, not throwing one away. Throughout, he watches Emily's face for a reaction. He gets none. He had expected her to be unhappy at first, but he had also thought that once he explained the reasoning she would see it for what it was. Now, watching her stillness, he is less certain.

'So you'll be living at home still?' she says.

'Well — no. I start at Catterick. Basic training. Then Abingdon for Parachute training after that.'

'And after that?'

'Aldershot.'

'So we won't get a lot of time together.'

'Basic is eight weeks. We get leave most weekends.'

'Oh, Keagan.' She looks at him. 'The army. Why?'

'It's good training, Em, the money's decent, and after the first stretch it sets us up properly. People come out of the forces and get great jobs — companies value military experience.'

'He's right,' Peter says, doing his best. 'It's a genuine career path.'

Emily says nothing more. She gets up from the table quietly, without a word, and walks straight out through the door to the beer garden.

'Well,' Jenny says. 'That went brilliantly.'

'Give it a rest,' Keagan says.

'Why didn't you talk to her about it before you went and signed up? Oh — wait. Maybe because she might have said it wasn't a good idea?'

She looks at him steadily. 'Are you going after her, or would you like me to sort out your mess?'

'Jen, leave it,' Peter says, and Keagan is already on his feet.

Outside, Emily is sitting on one of the wooden benches in the beer garden, her arms folded, looking away. Keagan sits down next to her, a little sheepishly. He touches her arm.

'I'm sorry. I didn't mean to upset you.'

She turns to look at him and her eyes are bright. 'These aren't upset tears, Keagan. These are anger tears. Don't confuse the two. How dare you.'

'I'm sorry.'

'There it is again. Sorry fixes it all, does it? How about thinking first, before you do something that affects the people who care about you? It's not about the army. It's about doing it without a word to me. And then telling me on the first night of our holiday with Peter and Jenny sitting there.'

'I thought once I explained, you'd see it made sense. I don't want to be a builder my whole life. This is a way to better myself. It's for us, Em.'

'It's not my place to tell you what to do with your life. I don't want that. I just want to be part of it — which means you give me the chance to talk about things that affect us both.' She pauses. 'For what it's worth, I don't think it's a completely terrible idea. But it's the army, Keagan. Will you have to go to Northern Ireland?'

'Paras do tend to get posted there, yeah. It'd be luck of the draw.'

She closes her eyes briefly. 'I wish you'd talked to me. We might have thought about the RAF — I know you've always wanted that, and I'm sure if you put your mind to it you could sit the exams.'

'Peter thinks the same. But be honest with yourself, Em. I'm working class. When are they going to let someone like me fly a fighter jet? It's always been the dream, and maybe I'm bright enough, but I'm also a realist. People like me don't get to be officers and pilots. In the army it's different — you're respected for what you do, not who your father is. I want this.' He looks at her properly. 'And I want you to be happy for me. I want this to be the start of something real for us. The married quarters are meant to be very nice actually.' He lets that land carefully.

'If that's a proposal, first: you can do it properly, not as a throwaway comment. And second: if you think I'm living on an army base in the middle of nowhere, you are very much mistaken, Keagan Devlin. Not a chance.'

'Message received,' he says, and pulls her into a hug. 'I'll be safe. I promise.'

'No, you won't. You'll be the first one to take risks — that's just who you are. But maybe being in the military will teach you something about discipline and following the rules.' She rests her head against his shoulder. 'I hope so. Now let's get back in there and face the music.'

'What does that mean, exactly?'

'It means I might forgive you before the week's out. Jenny won't.'

He considers this. 'How long are we talking?'

'A very long time.'

They go back inside together. The jukebox is playing Fantasy by Earth, Wind & Fire, and Keagan dances his way back to the table, which earns him a look of pure disbelief from Jenny and a quiet smile from Peter.

Jenny watches him sit down. Her expression says everything.

'Another round?' Keagan asks.

'Just a half,' Peter says.

'Lightweight.'

'Bloody navvy.'

'You cut me to the bone.'

Before he goes to the bar, Keagan leans across and kisses Emily, then turns and pulls Jenny into a hug. She reacts as though she has been grabbed by something unpredictable and vaguely damp.

'He is far too tactile,' she says to Emily, once she has recovered herself.

'It's the Irish in him,' Peter says. 'He hugs my mum when he comes round.'

'He hugs my mum,' Emily says, laughing. 'And my dad.'

'Your dad lets him?' Jenny says.

'My dad loves him,' Emily says. 'Which tells you everything.'

~

THEY LEAVE BEFORE CLOSING, the previous night's crossing finally catching up with all of them. Keagan guides Emily back to the chalet by the hand, and the cold air hits them the moment they're through the door. They stand there looking at each other.

'Right,' Keagan says. 'Pyjamas and jumpers, or just sleep in what we're wearing?'

The heater on the wall is a dial and a mystery. He crouches in front of it for a couple of minutes, turning the dial experimentally, achieving nothing of consequence. Emily watches him from behind.

'Bathroom first?' she says.

'Go on then.' He has another go at the heater dial. It clicks once and then is silent.

The evening had turned out much better than it had started. Over dinner, Emily had softened — not surrendered, but thought it through and found a version of it she could live with. Even Jenny had been grudgingly less hostile by the end of the night, though she had made sure Keagan understood that her generosity was not to be mistaken for approval. Peter had been, as always, steadfast and warm in his support — so convincing, in fact, that Keagan had left the bar feeling more certain about his decision than when he had walked in.

Emily comes out of the bathroom. She is wearing a new nightdress, dark red silk, and she is already shivering in the bathroom doorway.

'Can you get me a jumper out of the drawer?'

'I don't think so,' he says.

She laughs, grabs the nearest pillow and throws it at him, then makes a run for the bed, diving under the covers in one movement.

'Your turn,' she says from underneath them.

'That's not fair.'

'Bathroom. Go.'

He goes. When he comes back she has resurfaced from beneath the covers, and she is watching him with that particular expression that means the argument is over.

'So,' she says. 'Where are you planning to sleep?'

'Well. I could take the sofa.' He looks at it. It is small, stained in ways that suggest a long and complicated history, and lists slightly to the left.

'Although I don't think I'd survive it. I'm fairly sure something is living in it.'

'Then you'd better be nice to me.'

'I'm always nice.'

'Huh,' she says, which covers a lot of ground.

He sits on the edge of the bed and she lifts the covers to let him in, which he takes as the full amnesty it is. The room is cold enough that they press together without ceremony, and after a while the cold stops mattering.

He brushes her hair away from her face. In the low light from the bedside lamp, he looks at her properly.

'I love you, Emily Callison,' he says. 'I always will.'

She looks back at him for a moment before she answers. 'I know,' she says, quietly. Then, softer: 'I love you too.'

They had come into this relationship knowing very little about love and finding their way as they went, and their time together had always been rushed — someone's house, someone's parents downstairs, always half an ear on the door. Tonight is different. Tonight there is no one to listen for, no particular hurry, no interruption waiting in the hallway. She feels it, and she wants the night to be different. To stay in it.

He is careful with her. Patient in a way she is not always sure he knows how to be, and the surprise of it stays with her. Afterwards, they lie together in the cold little chalet with the wind still moving outside, and he holds her as though he has no intention of going anywhere.

They talk for a long time in the dark — about the future, about what comes next, about the shape of things once basic training is done. He talks about what he wants for them. She listens, and she lets herself believe it.

At some point he falls asleep mid-sentence. She lies there for a little while longer, listening to him breathe, looking at the ceiling.

She reaches across and turns off the lamp.

She knows he is not perfect. She has never needed him to be. She loves him for what he reaches for, not what he always manages to be, and in the dark she makes her peace with that again, as she has before, and as she expects she will again.

She closes her eyes.
Whatever comes next, she thinks, they will get through it.

CHAPTER

NINE

TOTAL ECLIPSE OF
THE HEART, APRIL 1982

Leaving Bank station and walking up Threadneedle Street, Emily feels the nerves churning in her stomach. She is excited about starting the new role — genuinely, properly excited — but the anxiety is there too. How will the day go? What will the people be like? All the usual concerns of a first morning, amplified by the fact that she feels, underneath everything, a little lonely. Keagan has been tied up with extra training for the past few weeks and has not been home, and she is missing him more than she would readily admit. The news that Peter and Jenny have decided to live together and are currently looking for a flat together only adds to it. Everyone is moving on to the next thing. Today, she supposes, so is she.

She spent the last eighteen months working within the training facility at Allie Street, and the transfer she has worked for has finally come through. She would work out of one of the City of London branches, and although it is a probationary move, it puts her exactly where she wanted to be: the Investment Division.

72

She sees the sign above the imposing Edwardian building ahead of her. NatWest. She pauses on the pavement, takes a breath, and goes in.

At the reception desk she introduces herself and explains it is her first day. The two women behind the desk welcome her warmly, and the younger of them — Patricia, she says her name is — comes around the front and takes Emily through a substantial set of oak doors marked Staff Only. Patricia has an easy, friendly manner, and Emily likes her immediately. She is from the west of London by the sound of her voice, wearing a conservative floral dress with a pink cardigan tied loosely around her shoulders, her blonde hair long with a slight wave that frames a pretty face. Emily makes a mental note to ask her where she shops.

Patricia taps a code into the entry pad, takes her through the back offices and into the staff room, which runs the length of the building behind frosted glass panels and is bright enough to feel welcoming. A small group of staff are gathered around the tea area, catching up on their weekends. Patricia brings Emily over, introduces her as the new girl and asks everyone to help her settle in.

The group seems pleasant enough. As they exchange names and small talk, Emily notices a young man standing slightly to the side of the group — mid-twenties, she would guess, wearing an immaculate blue pinstripe suit and black shoes. His hair is dark brown, almost black. There is a confidence about him in the way he holds himself, the way the others respond to him, and after a moment he steps across and extends his hand.

'Hi, Emily. I'm Stephen. Stephen Thompson. Good to meet you.'

She catches the briefest flicker from Patricia — a slight smirk, eyes going briefly skyward — and files it away. She takes his hand carefully.

'Hello, Stephen. Good to meet you too.'

'You've been assigned to my team, I believe. Mr Gibbons is our manager — he's all right, but a bit old school. If you need to know how things actually work, I'm always about.'

'Thank you.' She withdraws her hand.

'So where are you from?'

'Barkingside. Grew up there.'

'Oh, you're practically near me — I'm in Upminster. East End, both of us. That makes three now, with John in accounts.'

'Right,' Emily says, not entirely sure what he is getting at, and not sufficiently curious to ask.

'Anyway, good to meet you. I've got a meeting now, but we'll catch up later.' He moves off.

She watches him go. There is something about the way he looked at her — not quite right, though she could not explain it precisely — and she makes a note of it.

Patricia appears at her elbow. 'You've met Stephen, then.' The tone has a follow-up built into it.

'Yes. Should I know something?'

'Just — be careful of him. Don't be taken in by the charm. Trust me, it's only skin deep.'

Emily nods. There is clearly more to that statement, and she would like to hear it, but not today. She follows Patricia towards her department and gets to work.

~

ON THE PACKED UNDERGROUND HEADING BACK from barracks, Keagan is looking forward to his weekend at home. He has not managed to get back much over the past few weeks — there has been extra training to sit, and he is working towards his Lance Corporal stripe, which takes up time he would rather spend elsewhere. He is looking forward to seeing Emily. They speak on the telephone almost every day, but it is not the same, and the distance shows in both of them at times, in the shortness that creeps into their voices when one of them is tired.

He is sitting in his combats, quietly reading the Evening Standard along with what appears to be most of the carriage. The cover story stops him.

Argentine forces today invaded the Falkland Islands, a Government broadcast in Buenos Aires announced.

Like most of the people around him, his first thought is that the Falkland Islands are somewhere off the coast of Scotland. The article sets him straight quickly enough — eight thousand miles away, off the

Argentine coast, disputed territory for over a hundred years. The invasion has apparently taken almost everyone by surprise.

He reads on, turning the pages, looking for more detail: the scale of the invasion, the political response, what might happen next. Whether there will be a war. Whether he might be involved. It will be cold down there, he thinks, which strikes him immediately as an odd thing to notice first.

As the train pulls in towards Gants Hill, the man sitting opposite gets up. Middle-aged, compact, the quiet look of ex-military about him. He pauses on his way to the doors and looks at Keagan's combats, then at the newspaper in his hands.

'Go and give them hell, son,' he says.

'Yes, sir,' Keagan says. He is not entirely sure whether that is his conditioned army response or something he actually means. He suspects both.

He folds the paper and stares at the seat back in front of him as the train pulls away again. He has a tour of Northern Ireland scheduled later in the year. He has never joined for a war — no one in peacetime really does — but he is honest enough with himself to recognise the feeling sitting in his chest now, and it is not entirely dread.

Peter has the deckchairs out on the patio. They are sitting with cans of Foster's, the April evening carrying a slight chill, while Emily and Jenny are in the pool. Jenny's parents are away for the weekend, and with the house to themselves Jenny has had the heating at maximum since they arrived. The pool is warm enough; it is the sitting out here in the cold that is the question, but neither of them has moved.

'So will we go to war?' Peter asks.

'I think we might. Normally something like this gets sorted diplomatically before it comes to that, but it's Maggie. She won't stand for this.'

'Will they send you?'

'Most likely a Marine-led operation, I would have thought. If she goes all-out, there's a chance — Three Para are on standby — but we're still scheduled for Northern Ireland later in the year.'

'Good,' Peter says.

'Yeah.'

Peter watches him from behind his can of Foster's. He knows Keagan well enough to read the conflict in his face — the part of him that would want to be involved, because it is what he has trained for, sitting alongside the part of him that is thinking about Emily. He does not press it.

'Have you found a flat yet?' Keagan asks, shifting ground.

'Think so. There's a conversion in Ilford — quite nice, not too far from everyone. If we can get it, we'd be moving in next month.'

'That's brilliant. Your mum all right with it?'

'She likes Jenny, but no, not really. I expected that. She just wants to keep me close so she can look after me. I understand why. But it's something Jenny and I need to do.' He pauses. 'I don't know how long I have, and we don't want to waste time we don't need to.'

'Don't think like that,' Keagan says. 'The advances they're making in medicine — who knows. You'll probably outlive me, like you said.'

'That was before you took up soldiering as a hobby. You still smoke. You're potentially going off to fight a war.' Peter considers this. 'Yeah, all right. Scrub what I said. I'll definitely outlive you.'

The doors slide open and Jenny and Emily appear with towels around their shoulders, deciding they are beginning to wrinkle.

'Who's going to war?' Jenny says.

'Nobody. We were talking about the Falklands.'

'Is there going to be a war?'

'Who knows,' Keagan says, a fraction too quickly.

Jenny gives him a look but lets it go. The girls disappear inside to change, and Keagan and Peter carry on talking about the flat — what needs doing, who could help, Keagan offering his family if there is any work to be done. Peter is hoping the conversion company will deliver what they have promised and it will be ready to move into. Within a few minutes the girls are back with takeaway menus and they spread them out on the garden table, arguing cheerfully about Chinese versus Indian until the Chinese wins by two votes and a veto.

~

THE MV NORLAND sits at dock, twenty-seven thousand tons of North Sea ferry doing its best to look purposeful. Two temporary helicopter decks have been bolted to the rear. She still has the look of something that usually carries lorries and package tourists across the English Channel. Today she will carry Two Para south.

Lance Corporal Marks stands beside Keagan on the dock, looking up at her.

'We're Paras,' Marks says. 'We're supposed to drop out of the bloody sky. What are we doing boarding a ferry? That's for the Marines. Those lot always arrive second.'

'We really do need to work on your vocabulary,' Keagan says.

'Get stuffed with your posh London talk.'

Keagan laughs and shakes his head, turning away from Marks to scan the crowds. He knows Emily is in there somewhere, along with Peter and Jenny. Emily had rung last night to say she had booked the day off work, her line manager unhappy about it but not happy enough to actually stop her. Peter was driving them down to Portsmouth during the early hours.

The crowds are enormous. Thousands of people pressed together on the dockside — relatives, friends, well-wishers who have come simply to show up and be counted, to wave off the men the papers have been calling their heroes all week. Finding three specific faces in this is not a realistic proposition.

Marks grabs his shoulder. 'Come on, Devlin. Time to board. You've got the whole voyage to stare into the distance.'

Nobody came to see Marks off, Keagan notices, but keeps the observation to himself. He picks up his gear and heads for the gangplank, already streaming with troops.

The civilian crew who welcomes them aboard are volunteers, he has been told — the original Norland crew, who chose to stay on for this rather different crossing. Normally she carries freight and businessmen and families starting their holidays. Today the corridors smell of kit and boot polish and something underneath that no one is naming.

He leaves his kit at the bunk he has been assigned and makes his way up to the top deck, where colleagues are already three-deep at the barriers, all of them doing the same thing he is doing — leaning out, scanning faces, trying to find one particular person in the impossible crowd below. He reads the homemade banners. He watches people laughing and crying at the same time, the way people do when they do not know what else to do with their faces.

He has not felt nervous until now. Standing here, ship engines beginning to pulse below his feet, he feels it properly for the first time.

THEY SET off from Ilford in the middle of the night, Peter at the wheel, and arrive on the outskirts of Portsmouth to find traffic barely moving on every approach road into the town. They follow the signs for the docks, crawling forward in a long, slow queue, and at the dock entrance run into barriers, diversion signs, parking signs directing them away from the waterfront and into what appears to be an industrial estate. A man in a high-visibility jacket waves them into a space at the far end of a large car park.

They walk back towards the docks with a stream of other people, all of them heading the same way.

'You all right, Em?' Peter says as they turn the corner and the entrance to the Naval Dockyard comes into view.

'She's fine,' Jenny says, which is the kind of answer that is not an answer.

Emily had been quiet for most of the drive down, sharing the odd quiet moment with Jenny in the back seat, and Peter had left them to it. He knows what she is carrying. He also knows she is right about Keagan — he had tried to reassure her on the phone last week, telling her that Two Para were the backup regiment and that it was unlikely they would see real action. She had told him, gently, that he should know better, and she was not wrong.

He keeps that to himself now and steers them through the security checkpoint.

They follow the signs for visitors, joining the compressed mass of people being channelled along the dockside to a temporary observation area. From behind the safety barriers they can see the bow of the Norland across the water.

'How are we going to see him in all of this?' Jenny says.

'Get the banner out,' Peter says.

Jenny reaches into her bag and pulls out the sign they put together on the kitchen table the night before — a bedsheet, really, with the words painted on in black emulsion because it was the only paint in the house. It is not elegant, but it is large.

The ship's horn sounds, loud enough to feel in the chest. The ropes are hauled back. The horns of every vessel in the dock seem to answer at once, a vast, clattering echo, and the crowd on the dockside erupts — cheering, waving, shouting names into the noise. On the decks above, the troops shout back.

Emily holds one end of the banner. Peter and Jenny hold the other. She is scanning every face along the ship's railing, looking for one that is his.

KEAGAN SEES IT.

He is not sure how, in all of this — the noise, the crowds, the ship pulling slowly away from the dock — but his eyes find it. A bedsheet held up between three figures on the observation platform.

Keagan Devlin, get your arse back safe.

His heart kicks hard. He can see them. Emily at one end, Peter and Jenny at the other. Emily is crying and scanning the ship's rail, methodically, face by face. He waves, knows she cannot see him yet, grabs a flag from the Para beside him and waves that too. He is shouting her name into the noise, which is pointless but he cannot help it.

Then her eyes find him.

He can see the moment it happens — the way her whole face changes.

He mouths it: I love you.

She says it back. He can see the shape of it even from here.

He stays at the rail until he cannot see the dockside anymore.

TEN

SOMEWHERE, SOMEHOW, APRIL 1982

Stephen stops at Emily's desk with his hands on the back of her chair, as is his habit.

'Where were you Friday?'

'Portsmouth, actually,' she says, a small edge in her voice. 'I went to see Keagan off.'

'Oh — I'm sorry. You all right?'

'I'm fine, thank you. It just feels a bit strange.'

'Of course it does. Listen, a few of us are going out after work — why don't you come along? Take your mind off things.'

'I don't think so. I'm quite tired, honestly.'

'Pat's going, and all the crew from personnel will be there. Never a bad thing to have them on your side.' He says it with a wink. 'Just for one.'

'I'll let you know later.' She turns back to her terminal. 'I really need to get on.'

He moves off and she logs in and starts the morning tasks. She has been thinking about Stephen for weeks, trying to square the two versions of him: the man all the girls in the office have warned her about, and the man who has only ever been polite and genuinely helpful with her. Perhaps the difference is simple enough — she has no interest in him beyond friendship and never has had, and maybe he understands that. He always wants her to join them for drinks after work, but it is always in a group, always other people there. It is not as though he has ever overstepped.

But today, Stephen is only half her mind. Today is her performance review.

She knows she has done the work. She knows her numbers are good. She will not be completely certain until she is sitting across from the department head and someone from personnel at two o'clock, but she is confident. More than confident — she is invested. The Investment Division is opening up and she wants to be in it.

She spends the morning going through her files, running back through anything that might catch her out. By noon she closes the last one, picks up her raincoat, and goes to meet the girls for lunch.

THE SHIP and Anchor is the reliable choice for bank workers in this part of the City — a Victorian pub that has been trading since the 1800s, all dark wood and sawdust on the floors, doing its best to feel like the past while the modern speakers above the bar play whatever Capital Radio is currently blasting out. Today it is something loud and cheerful that makes conversation an effort.

Emily and Patricia order at the bar — tonic water with lime for Emily; she never drinks at lunchtime — and find a table in the corner with Debbie and Janet from personnel.

'So,' Patricia says, once the waitress has put the food down, 'ready for your interview?'

'Hopefully.'

'You'll be fine,' Debbie says with the air of someone who has processed many of these. 'You know the score by now.'

'You look like you're about to be executed,' Patricia says.

The table laughs. Emily smiles despite herself.

'I know. I want the transfer to the new department, and for that I need a strong review. That's all.'

'What, you want to work up there with all those jumped-up lot?' Janet says. 'I have worked with them. If you didn't go to Eton or Cambridge, you're simply not good enough in their eyes.'

'It's not about wanting to work with any particular person. I think Investment Banking is where the bank grows over the next decade. It's a career move.'

Something passes around the table. A look, quiet and loaded. Emily catches it.

'What?'

'You don't know, do you?' Patricia says carefully.

'Know what?'

'About Stephen.'

Emily waits.

'He's got a team in Investments. He'll be running one.'

Emily absorbs this. He had never mentioned it, not once — and he knew perfectly well it was her preferred move.

'I didn't know, no. But that doesn't matter, surely. It would be good to have a friend there if I get the transfer.'

'Yes,' Debbie says, with a dryness that carries its own meaning.

'What's that supposed to mean, Debbie?'

Silence settles over the table.

'Emily, he fancies you. Everyone can see it.'

'No, he doesn't. He's a friend. Patricia, you know that.'

'I know you think of him that way,' Patricia says gently. 'That doesn't mean he sees it the same way.'

'He doesn't,' Emily says, though she sounds less certain than she means to.

'Emily, I've known Stephen a long time.' Patricia sets her fork down. 'He doesn't have girl friends. He has women he wants to sleep with and women he has slept with. I'm not saying this to upset you. I'm just telling you how it is with him.'

The conversation moves on after that — Debbie has stories that are always eventful, and the table ends on lighter ground. But the walk back to the office is quieter for Emily. She turns it over as she goes. Is it the interview she is unsettled by, or the thing about Stephen? If she is honest, she has probably known it for a while. She thought she was managing it. The fact he never said a word about his transfer to Investments makes her wonder whether she has been quite as in control of the situation as she believed.

IT COULD ALMOST BE a summer cruise.

The MV Norland basks in sunshine crossing the equator, troops and civilian crew stretched out on the decks, a football match going between two loose teams on the makeshift pitch aft. The diplomatic effort is still running — the Americans brokering, the news filling each day with talk of a possible deal — and the mood on board has settled into something that does not feel much like going to war. Many of the lads are convinced they will turn around and come home before they ever see land.

Keagan and Marks are on the top deck, watching the football from a pair of loungers. Keagan has a blank piece of paper in front of him.

'Better than a tour in Northern Ireland,' Marks says.

'You might think differently when we actually get there,' Keagan replies, looking down at the paper. 'I'm not convinced Maggie accepts any deal. I don't think that's what this is.'

'What are you writing? Or not writing, by the look of it.'

'Death letter.'

'Ah, for God's sake, mate. Don't. You know it's bad luck.'

'That's bollocks.'

'It is not bollocks.'

'I can't do it anyway,' Keagan says, putting the pen down, 'especially with people banging their gums in my ear every two minutes.'

'That's no way to address a superior,' Marks says, tapping his arm where the Lance Corporal stripe would sit if he were in uniform.

'What are you wearing, Marks?'

'My favourite T-shirt.'

'Then do me a favour with your superior shit until you've got the uniform to back it up.' Keagan grins at him.

Marks grabs for a headlock that Keagan slips easily. They have been close since Keagan's first weeks in the regiment — an unlikely pair on paper, Keagan from Essex and Marks from a mining village in Merthyr Tydfil, with not much in common beyond a shared preference for mid-week pints in Aldershot. Marks's background is not what it first appears: his parents are wealthy, his father having built an international business from nothing. His father had wanted him in the company. Marks had wanted to be here. Keagan had backed him through the early difficult months as a newly made Lance Corporal, and that had cemented it. On a couple of weekends Keagan had taken him back to Essex, and Marks had met Emily and told Keagan, each time, that she was far too good for him. Keagan did not argue the point.

'You know if we see action, I'm sending you over first,' Marks says.

'Have you sorted the rations for tonight yet, Corporal?' Keagan asks, meaning the alcohol vouchers — two pints per man per day, and a trading economy established within the first forty-eight hours on board. Those who weren't drinking were swapping their vouchers for cigarettes.

'We're on eight pints. I've told Shelly you'll share your bunk tonight and he said that was worth two more.'

'He only has eyes for you, mate. You've probably already sorted him out.'

Shelly — real name Wayne — had stayed on the ship for the extra pay and the adventure, stewarding during the day in his cruise-line uniform and transforming each evening into Shelly: full make-up, flowing gowns, a cabaret vocabulary that made seasoned Paras pause. He had been mocked in the first days and become a kind of battalion mascot by the end of the first week. His evenings in the ballroom drew most of the ship.

'I'm going back to the cabin,' Keagan says, getting up. 'I might actually get this written in peace.'

'Cursing yourself,' Marks says. 'Your funeral. Literally.'

Keagan heads below. The shade of the cabin is a relief after the glare of the deck. He sits on his bunk and uncaps the pen and after a moment writes the first line of the three letters he needs to write, whatever else he can or cannot say in them.

Dear Emily...

The afternoon goes. When Marks comes back through the cabin door, the light outside has changed and Keagan has folded the last of the three letters into its envelope and tucked all of them into his pack.

'Let me grab a shower and we'll get that beer,' Keagan says.

'No rush. Apparently crossing the equator today means a celebration, so it's going to be a big one.'

∼

'YOU'LL NEVER GET that up there on your own,' Jenny says as Peter jams himself into the foot of the stairs, both arms around his desk.

He has decided it is a one-man job. It becomes clear within about thirty seconds that it is not.

'Let me help,' Jenny says, taking the bottom end, and between them they have it up without much effort.

They have found a flat in Ilford — refurbished, spacious, with the high ceilings and ornate plasterwork of the 1920s building it was carved out of. Affordable on two incomes. Peter, with help from his father, has got the butcher's shop running well, and Jenny has joined the ambulance service. They were determined to do this on their own terms, and the flat fits.

'Emily's coming over tonight after work,' Jenny says, standing back to look at where the desk sits in the second bedroom they have decided will be a study and occasional guest room. 'She said she'd help unpack and we could get a takeaway.'

'Has she heard from Keagan?'

'Not recently. The letters take time coming through — they check everything apparently. He tried to ring last week but she was late home from work and missed him. She was upset about it.'

'Hopefully they turn around and come home soon. The news keeps saying a deal's close.'

'Let's hope so.' Jenny glances at him. 'You never said — how was your mum this morning?'

He says, simply, 'Tearful.'

Jenny nods. She knows what it has taken from Peter's mum to let this happen — fifteen years of caring for him, of being the person who understood exactly what he needed and when. That does not simply stop because he has packed a van and moved two miles away. Peter and Jenny both know this, and they have made the guest room with her in mind.

'Invite them both over this weekend,' Jenny says. 'Do a proper dinner. If they stay over I'll take her into town Sunday — she'd enjoy that. Your dad can go down the pub with you while we're out.'

'Yeah, he'd like that. He doesn't get much chance at home.'

'Right then — let's get the last boxes up, then we need food in for tonight.' And she heads back down the stairs.

They had not deliberated long over the decision to move in together. Both of them understood the arithmetic of time without ever saying it plainly: that they would have fewer years than most young couples starting out, and they were not going to lose any of them to waiting. They had talked about getting married, and while Jenny's parents preferred that, a long engagement spent planning a white wedding felt like the wrong use of what they had. The flat came up, they were accepted, the paperwork was done within four weeks.

By the time Emily arrives, the supermarket run is done, the cupboards are roughly stocked, and both of them have earned a rest on the sofa. Jenny gets up to answer the doorbell, giving Peter the look.

'Only because I know it's Emily. Next time it's you.'

Emily comes in with her coat still on and immediately begins assessing what needs doing, which turns out to be most things. Peter quickly discovers he has no meaningful say in where anything goes and volunteers to collect the Chinese instead. He takes the order written on the back of an envelope and lets himself out.

'Let's get the stereo working,' Jenny says, rooting through boxes.

They find the Pioneer system in the third box, manhandle it free and get the speakers connected. The records are in a box they have not located yet.

'Just put Capital on,' Emily says.

The radio finds the station and with the music playing they agree the stereo is enough unpacking for the evening, and Jenny opens the vodka she has had chilling since the afternoon.

'So how are you?' Jenny says, once they are settled with their drinks.

'I'm all right. I miss him.'

'Course you do.'

'It's different, Jen. He's been away before, but knowing he might be — it's different.' She looks at her glass. 'It scares me a bit.'

'We don't know it comes to a fight. Could all be sorted by tomorrow and he'll be on his way home.'

'And if it isn't sorted?'

'Then he'll be fine,' Jenny says. 'He's trained for this, Em. He's not some kid getting into trouble outside the Palais on a Saturday night anymore.'

Emily smiles, but only just. 'He's a hothead. You know he is. Whatever they're doing, whoever's giving the orders — if there's a chance to be first in, he'll take it.'

'He cares about you. He'll have that in his head.'

'Jen,' Emily says, with mild surprise, 'are you defending him?'

'I wouldn't go that far.' Jenny takes a sip of her drink. 'Look — I know I've been hard on him. But it's not because I think he's wrong for you. Peter's told me a lot about him and honestly, underneath all the performance, he cares about people. He really does. You and Peter are at the top of the list.' She pauses. 'It's the bit where he doesn't seem to care about himself that worries me. That's when he ends up hurting you, and that's why I'm always on his back.'

Emily is quiet for a moment. 'I didn't know that. I always thought you just thought he wasn't good enough for me.'

'I care about both of you. He's good for you, Em. Most of the time.'

'Thanks, Jen.' Emily turns her glass in her hands. 'I hope he's changed enough. I have nightmares most nights. I just want this to be over.'

They hear the door below and let the subject drop. Jenny knows Peter has been carrying the same weight and she does not want it laid out on the table when he walks in.

'Dinner's here.' Peter comes through to the living room with two carrier bags. 'Oh. You've already started on the vodka.'

They eat off their laps on mismatched plates — the crockery box has not been found yet — with trays balanced and the radio still on in the background. Peter asks about Emily's new job.

'Really good. The work's interesting and my review went well today.'

'How are the people?' Jenny asks.

'Mostly fine. The manager can be tricky, but the girls are a good laugh. Stephen — the team leader — is helpful enough. We all went for a drink the other night.'

The radio shifts and a news bulletin cuts in, leading with the latest on the Falklands — Argentine positions, British fleet, the breakdown of the American-mediated talks. The words move through the room and Emily's gaze goes elsewhere.

'He'll be all right, Em,' Peter says quietly.

'I know.'

Peter sets his tray on the floor and looks at his hands for a moment. 'I've never told anyone this. Even Keagan doesn't know I told you. He'd probably kill me.' A pause. 'He only joined the Army because of me.'

Both of them look at him.

'He got expelled because of me. And he got expelled because of what happened to me.'

The radio continues. Nobody touches the food.

'Peter,' Emily says carefully, 'he lost his temper. He nearly put that boy in hospital. That's not your fault.'

'I was there. He never told you that?'

He tells them what happened that day in the library — the part of it that Emily had never quite been able to piece together. Keagan had always shut down if she tried to raise it, walking away from the conversation before it got anywhere. Now the gaps fill in.

When Peter finishes, Jenny says nothing for a moment.

'None of it is your fault,' Emily says. 'You were being attacked. Keagan came in and defended you, and that's who he is and he wouldn't have had it any other way. But he didn't have to half-kill the boy. He could have stopped him and walked away. That's why they expelled him — not because he stood up for you, but because he didn't know when to stop. That's Keagan. That's nobody's fault but his own.'

'But if I hadn't been there—'

'Peter.' Emily's voice is firm but not unkind. 'It's not your fault. It never was. Don't carry that.'

The room settles. The subject does not come up again. They spend the rest of the evening moving between boxes and the sofa, the girls directing and Peter transporting, the flat gradually beginning to look like somewhere people actually live. Coffee is made. Emily says eventually that her taxi is booked and she should go. She gives Peter a long hug at the door and kisses Jenny goodbye, telling them she will be back at the weekend to help with the rest.

When the door closes, Jenny takes Peter's hand as they go back up the stairs.

'I wish you'd told me,' she says.

'I know. Keagan asked me not to tell anyone and I never did, until tonight. I think he always felt like he was protecting me — in his own strange way. And I suppose I felt I owed him.' He stops on the landing. 'I just don't want anything to happen to him out there. Honestly, I don't think I could forgive myself.'

'That's daft, Peter. You didn't start any of it and you never asked him to do what he did.' She squeezes his hand. 'And nothing is going to happen to him, so stop worrying yourself.'

'I love you, Jen.'

'I love you too,' she says. 'But if you ever keep anything from me again, Peter Chubb, I will kill you myself and save the Argentine Army the trouble.' She kisses his cheek. 'Now. Do you want to try out this new bed or not?'

ELEVEN

HAMMER TO FALL, MAY 1982

The mood on the MV Norland shifts as she approaches San Carlos Bay. The joking has stopped. The music has stopped. Men who spent the crossing playing cards and trading vouchers for beer are now going through kit they already checked twice, because it gives their hands something to do.

It is bitterly cold. The temperature has dropped day by day since they crossed the equator and tonight it is sharp enough to make your eyes water. The diplomatic options have quietly run out, and everyone on board knows it. The war is happening. The ships around them in the darkness make that plain enough.

Shelly is on the top deck in full evening wear, make-up done, as though tonight is a performance night. He is standing at the rail watching the dark water when Keagan and Marks pass on their way below.

Marks stops and offers his hand. 'See you, Shelly.'

Shelly ignores the hand entirely and pulls Marks into a crushing hug, kissing the side of his head.

'Keep safe, you big brute,' he says.

Marks pulls back looking slightly dazed, his face colouring. He mumbles his thanks.

'Hugs, no kisses,' Keagan says, stepping forward.

'I know.' Shelly smiles for the first time. 'You just can't help yourself around me, can you.'

He hugs Keagan and then takes a small step back, composing himself.

'Take care of my brute for me. I want him back with all his parts intact.' His eyes drop meaningfully to Marks's general direction.

'Oh, for fuck's sake,' Marks says, and turns to leave.

Keagan can see the pain underneath the performance. Whatever anyone thought of Shelly when they boarded at Southampton, something has formed during the voyage that none of them had a word for and did not need one.

'Keep that bar stocked for when we get back,' Keagan says, patting his shoulder. Then he follows Marks below.

THE LOWER DECK IS PACKED. Hundreds of men in full battle dress, each carrying close to a hundred pounds of kit, crowded into the space in the hold. Some are talking, telling jokes. A few are doing final checks on equipment already checked a dozen times. The lucky ones have found somewhere to sit.

Keagan and Marks find their platoon around a pallet of equipment and settle in to wait. Officers and NCOs move through the crowd, calling platoons forward by company.

The transfer to the landing craft is awkward. The smaller craft sit about four feet below the doors in the ship's hull, and with the waves moving them, the gap keeps changing. Nobody wants to be in the South Atlantic in full kit — survival in that water is measured in minutes. The officers are frustrated by the slowness of it.

When B Company's shout goes up, Keagan and Marks go with the troop. The drop sends a bolt of pain up through his ankles but nothing serious, and he is herded into the middle of the craft as the engines power up and they move towards Blue Beach.

'Can anyone up front see where we're going?' a voice calls from the back.

'Sorry mate,' comes the reply. 'Some bugger's boarded up the patio doors. Can't see a thing up here.'

Laughter runs through the craft. Someone else pipes up. Then someone else. The humour passes through the packed bodies like a current and for a moment it feels almost manageable.

The door drops at the front with a crash of water.

The troops at the front step off and the cursing starts immediately.

'Shit. This your idea of a joke, bootneck?'

'Jesus fucking Christ.'

'How about you take us to the actual beach? It's shoulder-deep here.'

The landing craft has stopped short of the shore. The slope means three feet of freezing water at the exit point, in full combat kit, in the South Atlantic in winter.

'Fucking bootneck driver,' Keagan says as the cold hits him below the chest and instantly removes any feeling from the waist down.

They wade through as fast as they can. Numbness slows the legs but they reach the beach and the Para NCOs are already calling companies together. Corporal Buckley gathers B Company and runs through the plan. Two Para are to tab four miles up to Sussex Mountain and take up position covering the landings from the south. No confirmed intel on Argentine positions there — the SAS and SBS units already on the island have reported no movement, but Buckley makes it plain enough that assumptions cost lives.

They move off as part of the battalion, heading up steep frozen terrain. The weight of the kit at least keeps them warm. Being soaking wet from the landing, with Antarctic winds driving across the hillside, helps considerably less.

'DOWN.' The shout passes back from the forward units as they encounter dug trenches cut into the mountainside. The company holds. Weapons up.

'Clear.'

Buckley gets them moving again.

'It's so cold my nuts have disappeared,' Marks says as they climb.

'Shelly said you didn't have any to start with,' Keagan says.

'Knock it off with the Shelly comments.'

Keagan grins and they continue up.

'Keep it down.' Buckley's voice cuts through from ahead.

~

THEY REACH the summit of Sussex Mountain as the sun rises across the bay. From up here the scale of the operation becomes visible all at once — more than twenty ships sitting in the inlet below, Royal Navy grey mixed in with the civilian troop carriers. Landing craft still moving between ships and shore. The Royal Engineers starting work on a jetty. All of it, for the moment, quiet.

Their job is to protect the landings from the south. Two Rapier anti-aircraft missile systems are set up as they dig in. To the north, Three Para and the Marines are doing the same.

'Dig in, lads,' Buckley orders, and nobody argues with him. Still wet from the landing and exposed to winds that have strengthened at the summit, the trenches offer the only shelter available. When the sun is fully up the burners come out for a brew and for a while it is almost peaceful — the fleet spread out below them, the sky clear, a mug of something hot.

The calm does not last.

'Incoming.'

The shout carries across the mountain and men grab weapons and drop into trenches before the word has finished echoing. The sound arrives a second later — Argentine jets, low and fast, streaking in across the entrance to the inlet.

The first wave of four aircraft comes in at water level, pulls up over the ships, releases its bombs and is gone before the Rapier operators have fully acquired the target. The frigates and destroyers fire missiles in return. The ships in the inlet are tightly packed — fighting vessels inter-mingled with the civilian carriers — and it is difficult from the moun-tain to track what is happening to what, only that the jets keep coming and the law of averages will not hold forever.

'Can you see the Norland?' Marks asks, the three of them scanning the bay.

'There — just right of centre,' Buckley says, pointing. 'That Navy frigate's putting herself between it and the planes.'

Whoosh... the nearest Rapier fires. Every set of eyes on the mountain tracks the missile across the sky. When it finds the Argentine A-4 Skyhawk — the jet buckling upwards, then dropping, vanishing below a hill beyond the inlet — the cheering erupts across the trenches.

'That's four I've counted,' Keagan says, watching the smoke rise.

'Ships look all right so far,' Marks says. 'Can still see fires on a couple of them.'

'I just hope the Norland's OK,' Keagan says. 'Those lads didn't sign up for this.'

The day continues with wave after wave of Argentine aircraft coming in through the gap in the hills, dropping their bombs and pulling out. In many cases not pulling out fast enough — more than a dozen kills confirmed from the mountain over the course of the afternoon. The frustration in the trenches builds steadily. Two Para went ashore expecting to fight and instead are watching the action happen to the ships and the people they sailed with. The Rapier crews are doing the job they were meant to do, but the infantry can only sit in their holes and watch.

'Nearly dusk,' Buckley says. 'It'll ease when the light goes.'

'Get those passenger ships out tonight if they can,' Keagan says.

'Next wave,' Marks says.

Four more jets come in low across the water. They watch the bomb releases — arching away from the aircraft — and one of them is heading for the frigate protecting the Norland. The explosion at the stern of the ship is enormous. Smoke immediately, then flame.

Nobody says anything for a moment.

'That's the Ardent,' Buckley says quietly.

More waves come in. The Argentine pilots have identified her as damaged and crippled ships draw fire. More explosions tear through her. Helicopters and small craft start moving towards her through the smoke. Then, through a gap in the smoke, the list is visible.

'Poor fuckers,' Buckley says.

They watch the crew going into the water. They watch the ship go down.

~

AFTER THE INTENSITY of the landings, Sussex Mountain settles into six days of nothing. Sub-zero temperatures, wind, and waiting. Rumours move through the trenches daily — targets, long marches, possible actions — and nothing materialises. Two days ago the orders came down for a raid on the Argentine airbase at Goose Green, and after hours of physical and mental preparation, the orders were withdrawn. Adrenaline that had nowhere to go. The return of the mundane was harder to bear than the cold.

Two Para trained for combat behind enemy lines, first in and straight into the thick of it. Sitting in a trench watching someone else's war through binoculars was not in any syllabus they had ever studied.

'B Company — to me.'

The company assembles at the ops centre. The orders are given without ceremony. Four hours to prepare for a tab to Goose Green. Two Para to capture and hold the facility, with naval gunfire support from a Royal Navy frigate and, weather permitting, Harrier air cover from HMS Hermes. Argentine forces defending the base estimated at between five hundred and a thousand troops — a range that tells you how reliable the intelligence is, but it is the best available.

The briefing ends with an announcement that the BBC World Service has broadcast the Goose Green operation during its news bulletin.

The silence that follows is remarkable.

The regimental commander is livid. The operation will proceed regardless — the belief being that the Argentines won't credit anyone with the nerve to advertise an attack they're actually planning to carry out.

The plan: B Company will advance on the initial target, a school-house at Camilla Creek held by a company of Argentine troops, flanking from the right along the coastline. A and C companies will come over the central ridge.

'That's nice,' Keagan says. 'A little stroll on the beach.'

'Just watch out for the mines,' Corporal Stevens from A Company says as he passes. 'And come on, you Spurs.' He grins at Keagan, referencing Tottenham's FA Cup win in the replay that week.

'You were bloody lucky,' Keagan says. 'Another replay to bail you out.'

Stevens laughs and moves on. Small moments of ordinary life, somehow still existing out here.

It is a four-mile tab to the start point across frozen ground — uneven terrain with crevices and holes that catch ankles in the dark. Moving in darkness gives cover, but the medics deal with turned ankles steadily on the way across. If twisted ankles are the worst of it, they will all be grateful enough.

B COMPANY REACHES their position facing the schoolhouse and takes up the line. Lieutenant Pitts moves along the troop with his NCOs.

'Buckley — your team takes the position right of the main building. Covering fire from the centre. Wait for the command. Clear?'

'Yes, sir.'

Pitts continues down the line. Minutes pass.

'Open fire.'

The night tears open. Tracer rounds cross the ground in front of them and for a few seconds the fire only travels one way. Then it comes back.

Thuds of incoming rounds hit the soil close by. This is no longer a training exercise. Everyone in the trench understands that simultaneously.

'Heads down,' Buckley shouts, which no one needed telling.

Keagan and Marks concentrate fire on their target — a machine gun position dug into the ground to the right of the schoolhouse. Tracer fire from the position stitches the soil around them. Keagan identifies two additional firing points flanking the main gun.

'Cover that gun,' Buckley orders. 'Keagan, Marks, Bishop — with me. We're going around on that position. Ready?'

'Ready, Corporal.'

'Go.'

The four men move off low and fast, taking an arcing route to approach the gun from the side. Buckley leads, Keagan and Marks either side, Bishop at the rear. They use the contours of the ground to close the distance. The position continues firing on the main body of B Company — they haven't been spotted.

Fifteen yards out, the rough terrain ends. Flat, low grass between them and the trench.

Buckley gives it in a quiet word. 'Marks, Bishop — on my go, constant fire on the target. Devlin with me. You take right, I take left. Straight into the trench. Clear?'

Everyone confirms.

'Go.'

Marks and Bishop open fire. Buckley and Keagan sprint.

The surprise buys them just enough. The Argentine gunners are swinging to meet the new fire coming from their side when Keagan and Buckley are on them. Three men in the trench. Rapid fire. It's over in seconds. They radio in and use the captured ditch as cover, turning fire on the schoolhouse windows.

The left-hand gun position has been taken simultaneously. The schoolhouse is under fire from all directions now. Tracer rounds tear through the walls. The windows go. The doors go. When the firing finally stops it is because there is nothing left coming back out.

Keagan and Buckley rise from the dugout and approach the building from the side with Marks and Bishop behind them. The silence is total. The side door opens onto a single room dark with bodies. Even in the darkness there is blood on the floor and up the walls. Nothing in there is still breathing.

The medics move in to find any survivors as more troops secure the building. Buckley gathers his team outside.

'Good work. Take ten, then we move. We need that ridge overlooking the airbase at Darwin before first light. Our company takes the left flank, A and C through the centre. Clear?'

Water canteens come out. The men sit.

Keagan sits next to Marks and neither of them speaks.

His first kill.

He can still see the face. The young Argentine — not much older than sixteen or seventeen, looking up at him in the second before it was over. The expression was surprise more than anything else. Fear underneath it. A clumsy attempt to bring his weapon around and then nothing. Whatever the boy had expected when he woke up this morning, it was not this.

Keagan had done his job. The job he trained for. It was automatic, exactly as the training said it would be. He would do it again — he knows this with certainty — and he probably will before this is over. As a young man he got satisfaction from a fight. But the person on the other end of it always got back up. The young Argentine, now laid out with the others in front of the building, would not be getting up. He would not be going home. He was simply on the wrong side, and that was Keagan's job, and that was the end of it.

What surprises Keagan, sitting in the dark with his canteen, is not that he feels bad. He does feel something — a sadness for the boy and whoever is waiting for him to come home. What surprises him is that the guilt is not there. He always thought it would be. He always assumed, after something like this, the guilt would come in like a tide. It doesn't. He doesn't know what that means or what to make of himself because of it. Maybe it will come later.

He reaches inside his combats for the crucifix and holds it in his fist for a moment. He says a silent prayer — for the young man who is not going home, and for his own part in that.

Then Buckley gives the word, and they move off towards the ridge.

CHAPTER

TWELVE

FATHER FIGURE, MAY 1982

The warm evening has brought the City workers out in their droves. Nobody wants to be crammed into a tube carriage on a Friday in late May, and The Ship and Anchor is packed to the doors. Emily is with a large group from the bank — colleagues, friends, the usual Friday sprawl of people unwinding after the week.

The discussion over lunch about Stephen has been on her mind since Tuesday. She knows what she feels. Whatever he wants or hopes for, they are only ever going to be friends, and she intends to make that clear whenever the right moment comes.

The bar is too busy to fight through more than once every forty minutes, so drinks arrive on trays at the outside table they have claimed. Emily has lost count of her vodka and oranges. She opens her purse.

'Right, my round,' she says. 'Who's drinking what?'

She heads inside with Debbie. They wait for a gap at the bar, working their way forward until they finally get served. The television screens mounted around the bar are showing the BBC early evening news. Emily is halfway through ordering when she hears Debbie go quiet beside her.

'Emily.' Debbie touches her arm and points to the screen directly above them.

Emily looks up.

'*...the area is under constant bombardment and an unknown number of troops from the 2nd Parachute Regiment are involved. The action started in the early hours of this morning and has continued throughout the day. Casualties are unknown at this time, but the field hospital is operational. I have seen several casualties brought in over the last couple of hours...*'

'Love?' The barman taps the bar in front of her.

Debbie reaches across, takes the money from Emily's hand and passes it over. 'There you go.'

Emily barely hears her. 'That's Keagan's regiment,' she says.

'I know. I'm sure he's fine. Come on, let's go back out.'

'Yes. Yes, of course.'

She carries the tray back outside, sets it on the table, and excuses herself for the toilet. She doesn't go to the toilet. She goes back inside and stands beneath the nearest screen.

Patricia notices and leans over to Debbie. 'Everything all right?'

'It's on the news. Keagan's regiment is in action.'

'Shall we go to her?'

'Give her a minute,' Debbie says.

The correspondent continues between studio cut-aways, careful not to breach operational restrictions but giving what he can.

'*...at approximately two this morning, troops attacked multiple positions approaching the airfield at Goose Green...Harrier jets were visible at first light...Argentine numbers defending the airfield have been estimated at around a thousand troops...*'

Emily watches, looking for anything — a face she recognises, a detail that tells her something. The news moves on to other stories. She stands there for a moment longer, not ready to move.

'Penny for them.'

Stephen. She didn't hear him come inside.

'Sorry — I was miles away.' She forces a small smile. 'I'll come back out, just give me a minute.'

She turns to go. Stephen takes her arm — not roughly, but firmly enough to stop her.

'I know you're worried. You don't have to pretend you're not. Come and sit down for a bit.'

'I'm not sure I'd make much sense right now, honestly.'

'You don't have to make sense. Come on.' He nods towards a corner table that has just come free. 'I'll get you a drink. You can tell me as much or as little as you want.'

She nods, and goes to the ladies' room while he goes to the bar.

'Pint of lager,' he tells the barman, 'and a vodka and orange. Make it a double.'

The corner is quieter than the rest of the pub. Emily sits, wrapping both hands around her glass.

'Don't keep telling me he'll be fine,' she says. 'Everyone does that.'

'All right,' Stephen says. 'I won't.'

She looks at him, a little surprised. 'I worry because I know him. When he's in it — really in it — he doesn't think about being careful or coming home safe. He just fights. It frightens me.'

'I've got a couple of mates over there. Navy, so not on the ground like Keagan, but it doesn't stop you turning the news on every hour.'

She nods.

'I grew up in the same area as you,' Stephen says. 'There were always those who used their brains and those who used their fists. My brother was the fighter. Didn't do him much good in the long run.'

'Keagan isn't stupid,' Emily says, sharper than she intends.

'I know that. I didn't say he was.' Stephen holds his hands up. 'I just meant — I understand what you're feeling. You've got all the worry and you're dealing with it here on your own. That's harder in some ways than being out there.'

'I'm angry,' Emily says. 'I don't know why. It was his choice. I've always accepted that. But I'm angry anyway and I can't explain it.'

'You don't have to explain it. You're a partnership. What one person does affects the other. The anger makes sense.'

She stares at the table. 'He didn't really give me a choice. When he joined up, I don't think either of us believed there'd actually be a war. Northern Ireland, yes, always that. But not this.'

'He's doing exactly what he wants to do,' Stephen says. He takes a sip of his pint. 'That's fine. I won't lose sleep over what Keagan Devlin does or doesn't do. But I care about you. I can see what this is doing to you, and that's why I'm here. For you.'

'Stephen.' Emily meets his eyes. 'I love Keagan. He is the only man in my life. I need you to understand that clearly, as a friend.'

'I do understand it.'

'I just want to be sure.'

'I'm not here for anything other than that.' He holds her gaze steadily. 'Some of the girls talk. I know what they think. But Emily, I just want to be your friend. That's it.'

She holds the look for a moment, then nods. 'Thank you. It's hard sometimes, at home — Jenny and Peter are so close to Keagan. There are things I can't say to them. So yes. Thank you for listening.'

Stephen reaches over carefully and puts an arm briefly around her shoulders. 'Always,' he says.

Emily pulls back gently. 'Come on. It's a team night.'

OUTSIDE, the sun is beginning to set over the city, the light breeze bringing the first real chill of the evening. The group is loud and in good spirits, and when someone suggests the nightclub on Cannon Street, nearly everyone agrees. Emily goes along with it. She has decided, consciously, to try to enjoy herself tonight. She needs it.

The club is already busy despite the early hour — the City clears out from five onwards, which means the clubs fill quickly and close at eleven to let people catch their trains. Emily and Patricia find a table near the dance floor and settle in. The floor is packed with men in loosened ties and women still in their office clothes, moving to Michael Jackson and whatever else the DJ decides he's feeling tonight.

Stephen arrives at the table with a loaded tray — beers, shorts, and what looks like a particularly generous vodka and orange that he hands directly to Emily.

'There you go.'

The night takes on its own momentum. Emily dances — properly dances, for the first time in longer than she can remember. Patricia, Debbie, strangers on the dance floor. She lets it go for a while, the worry and the news broadcast and the sick feeling that has been sitting in her chest since she saw the television screen. She lets it go.

Patricia catches her eye from across the table as they both take a break from the floor. There are more drinks on the table. Emily reaches for hers and takes a long sip, the room pleasantly blurry at the edges.

'We should start thinking about the last trains,' Patricia says.

'One more.' Emily says it with enough certainty that Patricia raises her eyebrows.

'You all right? I don't think I've seen you quite like this before.'

'I'm enjoying myself. That's all.'

'I know, I just don't want you stranded here.'

'Don't worry, Pat, I'll make sure she gets to the station,' Stephen says, appearing at the table.

Patricia looks at him. 'You're the reason I want to get her home,' she says flatly.

'Oh, come on. That's not fair.'

'It's all right, Patricia,' Emily says. 'Honestly. You get off. I'll have one more and get a cab to Liverpool Street. I'll make the last train easily.'

Patricia looks at her for a moment. 'You're sure?'

'I'm sure. Go. I'll see you Monday. Thanks.'

Patricia says her goodbyes, pausing at the door to give a small wave back.

One more drink becomes a slow dance that Emily immediately regrets agreeing to. The DJ has shifted the mood and Stephen's arms are around her before she has quite registered what is happening. The song is Heatwave, 'Always and Forever', and Emily goes rigid. That is Keagan's song. Their song, in the kitchen at home, in the car — everywhere.

'I've got to go.' She pulls away from him, goes straight to the table, picks up her bag and coat.

'Slow down, I'll come with you. I said I'd get you to the station.'

'It's fine. I can manage.' She's already heading for the exit.

Outside in the street, cooler now, the alcohol hits her properly when the warm air disappears. She pushes on a door that says pull and ends up on the pavement.

'Emily. Over here.' Stephen has his arm up, flagging down a black cab. 'Come on, I'll drop you at Liverpool Street and get over to Fenchurch Street for mine. It's a later train, I've got time.'

She weighs it up. She needs to get to the station. She nods and gets in, misjudging the step and landing inelegantly in the back seat.

They ride in silence across the city.

Liverpool Street is busy even at this hour. Stephen pays the cabbie and follows her inside. She doesn't argue this time. The floor feels less than entirely steady.

They head down towards the Central Line, and the gates are closed. The last tube has gone.

Emily looks at her watch and has to concentrate to read it. Gone midnight. She doesn't understand how that happened.

'The mainline,' she says, turning back. 'I'll get the Ilford train and a taxi from there.'

She finds the departure board in the main station — an old rattling thing, the flaps turning over in their slots — and scans it for the Ilford service.

12.10 DEPARTED.

She stares at it.

'I'll get a taxi,' she says, more to herself than to Stephen.

'Don't be daft. That'll cost you a fortune at this time of night.' He thinks for a second. 'Come on. Get my train to Upminster. I'll sort you a taxi from the station, it'll be half the price and you'll probably get home quicker.'

It makes sense. She can see that it makes sense. She agrees.

THEY MAKE Fenchurch Street with minutes to spare and board the last Southend service, an elderly Class 310 with manual doors and individual compartments — the Misery Line, as every commuter in east London calls it. At this hour the carriage they find is empty. Emily drops into the window seat and is asleep before the train has cleared the platform.

'Upminster. This station is Upminster.'

Stephen is shaking her shoulder. She surfaces slowly, the train already slowing.

'Come on.'

Outside, the taxi rank is empty. The office is closed.

'I'm sorry,' Stephen says, 'I live just around the corner. We'll go there and I'll ring for a cab.'

She is too tired and too disorientated to argue. He puts an arm around her shoulders as they walk, steadying her. His flat is a short walk — a converted house, studio on the upper floor, a narrow staircase. He unlocks the door and she goes inside.

'Sit down,' he says. 'I'll sort a cab.'

Emily sits on the edge of the bed. The room tilts slightly. She closes her eyes.

~

THE DARKNESS COMES and goes in pieces.

She is aware of movement, of hands, of weight. She tries to surface, tries to speak, and the words don't come. Something is wrong. Something is badly wrong and she cannot make her body respond. She tries to say stop, she tries to say no, and it comes out as almost nothing. His weight is on her. She is pinned. She tries again. No. Stop. She is crying and she does not know when she started. She calls for Keagan — not out loud, just in whatever part of her is still awake — and then the darkness takes her back down.

~

'GOOD MORNING, GORGEOUS.'

Emily opens her eyes.

A room she doesn't recognise. Pale curtains. Morning light. She sits up slowly and the events of the previous night rearrange themselves, disconnected.

Stephen is lying next to her. He is naked. She is naked.

She aches. She hurts in a way that tells her what happened and she doesn't want to understand it.

'Can I make some coffee?' He stretches, easy and comfortable. 'You probably need it, the state you were in.'

She cannot find a single word. She gets up, not looking at him, and finds her clothes in a heap on the floor. She starts to dress, her hands not quite steady.

'What's the rush? It's Saturday. I thought we could get some lunch, maybe a walk if it stays nice.'

She keeps dressing.

'Emily. What's the matter?'

She picks up her bag and coat from the table and goes to the door. There is a chain on it. She fumbles with it, her fingers clumsy.

Stephen is beside her. He is still naked. He puts his hand flat against the door.

'Would you calm down? I thought we had a nice time.'

'Get off me.' The words come out louder than she expects. She gets the chain off, wrenches the door open and she is on the stairs, then in the street, then just walking, as fast as she can, in whatever direction takes her away from there.

THIRTEEN

BROTHERS IN ARMS, MAY 1982

The shout goes up from the officers as the troops prepare for the next phase of the operation.

'Form up.'

They are to advance on Goose Green. To get there they will have to overcome Argentine defensive positions dug into the hills surrounding the town and airbase. B Company is to take a route around the ridge, using the shoreline before sweeping up from the left flank. A and C Companies will take the more direct route through the centre. After final checks on equipment and ammunition, they set off into the dark.

'You all good?' Buckley asks his team. He gets the necessary responses and they move.

It is four in the morning. They need to be in position and into the action quickly if they are to avoid being caught in the open when daylight breaks at half six. After a short tab around the shoreline, C Company is halfway up the slope and ready to take the two defensive positions they can identify. Instructions come down. Buckley's team are to take the heavily defended position to the left and provide cover for A Company pushing through the centre.

The open-fire command goes out across all companies at once, and the night sky lights up with tracer, the Argentine positions suddenly visible in the flickering orange lines but the Paras' own locations exposed in return. The gunfire is relentless — a constant symphony of cracks and thuds, the most unsettling sound being the soft percussion of rounds hitting the terrain just behind them. Progress stalls almost immediately under the weight of incoming fire. Cries for medics go up from positions across the slope. Buckley is trying to keep his team moving forward, but the ground offers almost nothing to hide behind. Tracer rounds come in thick and fast, tearing up the earth around them.

'On your left, twenty yards — cover!' Buckley shouts. 'Keagan, Marks, put down covering fire. Rest of you on my command.'

Keagan and Marks open up on the position ahead as the team moves — sprinting, dropping, crawling — across to a small rock formation that will give them the cover they need. Keagan fires in short controlled bursts, tracking the source of the tracer. Three rounds hit the ground inches from him. He drops flat, rolling hard away from the impact point, keeping low.

'Marks. You good?' he shouts.

'About five yards behind you,' Marks calls back. 'Keep firing, I'm coming up.'

Keagan opens up again, joined now by the team sheltered behind the rocks. A tap on his shoulder — Marks is in beside him. Together they keep the fire going, both scanning across to where the main group have taken up position ten yards further on.

'Cover us,' Keagan shouts.

Twenty guns open up from the rock formation, and the incoming fire drops just enough. Keagan and Marks are on their feet and sprinting before they have time to think about it. Marks hits the deck first. As Keagan throws himself across the last stretch of open ground, there is an almighty crack — a round hits the side of the rock directly in front of his face.

Keagan lands hard with a groan and lies there for a moment.

'You all right?' Marks asks.

Keagan rolls over and pulls off his helmet, turning it in his hands. There is a long gouge across the side of it.

'That bullet clipped my head,' he says, and then starts laughing. 'At least I know the helmet works.'

'Only on a ricochet. I wouldn't go testing a direct hit.'

'Sound advice, cheers mate.'

'Shut it, the pair of you,' Buckley blasts. 'Get some fire on those bloody guns if you don't mind.'

They crawl up to the rocks and open fire.

ALL ACROSS THE HILL, the Paras are being held up. Casualties are building. Orders and instructions crackle constantly over the radios. No matter what they try, they cannot break through, and more drastic measures begin to be considered. Finally the order comes for a co-ordinated mass advance across all fronts. It is a risk — they all know it will cost them — but staying pinned down in the open once daylight arrives would be worse. They could be picked off at will. The sun is already beginning to pale the eastern horizon.

They rise together. Over twenty guns lay down sustained fire on the position ahead, and for a moment the Argentines take cover to reload. In that moment the Paras sprint. Then the incoming fire surges back, and men start going down around Keagan — he sees at least three colleagues fall before the shout goes up.

'Down.'

They hit the deck and reload, faces pressed into the cold ground.

Ten yards to the machine-gun position now. The sun is coming. They are running out of time.

The command comes. Keagan is up, firing directly ahead as he runs, pushing hard towards the guns. Marks is to his right, matching him stride for stride, the two of them swinging wide towards the left side of the trench. Around them, tracer lights up the hillside. Men fall. Shouts for medics carry only a few yards in the noise.

Keagan closes on the trench, bayonet fixed. He drops into it, firing without pausing, and the occupants go down in front of him — some from his rounds, some caught by fire from above. He lands amongst the bodies. The gunfire all around them continues from positions not yet taken, so there is no time to stop and think. Others drop into the trench with him, and they push on.

'Marks.' He shouts it across the trench. No answer. He looks around the rim. Nothing.

He remembers the shots that swept past him as he jumped. The fear comes in quick and cold.

He pulls himself back up and out of the trench, staying low, moving back across the ground they had covered. And there, barely a yard from where Keagan had been running, a body is lying face down.

Keagan crawls towards him, keeping as flat as he can with fire still coming in from other positions further up the slope. He reaches Marks and turns him over.

Marks groans, his face tight with pain. Keagan looks down and sees why. He has taken rounds to the body. Through his uniform, part of his intestine is visible. Marks moves his hands towards it instinctively, trying to hold himself together.

'Medic.' Keagan shouts it as loud as he can manage. 'You're going to be all right, mate. Stay with me.' He throws down his own weapon and presses his hands where Marks's are. 'Medic. Here. Now.'

'Get your bloody head down,' Marks manages.

'You're going to be fine. We'll get you into the trench and they'll sort you out.'

'I'm done, mate.'

'No you bloody aren't. Don't be stupid. I'm not letting you die out here, all right?' He shouts for the medic again, scanning the ground around them, but it is clear that no one is coming. The battle is still going all around them. The trench they took is empty — the team has already pushed on to the next position further up the slope.

Then gunfire opens up on them from a bank fifty yards to the left. They have been spotted.

'Where are Keagan and Marks?' Buckley shouts as they continue up the hill.

'Keagan was in the trench with us. I saw him go back out.'

'For Christ's sake.' Buckley turns. 'Hold here.'

He moves back down the hill. Scanning the open ground, he picks them out — Marks on his back, Keagan flat on top of him, hands pressed to his stomach. Buckley spots the position to his right that is firing on them. He calls his troops and they attack it, drawing the fire away.

Keagan, with his hands freed for a moment, grabs his rifle and opens up, trying to reduce the incoming rounds. Buckley and his team close on the Argentine position fast. The soldiers manning it swing their fire towards the advancing Paras. Buckley rises from a crouch and goes forward firing from the hip, the team hard behind him. They take it quickly — two of the occupants killed, a third injured. The firing in this small corner of the battle stops.

Keagan does not wait. He shoulders his weapon, hooks his arms under Marks and drags him across the ground and down into the nearby trench. They land in the bottom with a heavy thud. Keagan calls for a medic as he raises his head above the parapet. Seconds later one drops in beside them and goes straight to work on Marks.

Buckley appears above the trench. 'Leave him to it, Keagan. With me.'

Keagan looks down at the medic. 'Will he make it?'

'I'll do everything I can. I've already radioed for an evac.'

He crouches close to Marks, near his ear. 'You're going to be all right,' he says quietly. 'And before you get any ideas — you still owe me a fiver, and you've still got that date with Shelly when we get home. I'm not letting you get out of either one.'

He isn't sure Marks hears him.

'He'll be fine, Keagan,' Buckley says.

'Yeah.' He says it like he means it, because the alternative is something he will not look at yet.

THE BATTLE ROLLS on for hours. The Argentines have positions dug into virtually every fold and feature of the hills surrounding Goose Green airfield. The original estimate of five hundred defending troops turns out to be considerably short of the truth. Progress is slow. The Paras are gaining ground but every position costs them, and with full daylight now upon them, each advance is more exposed and more expensive than the last. Three of Keagan's original section are dead or wounded, including Marks. Keagan himself has taken a round across the top of his arm — not deep, a graze really, though as the adrenaline has slowly reduced it has started to make itself known.

Word comes through during a brief pause in the firing that the Commanding Officer of 2 Para has been fatally wounded during the night's action. The news moves through the troops quickly and quietly. Men look at one another and say nothing much. Then they turn back and push on. The CO's death does something to them — tightens something. They will finish the job.

Now positioned along the top of the ridge and looking down over the main target, orders are being drawn up for the next phase. The attacks are running hours behind schedule, which means everything now has to be done in broad daylight. Keagan tries to get any information he can about Marks through the medics coming and going along the ridge, but nobody knows anything yet.

The orders come. B Company is to take the building to the right of the airfield that sits along the shoreline. Buckley gathers his men and points it out. 'On me.'

They move cautiously but with intent, working their way down from the ridge towards the target. Then, from somewhere behind the horizon, engine noise — growing, deepening. RAF Harriers sweep in low and fast over the battlefield and release their payload onto the airfield and the surrounding areas. The ground shakes. The distraction is immediate and total, and the troops use it to close the distance to the building with very little return fire coming at them. In position, they concentrate sustained fire on the structure. Very little comes back.

They are almost ready to move in when something appears at one of the shattered windows.

A white flag.

The order goes out to cease firing. Buckley confers with the CO, and together they begin to approach the building, the remaining troops covering them carefully. An Argentine officer emerges through the doorway holding the flag, accompanied by several men. They throw their weapons aside immediately, hands up, the gesture clear.

Buckley and the CO are still walking forward when it happens.

Crack. Crack. Crack.

Guns open up from the right — a position that apparently either hasn't received the order or has chosen not to follow it. Both men go down under the burst of fire and lie still in the open ground.

For a moment, nobody moves.

Then everything happens at once. British fire swings towards the gun position and silences it in seconds. Troops rush the bunker, surrounding it, the anger plain in every face. Medics and the remaining men move towards where Buckley and the CO have fallen. The NCOs begin marshalling the surrendering Argentine soldiers, who are themselves visibly shaken — fear clear in their faces, arms raised, wanting nothing more than it to be finished.

Keagan helps with the prisoners. He checks each one for concealed weapons with the kind of thoroughness that does not worry overly about being gentle about it. They assemble them in an open area in front of the captured building and post guards.

Then he makes his way across to where the injured men are being treated.

The medics are working on Buckley with everything they have — an IV line rigged above him, three of them working in close. Buckley is conscious. Keagan can hear him issuing instructions from the ground, which is either a good sign or entirely typical of the man. Beside him, the CO lies motionless. There is very little activity around him. A significant death, in a significant context, and no one quite ready to say it yet. The radios keep going. Hold the position taken. Await instructions. The British have secured all the ground surrounding the airfield. Negotiations for a formal Argentine surrender of the base are already under way.

Keagan takes up a position guarding the prisoners. Twenty or more men are grouped together in the open field, sitting or standing close to one another. He is one of five standing guard, rifle trained on them.

He looks at them. He thinks about the white flag. He thinks about Buckley going down. About the CO. About Marks, lying in the bottom of a trench somewhere behind him with a medic's hands keeping him alive.

For a moment he feels it — the cold impulse, the anger that wants somewhere to go.

Then he looks at the men in front of him properly. Cold faces. Exhausted. Some of them are very young. Their weapons and kit look poor, badly maintained, the kind of equipment that says these men have been badly supplied and badly led. Conscripts, most likely. Sent here for a cause they probably have little say in and even less understanding of. And now it is over for them, and the relief in their faces is not hidden. They are not celebrating. They are not defiant. They are simply glad to still be alive.

Keagan keeps his gun trained on them and says nothing.

The radio crackles. Argentine forces across the area have surrendered.

CHAPTER

FOURTEEN

CHINA IN YOUR
HAND, JUNE/JULY 1982

The telephone rings in the hall. Jenny picks it up.

'Hello.'

'Hi Jen. It's Emily.'

'Oh, hi Em's. Haven't seen you in ages — have you been busy?'

'Yeah, sort of. Jen, are you at home for a bit? Is Peter there?'

'I'm just doing housework. Peter's over at his mum and dad's. Everything all right?'

'Would it be all right if I came over? I need to talk.'

'Yes — yes, come straight over. I'll get the kettle on.'

'I'll be about thirty minutes. Thanks, Jen.'

'No problem. See you soon.'

She hangs up and stands in the hall for a moment. What could be the matter? She runs through the possibilities and then stops herself on one of them. Please God, not Keagan. No — she would have heard. His family would have told Peter. They would know by now. She heads into the kitchen and clears last night's plates from the side, trying to keep herself occupied.

Thirty minutes later, almost to the minute, the doorbell rings. She opens the door and Emily is standing there, pale as a sheet, tears streaming down her face.

'Oh God, Emily.' Jenny pulls her into a hug before she can even speak. 'Come on, come inside.'

She brings her up the stairs and into the kitchen. Emily sits down at the table and Jenny turns the kettle on without asking.

'I don't know where to start, Jen,' Emily says, her voice thin and unsteady. 'I just needed to see you. I didn't know where else to go. I'm sorry.'

'Don't be sorry. Talk when you're ready. No rush.'

She has never seen Emily like this. Normally so composed, so together — Emily is the calm one. The kettle boils and she makes the tea, sets the cups down and takes the chair beside her. Five minutes pass without a word. Jenny holds her hand and waits.

'I've done something terrible, Jen.'

The words bring a fresh flood of tears. Emily shakes and drops her cup. Jenny is already on her feet — she leaves the cup where it falls and puts her arms around her instead.

'Come with me.'

She leads her through to the living room, sits her down on the sofa and pulls her close. They stay like that. Jenny holding her, Emily just needing somewhere to feel safe.

'Last night,' Emily starts, and then stops.

'What happened last night, Em's?'

'You can't tell Peter. Promise me.'

'I promise. I don't like it, but if you don't want me to say anything I won't. Just tell me.'

Emily tells her everything. The news of the battle coming through and the fear she'd been carrying since. The night out with friends and the simple desperate wish to forget, just for one evening, to feel normal again. Then Stephen — his move on her, her rejection. And then, haltingly, the part that makes no sense to her even now: how she ended up back at his flat. How stupid she had been. And finally the worst of it. Waking up in his bed, naked, with no memory of how she had got there.

Believing for one brief moment it was a dream, and then the realisation settling in like cold water.

'My God, Em's. He raped you.'

'But did he? I was in his bed, I was naked. Did he rape me or did I just do something stupid and can't face up to it? That's what I keep going round and round — I just don't know.'

'Stop right there.' Jenny's voice is quiet and firm. 'You didn't know what was happening. You were out of it. You were in no position to make any kind of choice. You said yourself — you didn't take your own clothes off, you didn't get into his bed. He used you, and that's rape. Don't you dare try to make that your fault. I won't have it.'

'I wish I could believe that.' Emily breaks again. 'I hate myself.'

'You've done nothing. You're the victim here. The first thing you do is make sure he doesn't win.'

'But I went there, Jen. I got in his car. I went to his flat. I got on his bed. After spending a night out with him. That's on me. I didn't go out intending anything, but I made choices that led me there. What was I expecting? I'm either an idiot or—' The anger surfaces sharply. 'And what the hell do I tell Keagan?'

'I've told you — I won't have you blaming anyone but him. Keagan we'll deal with when the time's right. But first you have to go to the police. This is a crime, Emily, and he needs to be locked up for it.'

She keeps her voice steady with effort. Inside she is close to boiling — the urge to ring Keagan right now, to tell him what has happened and then step back and let him do what he does. She knows what that would mean and for one dark moment, she does not care. But that is not what Emily needs. Emily needs her friend, calm and clear.

'Have you been home?'

'Yes, I got a taxi straight there. But Dad was furious — I've never stayed out without letting them know. Mum could see something was wrong, but I just went straight to my room and called you. He won't speak to me for days, you know what he's like.'

'You have to tell them, Em's. And you have to go to the police. I'll call them, if that helps.'

'I'm so tired, Jen. I just need a bit of time to think. Please.'

'Listen. Go and have a lie-down in our room, get some rest, and we'll talk when you're up.'

'Just a bit, maybe. Yes.'

'And Em's—' Jenny hesitates. 'I know I said I wouldn't. But if you're going to report this, Peter has to know. I'll only tell him with your say-so. But I have to ask.'

Emily is quiet for a moment. 'Let me sleep, and then yes. If we're doing this, of course you have to tell him. That's all right.'

'Go on then. I'll be here.'

Emily settled in the bedroom, Jenny goes back to the kitchen and crouches down to pick up the broken cup and mop up the spilt tea. Her hands move slowly. The anger is still right there beneath the surface, barely contained. She holds it in. Emily needs calm and practical help, not someone falling apart beside her. She runs through the possibilities — Keagan coming home, being told, and what happens next. Every version ends in the same place. Peter has to be there. Peter is the only person on earth who might be able to hold Keagan back from something that would ruin both of them.

She hears the door go downstairs. Peter's home.

'Hello, babes.' He comes into the kitchen and wraps his arms around her as she stands at the sink. 'All right?'

'Shall I make you a brew? How were your mum and dad?'

'I'm gasping — yeah, please. They're fine. Mum was a bit tearful, misses me.' He raises his eyebrows. 'You know how she is.'

'Oh — don't go in the bedroom. Emily's asleep in there.'

'Emily? Is everything—'

'Late night. She needed to crash for a bit.' She says it without looking at him, hating herself for it.

They take their tea into the living room and talk about his visit, what his parents had said, how his dad is getting on. Peter is mid-sentence when Emily comes in. Her eyes are raw, her whole body carrying the weight of what she is holding. The conversation stops. Peter looks from Emily to Jenny, and the look on his face says he already knows this is serious.

Emily sits between them on the sofa. She puts her arms around Peter and then Jenny's arms go around them both. Emily's shoulders shake with fresh tears for a few minutes before she can start. With Jenny gently filling in the gaps when the words run out, she goes through the whole of it with Peter.

He sits throughout with Emily's hand held between both of his. He does not interrupt, does not react visibly — just listens, steady and still, letting her speak at her own pace. When she finishes, he looks at the two of them.

'Are we doing this then?'

Emily and Jenny, in the same breath: yes.

Peter gets up, walks to the telephone in the hall, and dials 999.

THEY SPEND the rest of the day and into the evening with the police. Two officers arrive first — a male and female — and Jenny stays beside Emily as she goes through the events again, the officers quietly noting everything down. They ask if she would consent to come to the local station to make a full statement and to be seen by a specialist doctor. Emily agrees, weary now and resigned to it. She gets her coat, and with Peter and Jenny alongside her, they head out to the waiting cars.

At the station, Emily is questioned again, and a medical examination follows. Her clothes are taken away as evidence. Peter waits in the corridor and the two women come back out and sit either side of him on the hard wooden bench.

'Will you both come home with me?' Emily asks.

'We're here for you,' Jenny says. Peter gives her hand a squeeze.

'I don't know how to tell Mum and Dad. And I can't even think about telling Keagan.'

'You leave Keagan to me,' Peter says.

The original female officer comes back to tell them a car is ready to take Emily home.

AT HER PARENTS' house, the story comes out again — halting and painful for the third time that day. Her mother's reaction is immediate

and overwhelming. Her sister Anna cries with her. Her father goes very quiet in a way that is somehow worse than the tears. Emily bathes — her mother staying close throughout — and then she goes to bed, with Anna and Jenny on either side of her.

Downstairs, Peter sits with George and Valerie. Tea has given way to something stronger. George pours whisky for himself and Valerie. Peter nurses a beer. The initial shock has settled into something harder.

'Peter.' George leans forward. 'We're all going to need your help with this. You know that, don't you?'

'Of course. Whatever you need — Jenny and I are both here for her. Always.'

'I know.' George passes the glass across to Valerie. 'But there's Keagan to deal with. When he gets back, we're going to have to tell him. Who knows what state he'll be in after what he's been through over there. And you know how he is. I just don't want him storming in and making everything worse. He loves her — I know that — but when the red mist comes down. You're his best friend. I need you to help us with him.'

'He's got a sensible side. I know it's not always on show, but he'll deal with this. He cares too much for Emily to risk hurting her further. I'm sure of it.'

George shakes his head slowly. 'I know you mean well. And I don't think badly of him. I respect him for the way he loves our daughter, I do. In other circumstances I could think of no better man to have in her corner. But when he hears this — and his first thought will be to go and kill this man, because mine is exactly the same right now — he needs to hold himself back. Him ending up in prison for it won't help Emily. She needs him with her, not locked away somewhere. That would break her.'

'George, I know.' Peter sets his bottle down. 'But don't worry about Keagan. I'll take care of him — that's a promise. You concentrate on Emily, she needs her family around her now more than anything. As for Keagan — he'll explode, yes. But he won't let Emily see any of it. I know him. He's spent his whole life hiding what's going on inside. He'll deal with his own feelings in his own way, and he will not make this harder for her. I'd stake everything on it.'

George nods, once, and stares into his glass.

~

KEAGAN SITS ON HIS OWN, his untouched rations in front of him, looking out across the low rooftops of Port Stanley. They have been told to hold their positions at the base of the mountains surrounding the town. The Argentine surrender is being finalised, the last arrangements being made for entering.

It has been two weeks since Goose Green, and there have been further actions since, pushing towards the final assault on the capital. The unit is in reasonable shape. The dark humour has come back, which is always a sign the worst is over. The talk among the men — officers included — is that they should march on Port Stanley now. Word has filtered through that the senior staff want the Marines to enter first. There is symbolic logic to it: the Argentines defeated the Marines in the original invasion, so the Marines returning in triumph would mean something. The Paras' view on this arrangement is short and unprintable. They have fought and bled across this island. They are not waiting for anyone.

The order comes down to form up. They will march on Port Stanley.

Keagan falls in with his unit, fully loaded, a Union Flag on a makeshift pole fixed to his bergen. The joy of finally ending it sits alongside something heavier. Marks had undergone surgery on the hospital ship Uganda but had been in a critical condition. Keagan has put in request after request for information. All he has been told is that the surgery went well but that complications have developed. It is not enough.

The sun is out, though the wind off the water keeps the cold in it. They descend the gentle slopes into the town in single file, talking, laughing — the particular laughter of men who have survived something and are only just beginning to believe it. They are not going to let anyone raise that flag before them. That much is settled.

The track leading into town is scattered with abandoned Argentine equipment and rubbish left where it fell, the whole scene suggesting a hasty and disorganised retreat. As the Paras reach the outskirts, residents start appearing from their houses — bringing beer, bringing wine, reaching out to shake hands or simply to touch them. Kisses from men and women of all ages. A bottle of Famous Grouse passed hand to hand along the column. These are the people they came for, and both sides know it.

At the Governor's residence — the building they all recognise from the television coverage of the initial invasion — the platoon forms up. The flag is raised. Cheers go up from the small gathering of islanders watching, and a long, collective exhale moves through the ranks of men. The job is done.

'Devlin.' A shout carries across the gardens. 'Private Devlin — are you here?'

'Yes, Sarge.' Keagan heads over towards Staff Sergeant Jenkins, the senior NCO of the battalion. 'Here, Sarge.'

'Stand easy, Devlin. Walk with me.'

Something cold moves through him. A walk. In his experience, a walk is never just a walk.

Jenkins falls in beside him as they move across the gardens, away from the group.

'There's no easy way to say this,' Jenkins says. 'I know you were close. Lance Corporal Marks didn't make it, son. The surgeons fought hard for him, but the wounds were too severe and infection set in and they couldn't get ahead of it. He passed at oh-six-hundred this morning. You've been putting in regular requests for information — that's why I wanted to tell you myself. I'm sorry.'

Keagan stands still. He says nothing. Something in his chest feels like it has been struck very hard and he is waiting for the sensation to reach the rest of him.

'I know it's tough,' Jenkins says. 'We've all lost people here. That doesn't make it any easier — I'm not going to insult you by saying it's part of the job, because that's worth nothing right now. You both fought well. Be proud of him. Remember him as the brave young man he was.'

'I will, Sarge.' It is all he can get out.

Jenkins looks at him for a moment. 'Don't go falling apart on me,

Keagan. And before you say it — it's Sergeant, not Sir. I work for a living.' He says it with a dry smile.

'Sorry, Sarge.'

'Here.' Jenkins holds out an envelope. 'Looks like Marks wrote you a death letter. Did you owe him money?'

Keagan takes it. The paper feels thin in his hand. 'The Welsh twat owed me. It's probably an IOU.'

'Get yourself back to your troop. The whisky's going round over there and from the look of it, it won't last long.' Jenkins puts a hand briefly on his shoulder. 'You've all earned it, son.'

'Yes, Sarge. I think we have.'

He waits until Jenkins has walked back towards the others. Then he stands with the envelope in his hand, looking out across the harbour to the cold grey water beyond. Somewhere out there, on a hospital ship, Marks has been dead since this morning. Keagan was laughing and sharing a bottle of Scotch with the islanders and Marks was already gone.

He looks down at the envelope. He does not open it yet.

He puts it carefully inside his jacket, close to his chest, and walks back to join his troop.

CHAPTER

FIFTEEN

FAITH, JUNE 1982

The atmosphere aboard the MV Norland is nothing like it was on the journey south. The excitement and apprehension of before have been replaced by something quieter — relief cut through with grief. The bombs, the tracer fire skimming overhead, the freezing nights in dug-outs: all of it has stripped away any notion of heroism these men might have carried with them. They came here young. They are going back different.

Keagan is lying on his bunk, hands behind his head, staring at the envelope from Marks. It sits on the small desk beneath the porthole where he placed it the day Jenkins handed it to him. That was ten days ago. He has not opened it.

The few days in Port Stanley kept him occupied — organising prisoners, collecting abandoned Argentine weapons, the practical business of ending a war. He told himself he would read the letter when he had the time, properly, and that time would be on the ship. He has been aboard two days now. He still has not opened it.

His roommate, Lance Corporal Jones, puts his head round the door.

'Coming for a beer, mate? Dinner's going down now. We should grab something first and get a table early — I hear Shelly's doing one of his performances tonight.'

'Yeah, sounds all right. What time is it? I've got a call booked for eight.'

'Only half six. Plenty of time.'

They head down together, speculating about what tonight's meal will be. The food on the Norland is generally decent — a significant improvement on ration packs — and tonight it turns out to be shepherd's pie. Keagan clocks the beef mince, notes the difference with the mild irritation of a man who has made this argument too many times before, and says nothing about it.

Shelly is working behind the counter. When he serves Keagan, he looks up with the same expression he has worn since Keagan told him about Marks — a quiet, wordless acknowledgement that sits between them every time their eyes meet. He was badly shaken when Keagan told him. More than Keagan had expected. He had never thought of Marks as anything other than straight, but perhaps he had missed something. He will never know now. The wounds took that away as well.

They settle at the Formica tables with some of the platoon and the conversation spreads out across the evening — the action, Shelly's act, plans for getting home. Word has come through today that the Norland will take them as far as Ascension Island and from there they will be flown back. There is something faintly galling about that. The ships carrying the Marines will sail into Southampton to a heroes' welcome. RAF Brize Norton will be a quieter sort of homecoming. The lads are not happy about it, though nobody is particularly surprised.

Keagan checks his watch, excuses himself, and heads up to the communications room.

~

'Hello, beautiful.' He waits through an unusual number of rings before she answers. 'Everything all right?'

'Yes — I was just upstairs having a bath.'

'We've got good news. We're being flown back from Ascension, so we'll be home sooner. We land at Brize on the sixth of July. It's a Tuesday — not sure what time yet. I don't know if you can get there with work?'

'That is good news. I'll have to check.'

'So how are you, my love? What have you been up to?'

Something is wrong. He can hear it in her voice — a flatness that is not just tiredness.

'Just been busy.'

'How are Peter and Jenny? Have they settled in all right? Is he keeping well?'

'They love the flat. He seems well. I went over when they moved in — it's lovely. I think for Peter it feels like a whole new life.'

'I'm glad for both of them. I know it's not something he ever expected to have. I hope they make the most of it.'

'What do you mean, make the most of it?' Her voice sharpens.

'I just mean — you know what I mean, Em's. He never thought he'd have this. I hope they enjoy every minute.' He pauses. 'Is everything all right? Really?'

'Of course. Why do you keep asking?'

'Because you don't sound like yourself.'

'I'm fine.'

'You've got an edge about you I haven't heard before.'

Silence. Then: 'It's been hard, Keagan. I don't think you realise how hard these months have been. Not hearing anything. Never knowing if you're all right.' She breathes out. 'I'm sorry. I'm tired and it's been a long day. Everything gets on top of me. It's not your fault — it's me. You'll be home soon. Everything will be fine then.'

'Yes it will. I've got leave when I get back and a fair bit of back pay.' He manages a laugh. 'Maybe we could get away for a bit?'

'Yeah — maybe.'

'Only if you can make it, obviously.'

'What's that supposed to mean?'

'Nothing, I just—'

'I do have a life, you know. I can't just drop everything because you've suddenly got time.'

'Sorry, shall I ask the army to plan their wars around your diary?'

'Don't be a smart-arse. Everything's always a joke to you, isn't it.'

'I wasn't joking, Em's. I haven't been away through choice and I know it's been hard. I've never thought otherwise. But I didn't ask for any of this. I was just excited to be coming home.'

'I know.' She says it quickly. 'I'm sorry. I know it's selfish and I didn't mean to have a go at you. I am glad you're coming home — I really am.'

'I know, my love. I miss you.'

'I've missed you too.' A beat. 'I love you, Keagan.'

'I love you too, Em's.'

'I'm sorry about before.'

'Don't be. I shouldn't have bit back.' He hesitates. She is still not telling him something, and he is almost out of time. 'Listen — how's Marks? How are all the lads?'

He hears himself say it and stops.

'Em's — Marks is dead.'

Silence on the line.

'Oh my God. Keagan, I'm so sorry. I know how close you were. Are you all right?'

'Getting there. I was with him when it happened. He left me a letter.'

'What did it say?'

'I haven't opened it yet. Listen, my time's nearly up. I'll call you from Ascension with the details. I love you.'

'I love you too. Bye, Keagan.'

'Bye, Em's.'

HE WALKS BACK through the ship towards the bar, turning the conversation over in his mind. Maybe it is just the strain of the months apart. It must have been hard on her, being at home with no news, waiting. It will all be different when he is back.

Music reaches him before he even gets to the door — Dexys Midnight Runners, "Come On Eileen", rattling down the corridor and the sound of men on the other side of something, properly letting go. He pushes through into the noise and the warmth of it. Sod all the rest of it. He has earned a beer.

~

EMILY GOES BACK UPSTAIRS to her room. She reaches under the bed and pulls out the small kit she had used earlier. She checks her watch. Two hours. The dark ring is there, unmistakeable. The walls close in.

She is pregnant.

~

KEAGAN STEPS down the ramp of the transport plane onto the tarmac at RAF Brize Norton and stands for a moment on British soil. Then he looks for Peter. He knows he is here — they spoke briefly yesterday from Ascension, a short and loaded call that did nothing to settle his nerves.

He had not slept on the flight. Every time he went back over the conversations — Emily, then Peter, then Emily again — the same unease came back. Something is wrong and nobody is telling him. Somewhere over the South Atlantic, he had finally opened Marks's letter. It was brief, just like him. Marks thanked him for his friendship and wrote about his family, his parents' disappointment when he chose the Paras over his father's business. And then the real reason for the letter: inside the envelope was a second, sealed letter addressed to his parents. Marks knew Keagan would find them. He knew he could count on him.

Keagan had folded both letters away carefully and sat in the dark with the engine noise all around him.

'Keagan!' Across the tarmac, Peter, arm raised, grinning.

He waves back and hauls his kit over. Peter pulls him into a hug and claps him on the back, solid and real. Keagan is glad to see him — more than he could have properly said.

'Come on. Let's get to the car — we can talk on the way. It's a good two hours.'

They make their way out through the security cordon to the car park. Peter's green Ford Cortina is parked nearest the gate. Keagan drops his kit at the boot while Peter finds his keys. As soon as the boot is open, he loads the bag in and lights a cigarette.

'You can smoke in the car,' Peter says. 'You know that.'

'I know. I still won't.' He takes a long drag and exhales away from Peter, a habit so old now it is barely a habit at all.

'You can't protect me from everything, mate.'

'I know. Works both ways, doesn't it.' Keagan looks at him steadily. 'So what's going on?'

'Get in the car.'

They pull out of the base and onto the A40. Peter is quiet through the first junction, watching the road.

'So how are you? How did it go over there?'

'Mate.' Keagan's voice is flat and even. 'I'll tell you everything. But first you need to tell me what's happening. Emily isn't right. She didn't come to meet me today. You're hiding something and I've known you long enough to see it from a mile away. Until you tell me what it is, I don't want to talk about the Falklands.'

'All right.' Peter keeps his eyes on the road. 'There's something you need to know. But I need you to listen to everything before you react. Can you do that?'

'What is this?'

'Promise me first.'

'Yes — fine — I promise. Just say it.'

'It's Emily.'

'I worked that out. What about her?'

Peter takes a breath.

'There's no easy way, mate. She's been hurt.'

'Hurt how? What kind of hurt? What does that mean?'

'I'm trying. Give me a second.'

'I know. I'm sorry. I've been through every possible thing in my head for the last twenty-four hours, so please — just tell me.'

Peter keeps his voice steady and level.

'Emily was having a night out with friends from work. Someone she knew from the office.' He pauses. 'I'm sorry, Keagan. She was raped.'

The road ahead is grey and straight. Keagan says nothing.

Peter glances over. Nothing — no shout, no fist through the dashboard. Just Keagan sitting very still, staring through the windscreen. Peter had braced himself for the fury, the instant violence, the full force of everything he knows his friend is capable of. He has never seen him like this. He is not sure it is better.

He waits.

'How did it happen?' The words come out quietly.

Peter goes through it — what he knows, what Jenny told him, the night Emily came to their flat, the police, the statement, the medical examination, everyone rallying round. He tries to be careful with the detail without losing the shape of what happened.

More silence.

'How is she?' Keagan asks.

'Not good. Jenny says she's never seen her this low. She has moments — brief ones — where she seems herself, but most of the time she's very tearful. She's blaming herself, mate. She needs everyone around her right now.'

'Has she been back to work? Seen him?'

'She's signed off. I don't think she'll go back to that firm.'

Peter's hands are steady on the wheel but his mind is not. This stillness is new. In all the years — all the fights and the close shaves and the times Peter has had to step between Keagan and something catastrophic — he has always known what he was dealing with. He knew how to handle the explosion. This is something he has not prepared for.

'You know what night that was,' Keagan says quietly, still looking ahead. 'Goose Green. I was in a trench with Marks trying to hold him together, trying to keep him calm. He died that night.'

Peter glances across. Keagan's face is hard and set, but there are tears on it.

'I'm so sorry, mate. I'm so sorry to be the one telling you. I thought it was better coming from me, before you saw her.'

'Don't apologise to me. You did exactly the right thing.' A pause. 'I heard it in how you told the story. Trying to make sure I understood Emily had no part in any of it. You didn't have to. I know her. She has the biggest heart of anyone I've ever met. I don't care what the circumstances were — it is not her fault. That's not a question.' His jaw tightens. 'What it is, is that some worthless piece of shit decided he could do that to her. And he needs to understand what that feels like.'

He wipes his face with the back of his hand.

'That night — while I was in a ditch with Marks, trying to take his fear away, trying to do something useful for someone — she was going through that. And I wasn't there. I wasn't anywhere near her.' He stops. 'I know it isn't my fault. But it is. It's the worst I've ever felt. Worse than anything over there.'

'Keagan—'

'I'm not arguing about it. I'm just telling you.' He is quiet for a moment. 'And I'll tell you something else. For him, I'll take my time. I'm in no hurry. I'll let him think it's done with. Let him get comfortable. And then I'll make sure he knows exactly what it is to be terrified of someone who can do whatever they want to you.' No heat in it. Just a fact. 'But that's later. Right now everything is Emily. She gets whatever she needs from me. I swear that on everything.'

Peter says nothing for a stretch of road. He had imagined this conversation many times on the drive down — the shouting, the need to physically restrain him. He had not imagined this. The coldness of it unsettles him in a way the fury would not have done.

'I need you to think about what that would cost,' he says carefully. 'For her sake, not yours. She needs you with her — not locked up somewhere. You know that.'

'Who said anything about getting locked up.' For the first time since Brize Norton, Keagan turns and looks at him directly. 'Are you taking me there now?'

'I wasn't planning to go straight there, but if you want—'

'I want to go.'

'She does want to see you. She's nervous, but—'

'Peter.'

'Yeah?'

'Put your foot down. You're driving like a bloody old woman.'

Peter presses the accelerator and lets out a slow breath. Perhaps things will work themselves out, in the end. They usually do. But he makes a quiet note to himself all the same, and keeps it close.

~

VALERIE OPENS THE DOOR. She stands in it for a moment, taking him in — still in his fatigues, kit at his feet, looking like a man who has been somewhere very far away and is not quite all the way back.

'Hello, Keagan.'

'Hello, Valerie. Can I come in and see Emily, please?'

'Let me just check if she's—'

'Keagan.'

Emily's voice, from the top of the stairs. He looks up. She is standing at the landing in the half-light, watching him with an expression he cannot entirely read.

He moves past Valerie and takes the stairs two at a time. He does not say anything. He just puts his arms around her and holds her, properly, the way he has wanted to for six months, and after a moment he feels her stop fighting whatever it is she has been fighting since before he even landed.

He eases back and takes her face in his hands.

'My poor girl. You've been through so much. I'm sorry I wasn't here. But I'm here now, and nobody is ever going to hurt you again.'

That is all he says. It is enough.

She has been running this moment in her head for weeks — what he would think, what he would say, whether anything would be different in his face when he looked at her. All of it dissolves in a second. He is sorry. She does not have the energy to question why that helps as much as it does. She knows there are things still to come, conversations still ahead, futures still to be worked out. But not this minute. She lets go of all of it and buries her face against his shoulder and cries — properly, without trying to stop herself, without trying to protect anyone.

He smells of travel and cigarettes and something she cannot name, and it is the best thing she has ever smelled in her life.

After a moment he says quietly, just for her, 'Come on. Let's get downstairs. I could murder a cup of tea.'

She gives a shaky breath that is almost a laugh. He tucks her under his arm and they go down together.

In the hallway, Peter and Valerie are standing slightly apart, watching. Peter looks at her. She puts her arm around his shoulders without a word.

'Come on,' she says. 'You can help me make it.'

CHAPTER

SIXTEEN

LOVE WILL SAVE THE DAY, JULY 1982

Emily sits in the living room of her parents' house — the place that still feels safest to her, even now. Valerie is beside her on the sofa with one arm around her shoulders. George stands in the doorway to the kitchen, arms folded, jaw set. Peter and Jenny are to one side. Keagan is closest to Emily, standing just behind her, and nobody is saying much of anything.

DC Wade does the talking. PC Coleman — the woman officer who sat with Emily the night she reported it — stands a little to his left. Wade has a practised tone: sympathetic, measured, professional. He explains the investigation, the steps taken, the evidence gathered. He takes his time about it. Then he gets to the part everyone in the room already knows is coming.

There will be no prosecution. The evidence is insufficient. Stephen denies the allegation and maintains it was consensual. In the absence of witnesses and with no physical evidence that contradicts his account, the case would come down to one person's word against another's. No jury, Wade explains carefully, could be expected to return a guilty verdict on that basis alone.

There is one potential witness — a station guard who recalls seeing a couple leave late that evening. He remembers the woman seemed unsteady on her feet and the man was helping her along. They looked, he said, like two people who'd had a late night in the city and a few too many drinks. When shown photographs, he thought the man could be Stephen. He thought the woman could be Emily. In Wade's considered view, this witness is more likely to support Stephen's version of events than Emily's.

Emily listens to all of it without moving.

PC Coleman watches her face and steps in before Wade has finished.

'Emily,' she says, 'I know what you're thinking right now. And I want you to hear me.' She waits until Emily looks at her. 'There's a world of difference between believing you and being able to prove it in a court of law. I've handled many cases like this. I've sat with women like you in rooms like this one and said words like these more times than I care to count. And I know what I saw when I came to you that night. I knew the truth then and I know it now. Every officer involved in this case knows it.' She pauses. 'The law is where it fails, not us and not you. Until something changes — in the courts, in the way juries are directed, in how this crime is treated as evidence — cases like yours will keep falling. I'm sorry. I genuinely am. But I need you to hear this clearly: we believe you. Everyone in this room believes you. That isn't nothing.'

'Thank you,' Emily says. 'I understand.'

She turns her face into her mother's shoulder and cries softly.

George straightens in the doorway.

'Thank you, officers,' he says. 'I think we've heard what we need to hear. Our concern now is for our daughter. If there's nothing further required of us, I'd like to give her some time.'

Wade and Coleman stand. Coleman crosses to Emily and rests a hand briefly on her arm — not quite a hug, but close enough. Then George walks them to the front door.

The room is quiet when he comes back.

'I knew I should have kept my mouth shut,' Emily says. She lifts her head from Valerie's shoulder. 'If I'd said nothing, it would have been mine to deal with. Now everyone knows. It's like I'm wearing it — like

I'll always be wearing it. The girl who was— ' She stops. 'I wish I'd never said a word.'

'Emily Callison.' Valerie's voice is firm but not unkind.

'She's right, Em's,' George says, coming back into the room. He doesn't sit down. 'You did the right thing. Don't let anyone make you think otherwise, including yourself. What happened to you was done to you. That's not yours to carry. None of it.'

'But if I'd kept quiet, nobody else would be hurting. I can see it in all of you. That's because of me. Because I was stupid and careless and—'

'Stop.' George's voice doesn't rise, but it lands. 'You don't believe that and I won't have you saying it. Not under this roof.'

Emily looks at him. She doesn't argue. She just says, 'I don't know what to do, Dad. I don't know what I'm supposed to do now.'

'You don't have to know yet,' Valerie says quietly.

'Could I have a minute with Emily?' Keagan asks.

Valerie glances at George. A look passes between them.

'Of course,' she says. She touches Emily's hand as she stands. 'We'll nip out for a bit.' George picks up his keys from the sideboard without a word. Peter catches Jenny's eye and tilts his head towards the dining room. They follow the Callisons out, the door pulling gently closed behind them.

Keagan moves across and settles onto the sofa beside Emily, turning sideways to face her. He takes both her hands in his.

For a moment he just looks at her. Then he says, 'This is going to be all right.'

She almost tells him not to say that, because people keep saying it and she doesn't know what it means anymore. But she doesn't.

'The prosecution — that's a blow,' he says. 'I'm not pretending otherwise. But for you, it needs to be over now. It's done you enough harm. It has to stop being the thing your life is built around.' He squeezes her hands. 'You've got a career, Em's. You've got people who love you. You've got me, and I'm not going anywhere. You just have to start getting your life back.'

'I can't go back to that office.' Her voice is flat. 'He's there. In the same building.'

'I know. We'll sort that. Nobody expects you to work in the same place as him. Personnel will deal with it — move him, or move you somewhere better, or sort something. And if they won't, I'll go in there myself and have a word.'

She pulls her hands back slightly.

'Keagan.'

'Not like that. I don't mean like that.' He looks at her steadily. 'I mean I'll go in and put pressure on them to handle it properly. Through the front door, during business hours.' A pause. 'I'm not going near him. I know what you need from me and it's not that.'

She holds his gaze. She wants to believe him. Part of her does. But she also knows Keagan — has known him since she was fourteen years old — and there is something behind the steadiness she cannot quite read. He has been quietly constant since he came home. No explosions, no raging, no mention of Stephen except when she has brought it up herself. For another man she would call it maturity and be grateful for it. For Keagan, it feels like the eye of something.

'Promise me,' she says.

'I promise.'

She holds the look a moment longer. Then she nods. She does not ask again, because she cannot afford to pull at that thread right now. There are too many other threads.

She thinks about the pregnancy test under the bed upstairs — the little kit she cannot bring herself to throw away, as though disposing of it would make the result more real rather than less. She has told nobody. She does not know how to begin. She is going to have a child. The child will be Stephen's. She has been through it many times already, in the dark, lying very still and very quiet, and she arrives at the same place every time: she will keep it. It is not about religion. She was baptised into the Church of England and never really grew into it. It is simpler than that. She cannot end a life because of how it started. It will be a disaster — she knows that as clearly as she knows anything — but it will be her disaster, and she will face it when she faces it. Not tonight.

She pushes it back down.

'I think a break would help,' Keagan is saying. 'You've still got a week and a bit signed off, and I'm on leave until the end of the month. What if we got away? The four of us — you and me, Peter and Jenny. A few days somewhere different.' He rubs the back of her hand with his thumb. 'I need to go to Wales at some point. To see Marks's family. He asked me to in his letter, and I'm not going to let him down on that. But we could make a trip of it. Fresh air, bit of countryside. What do you think?'

She is quiet for a moment.

'It would be nice,' she says, 'for the four of us to have some time together.'

'Then we'll do it.'

She leans her head against his shoulder. He puts his arm around her. They sit for a while without speaking.

IN THE DINING ROOM, Peter is standing at the window. Jenny is at the table — the big family table where she has eaten Sunday lunches and birthday dinners and sat up past midnight with Emily and Anna talking about everything and nothing. Today the house has a different weight to it entirely.

'Penny for them,' she says.

He turns. 'Sorry. I was thinking about Keagan.'

'You're always thinking about Keagan.'

'Ha.' He manages the ghost of a smile. 'Fair. But this is different. Something's not right. I saw it on the way back from Brize and I've been watching him ever since and it's still there.'

'I think he's been incredible,' Jenny says carefully. 'Not once has he lost it, not once has he made this about himself. You've been wanting him to grow up for years, love.'

'I know.'

'But?'

He looks at her. She knows him too well.

'He's too calm, Jen. That's not him. He doesn't do calm when it matters — he does calm when he's working something out.'

'You think he has a plan.'

It is not a question.

'I think he might.'

'A plan for what, exactly?'

Peter doesn't answer straight away. He turns back to the window and looks out at the small back garden — the tidy borders, the empty bird table.

'In all the years I've known him,' he says quietly, 'he hasn't let go of a single thing that was done to someone he loved. Not once. And this is the worst thing that has ever happened. So yes. I think he has a plan.'

'He promised her,' Jenny says.

'I know he did.'

'And you don't believe him.'

'I believe he meant it when he said it.'

Jenny is quiet for a moment. She has known Keagan long enough to understand the distinction.

'So what is it you think he'll do?' she asks, though something in her voice suggests she already half knows.

Peter says it plainly.

'Kill him.'

The word sits in the room.

Jenny takes a slow breath. She does not laugh it off. She does not rush to argue with it either. She has had enough conversations with Peter over the years — about Keagan, about his temper, about the times Peter has had to physically step between him and something irreversible — to know that this fear has always been somewhere in the background. But planning was never Keagan's way. His violence was always instinctive, immediate, something that happened before he'd finished the thought. This patient, measured version of him is new.

'I think you're wrong,' she says at last. 'But I think I understand why you're not sure.'

'Yeah,' Peter says. 'That's about where I've got to as well.'

He doesn't say anything else. There is not much else to say. He will watch. That is all he can do.

The dining room door opens and they both turn.

Keagan comes in first, one hand in his jacket pocket. Emily follows, her face still carrying the afternoon — eyes a little swollen, the careful, composed look of someone who has pulled themselves back together through effort rather than feeling better. She takes the seat next to Jenny without a word and Jenny takes her hand.

Keagan crosses to Peter and drops an arm around his shoulders.

'Right,' he says. 'Change of plan. How do you two fancy Wales?'

Peter blinks. 'Wales.'

'Countryside. Fresh air. Sheep. The full experience.' He grins. 'I need to take a letter to Marks's parents — he asked me to see them. I thought we could make a few days of it. The four of us. Get out of here for a bit.' He glances at Emily. She gives a small nod. 'I've just spent three months being shot at,' he adds. 'I think I've earned a few days somewhere quiet.'

The laugh comes before any of them quite decide to allow it — not loud, not long, but real. Jenny shakes her head. Peter raises an eyebrow. Emily, still holding Jenny's hand, looks across at Keagan with something that is not quite a smile but is somewhere near it.

'When?' Peter asks.

'Give it a few days. Let me sort a few things first. But soon.'

'All right,' Peter says. 'Wales it is.'

CHAPTER

SEVENTEEN

NEVER GONNA GIVE YOU UP, JULY 1982

The four of them sit around the small table in the B&B dining room, bright morning light coming in off the bay through the big bay windows. The place is dated but clean, and the view makes up for most of it. They'd agreed on that when they arrived.

'So what's the plan?' Peter asks, pouring from the stainless steel teapot.

'Keagan goes up to Merthyr this morning,' Emily says, 'and the three of us can have a look around, maybe get down to the beach.' She looks more like herself than she has in weeks, though there is still something held back behind the eyes.

'Sounds good,' Jenny says.

'I should be back by mid-afternoon,' Keagan says. 'Mr Marks mentioned a pint at the working men's club. The family are well known there, apparently.'

'Don't have too many,' Emily says. 'You're driving.'

'The all-new sensible Keagan, remember.'

141

That gets raised eyebrows all round, and a laugh that feels like the first real one in some time.

~

THE ROADS into Merthyr are the best thing about the drive — tight bends, long drops, the kind of roads the Ford XR3 was built for. He'd bought it from a sergeant in the regiment; it had been sitting at his parents' while he was deployed and this is the first proper run out. He has the Pioneer going at full volume and it helps, though not entirely. He is enjoying the car and the road and the fact that for the moment nobody needs anything from him. But underneath that is something he can't quite switch off. That bastard will not get away with it. He has been calm and steady for Emily's sake, and he will keep being calm and steady, but the thought is always there — patient, waiting.

He goes through the route from memory. Maps have always been his strongpoint.

Dai Marks had talked about his parents' place. The biggest house in the town, he'd say, and laugh as though embarrassed by it. His father had started out as a miner's son, got himself a labour-supply business, built it into something much larger. Keagan pulls onto the gravel drive and cuts the engine. His watch says eleven exactly. Military punctuality. He's pleased with himself.

He finds the old pull-bell beside the front door and waits. The door opens and a short, round woman in her fifties looks up at him.

'You must be Keagan, love. I'm Gwyneth. Come in, Roger's in the study. I'll get the tea on.'

She shows him to the study door and disappears towards the kitchen. He knocks and enters. Roger Marks is at the desk, reading through papers. He stands when he sees Keagan.

'There you are, Keagan. Good to meet you, son. Gwyn'll have the tea sorted in a minute.' He shows him to one of two sofas facing the fire-place, a vase of flowers standing where the fire would be. They sit across from each other and within a minute Gwyneth is back with a tray — pot, cups, biscuits.

Keagan reaches into his jacket for the envelope.

'Dai left this inside his letter to me,' he says, handing it to Roger. 'He wanted me to bring it to you in person.'

Roger takes it and passes it straight to his wife without opening it. 'That's him all over,' he says. 'Never the prolific writer, but he always wanted to do things properly. In his own way.' He uses his son's actual name — Dai — naturally, easily, and Keagan finds he prefers it. More real than Marks.

Gwyneth opens the letter. It is two pages. Keagan watches her read without watching too closely, giving her that much. He can see the moment the tears start to gather. A proud woman — she is keeping herself composed by sheer force of will, and he respects her for it. When she finishes, she passes the letter to Roger and thanks Keagan for making the journey.

'He speaks very highly of you,' she says. 'You must have been good friends.'

'We were,' Keagan says. 'Yeah. We were.'

Roger reads while Gwyneth talks — stories about Dai as a boy, pranks he'd pulled, the particular stubbornness he'd had since childhood. Keagan can hear Marks in all of it. The same grin behind the same stubbornness. He finds it very difficult to hold onto himself. He had not had the time to grieve properly, and sitting here with these two people who loved him is making it harder to hold at arm's length.

Then Gwyneth asks the question he knew was coming.

'Can you tell us how it happened? The letter from the Army doesn't say very much. Only that it was combat injuries. If you were with him, it would help us.'

'I was with him,' he says.

He takes his time. He keeps the description of the injuries simple — they don't need those details, and he is not going to give them. What he focuses on instead is Dai's bravery, his steadiness under pressure, the kind of soldier he had become. He is finding, as he talks, that it is doing something for him too. He has not spoken about it properly until now. Having two people in front of him who need to understand it — who have every right to understand it — makes him go through it clearly, without flinching away.

Roger listens to all of it without interrupting. When Keagan finishes, he says, 'Thank you, son. You've given us more than the whole of the MoD put together. Knowing it was real, knowing he had someone with him — it means a great deal.'

They move on after that, to stories, to laughter. Keagan tells them about Shelly — the steward-turned-cabaret act on the MV Norland, and the attention lavished on a deeply uncomfortable Dai Marks — and both parents laugh, really laugh, and for a few minutes the room feels almost warm.

Then Keagan finds himself answering Roger's question about his own plans after the army, and the honesty that comes out surprises him.

'I miss him,' he says. 'He was the best of us, and I feel such guilt about losing him that I'm not sure I want to go through all of that again. I was yards from him when it happened and I couldn't do a thing. Those rounds could have hit me just as easily, and then your son would be here instead, telling stories about what a dodgy cockney bastard I was.' He stops. 'Sorry about the language. That's what he used to call me.' He tries to smile but it doesn't quite reach. 'Damn, it's not fair. He didn't deserve it. And I killed the man who fired the shots, and I'd do it again.'

He goes quiet. Roger and Gwyneth look at each other and give him the space.

'I'm sorry,' he says. 'That was uncalled for. You have your own grief. You don't need my anger on top of it.'

'It's all right, boy,' Roger says. 'Your anger is the same as ours. It's normal. And hearing it from you — from someone who was actually there — helps us more than you know. Never be embarrassed about it.'

'Thank you.'

Roger glances at Gwyneth, and she gives a small nod.

'Keagan,' he says, 'there's something in Dai's letter I want you to consider. Before he left, we had spoken about him coming to work with me after his three years were up. I had a role for him heading up a new operation we've been establishing in Pittsburgh — training and management development, applying military discipline to commercial practice. He was going to start later this year.' He pauses. 'His letter asks me to offer you the role instead. Now, don't think I'd have mentioned it if you'd walked in here today and been an idiot. I wouldn't have insulted my son's memory with that.' He says it without a smile, then adds: 'But I've spent two hours with you, and I like what I see. It was his last wish, and I intend to honour it. I'd like you to consider it.'

Keagan sits back.

A job reference. His friend's last letter is a job reference. The thought makes him laugh, internally, and then it touches him more than he can easily say — because Dai Marks had thought about this while they were dug in on a hillside in the South Atlantic, and had written it down, and meant it.

'Roger,' he says, 'I wasn't expecting that. Not even a little.'

'I know. I'd normally never ambush someone like this — but that was Dai's doing, not mine.'

'Typical of him.'

'Yes. Please take whatever time you need. If you decide it's not for you, no hard feelings. But I think you'd be an asset, and I don't say that lightly.'

On the drive back to Barry, Keagan's head is full of it. Pittsburgh. America. He knows almost nothing about the city, but he knows enough about the offer — the role, the money, what Roger had outlined. He had barely let himself think about life after the regiment. Now he has something to think about, and for the first time in a long while it feels like a forward direction. He and Emily. A fresh start. Away from all of it. He allows himself to get ahead a little — in a good way, just this once.

PETER GOES BACK to the B&B with the bags after the shopping, saying he'll have a lie-down for an hour. Emily and Jenny find a pair of deckchairs near the back of the beach and settle into the early summer sun. It is the first time the two of them have simply sat together, just the two of them, in what feels like months.

'How's he doing?' Emily asks. 'I've been so wrapped up in every-thing. Peter's colour hasn't been good these last few days and I haven't said anything.'

'He's tired,' Jenny says. 'I'm keeping an eye on it. This break might help, actually. Fresh air, a bit of rest. He's been carrying a lot of worry about you. About Keagan.'

'It must be so hard. For both of you.'

'He's lived with it all his life. He copes.' Jenny is quiet for a moment. 'It's hardest when we try to plan for the future. He'd love a family. We both would. But it's almost impossible with his condition — the doctors have been straightforward about that. And even if it weren't — ' She doesn't finish the sentence. She doesn't need to.

'And you?'

'I knew all of this before I fell in love with him. He hid nothing.' Jenny looks out at the sea. 'I don't pretend I don't wish for more. But I wouldn't want anyone else. I just want as much time with him as possible, and I want it to matter.'

Emily takes her hand and holds it for a moment, and doesn't try to find the right thing to say because there isn't one.

After a while, Jenny looks at her. 'And you and Keagan. He's been incredible. I'll admit I didn't always give him enough credit, but he adores you. The way he's handled all of this — '

'I know.' Emily doesn't look away from the water. 'He's been brilliant.'

Jenny waits.

'But,' Emily says.

'But?'

'It's not over yet, Jen. Not all of it.'

'The intimacy? I hadn't thought about it properly, but — '

'It's not that. I know we'd get through that. I've always felt safe with him. I know I would still.' She stops. Then she says it. 'Jen. I'm pregnant.'

Jenny goes still.

She doesn't need to ask. She already knows. Keagan has been on the other side of the world since long before any of this happened. She turns in her chair and reaches over to take Emily's hand.

'Oh Em's. I'm so sorry. When did you find out? Does anyone know?'

'No one. You're the first. I did a test, then I went to the doctor on Monday. It's confirmed.'

'What are you going to do?'

'If you mean am I going to have an abortion — no. I can't, Jen. I just can't. That's not about religion or anything like that, it's just — I can't end a life for what its father did.'

'I understand that. I do.' Jenny is careful. 'But Emily. Keagan. Have you thought about — '

'I've thought about almost nothing else.' Emily's voice is steady, and that is somehow the most heartbreaking thing about it. 'I keep telling myself it will be all right, that Keagan is a good man, that he'll find a way to accept it. But then I think about if it's a boy, and he looks like Stephen. How could Keagan look at that child every day? How could anyone? And the child can't suffer for what its father did. That's not fair.'

'And Stephen—'

'Stephen will never know. I'm leaving NatWest anyway. He'll never be any part of my life or this child's.'

'Emily.' Jenny looks at her directly. 'You've already decided, haven't you. Not just about the baby. About Keagan.'

Emily doesn't answer straight away.

'I love him,' she says at last. 'I want you to know that. And the thought of it — ' Her voice catches, just once. 'But I'm thinking about the next twenty years, Jen. Not tomorrow. I know him. I know us. And I think if we try to push through this, we'll spend years resenting each other, and it will end badly, and whatever was good between us will be ruined. I don't want that. He deserves better than that. So do I.'

Jenny is quiet for a long time.

'I won't tell you you're wrong,' she says finally. 'I disagree with you, but I won't tell you you're wrong. Just don't shut me out. Now more than ever.'

'I won't.' Emily squeezes her hand. 'Now will you please hug me, and can we agree that for the rest of this trip we're just four friends on holiday? I want to remember it that way.'

Jenny hugs her, hard. And they sit like that for a while, with the sun on their faces and the sea going in and out, and neither of them says anything more about any of it.

THEY FIND an Italian restaurant for dinner and the evening opens up into something approaching normal — football, the shopping trip, the state of Barry Island's nightlife, Peter doing a surprisingly good impression of the B&B owner. Keagan talks at length about the visit to Merthyr, telling them about Roger and Gwyneth, about Dai as a boy, about the story of Shelly on the Norland. He keeps the Pittsburgh offer back. He wants to think it through more carefully, and he wants to have the right conversation with Emily before he mentions it to anyone. On the drive back he had half-planned the proposal in his head. He pulls back from it now and lets the evening be what it is.

They find a bar along the seafront — The Friars, says the painted board above the door. Inside: sticky floors, dim lights, a dance floor playing something synthy and new romantic that is not quite their sound, but danceable enough.

The men go to the bar. The women find a table near the back, away from the speakers.

'Need to tell you something later,' Keagan says to Peter as they're waiting to be served. 'Something happened today.'

'That's always a comforting opening,' Peter says.

'Nothing bad. Just — something I want to run past you.'

Peter gives him a measured look. 'All right.'

They carry the drinks over. The conversation runs easily. Keagan is aware, in the way he always is in an unfamiliar pub, of the looks coming their way. Cockney in Wales. He's had worse. Not tonight, he tells himself. Not tonight.

Then someone walking past catches his raised pint glass with an arm. Beer down the front of Keagan's shirt.

He stands.

'I think sorry's the word you're looking for,' he says.

The man — local, well-built, somewhere in his thirties — stops and turns. 'Accident, boyo. What's the problem?'

The table goes quiet. Emily stands and puts a hand on Keagan's arm.

'Leave it,' she says quietly. 'We don't want any trouble.'

'And there won't be any,' Keagan says, not looking away from the man. 'Because this fella is going to apologise and offer to buy us all a round. Aren't you, mate.' It is not quite a question. He keeps his voice flat and even, and keeps his eyes on the man's eyes.

There is a flicker there — uncertainty, calculation — and then the man nods.

'Fair enough. Accident, mate. Let me get you all a drink.'

Keagan sits back down. 'The man's a gent,' he says to Emily. Then, to the man: 'Very kind of you, but we've just got one in. Appreciate the apology though.'

The man moves off. Emily breathes out. Peter watches from across the table with a dry half-smile. Jenny stares at Keagan with an expression that could strip paint.

'What?' he says.

He blows her a kiss. Her mouth twitches, and she can't quite hold it back.

'Come on,' she says to Emily, 'let's have a dance.'

As the girls move towards the floor, Peter looks at him across the table.

'Go on then,' he says.

'Roger — Mr Marks — offered me a job today. Dai's job. He was leaving the regiment this year, apparently, and his father had a role lined up for him. In his letter, he asked Roger to offer it to me instead.'

'That's — ' Peter pauses. 'Is that good?'

'Yeah. Yeah, I think it is. It's a management development role, building up a new operation from scratch. Good money. And it would mean getting out when my three years are up.' He looks at Peter. 'Emily doesn't need another war, does she.'

'No,' Peter says. 'She doesn't.'

'There's a catch,' Keagan says.

'Of course there is.'

'It's in Pittsburgh.'

Peter says nothing for a moment. 'America.'

'America. I know it's a long way. But I think — she needs to get away from here, Peter. From all of it. Different city, different life. And I'm going to propose before we go. I don't want you missing my wedding.' He grins. 'That's the only reason I'm keeping you in the loop.'

Peter gives him a long look. Then he says, 'And Jenny.'

'The flights are included. Four return trips a year. I'll make sure you get over there. The money's good enough that I could pay on top of that if needed.'

'I'm pulling your leg, you idiot. Don't worry about us.' Peter sits back. 'I think it sounds right. The job. The proposal. Going somewhere new. I think it might be exactly what she needs, and you too.' He looks at the table a moment. 'You'd have told her all of this even without Roger's offer, you know. About the proposal. About getting out.'

'Yeah,' Keagan says. 'I know.'

'Then that's your answer, isn't it.'

Keagan is still thinking about that when he excuses himself for the gents. He's standing at the urinal when the door opens and someone takes the spot beside him.

It is the man from earlier.

'That a Para totem?' he says, nodding at the tattoo on Keagan's right forearm — the full Parachute Regiment totem pole, chosen specifically because he wanted to be different from everyone else who'd just got the wings.

'Two Para,' Keagan says. 'You serve?'

'Welsh Guards.'

'You in the Falklands?'

'Sir Galahad.'

A beat.

'Bloody hell,' Keagan says quietly. 'I'm sorry, mate.'

'I was at the right end of the ship. Walked off. But I lost a lot of friends that night.'

'Let me buy you that beer. Properly this time.'

They come out together and Keagan joins him at the bar with his group — all Guards, all veterans, some of them carrying it differently from others. They talk for ten minutes or so: frank and direct, the way men who've been in the same kind of places talk, with the banter still running underneath the harder things. Keagan buys the round and heads back to his table.

'Ten minutes ago you were about to start a war,' Peter says. 'Now you're best friends.'

'Welsh Guards,' Keagan says. 'Good lads. They were on that ship that got hit. Lost over fifty of their regiment that night, those were a few of the ones who walked away.' He picks up his pint. 'I was glad to buy them a beer.'

Emily looks at him across the table. 'I'm sorry, Keagan. For all of it. We haven't given you much space to deal with any of what you went through.'

'Stop.' His voice is gentle but firm. 'Don't. I don't need space, I need a normal evening with three people I love. So no more war talk.' He looks at Jenny and Emily both. 'What are we doing tomorrow, then?'

EIGHTEEN

A DIFFERENT CORNER, JULY 1982

Peter appears in the kitchen doorway.

'Big night tonight,' he says.

They're back home, the Wales trip behind them — a few days that felt, for the most part, like something close to ordinary life. Peter had spoken to Keagan earlier in the day. Tonight is the night.

'What do you mean?' Jenny calls from the kitchen. 'It's only eggs.'

'Not dinner.'

She comes through into the living room, wooden spoon in hand. 'What are you talking about?'

'I'm not supposed to say anything,' Peter says, 'but you won't be speaking to Emily before tomorrow anyway, so.' He pauses. 'Keagan's going to ask her to marry him tonight. He's accepted the job — the one Marks's dad offered him in Pittsburgh. Head of a department. Great money, great role. And it was in the letter, apparently, the one he had to take to them in person. He wants Emily to go with him. Fresh start, away from everything.' He watches her face. 'I know I said I'd keep it quiet, but it's good news, Jen. That's all right, isn't it?'

Jenny stands very still.

She knows, of course, what tonight will actually bring. She knows about the pregnancy. She knows about the decision Emily has already made, quietly and alone, and brought to shore on a deckchair in Barry in the early summer sun. And she knows now that Keagan is walking into that house tonight with a ring and a job offer and a future all planned out, and Emily is going to take it apart.

How does she explain any of that without explaining all of it?

'Jen.' Peter is watching her. 'You all right?'

'Peter,' she says, 'sit down. Give me a minute, I'll turn the dinner off.'

She goes to the kitchen and clicks off the cooker. She stands there for a moment looking at the wall. Then she goes back in, sits beside him on the sofa, and tells him everything. The pregnancy. What Emily said on the beach. Her reasons for ending it, the baby, her certainty that she won't change her mind. She tells him she disagreed, she still does, but she understood why Emily swore her to silence. She tells him she's sorry she didn't say anything before now.

'Shit, Jen.'

'I know.'

'You should have told me.'

'And you would have told Keagan. You know you would.'

He doesn't answer that.

'It wasn't ours to fix,' she says. 'Whatever we did would only have made it worse.' She leans forward. 'I'm sorry, love. I hated keeping it from you.'

He's quiet for a moment. Then he says, 'That bastard's going to walk away from this without a scratch. No charge, no trial, nothing. And if this goes the way you're saying — ' He stops. 'Emily is everything to Keagan, Jen. Everything. The only reason he's kept himself together this long is because of her. You take that away and I genuinely don't know what he'll do.'

'Don't,' she says quietly.

'You know what he's capable of. I know him better than anyone.'

'Let's not go there yet. Let's just see what happens tonight.' She takes his hand. 'Maybe it'll work out. Maybe against all odds they'll find a way through. I hope so. God knows I hope so.'

Peter nods, but his eyes say something else entirely.

~

KEAGAN ARRIVES to find the house in full swing. Valerie had promised toad-in-the-hole, his favourite, and she hasn't let him down. The whole family has made the effort — table set, the good plates out, the sense of a deliberate return to something normal after weeks of difficulty. They think of Keagan as one of their own, and tonight feels like a celebration of that.

Emily had wanted it quieter. She'd thought having her family around would make it easier. Now, watching Keagan come through the door full of life and laughter with Anna already pulling him towards the sofa, she's not sure she thought it through.

Anna is completely in her element. She has missed him, and she makes no effort to hide it. He sits there with her perched beside him, laughing at everything he says, and Keagan is glowing. Emily watches him and loves him and hates herself for what she is about to do.

'Can I help with anything, Valerie?' he asks, as they carry the food through to the dining room.

'No, sit yourself down. You and the girls go on through.'

You and the girls. Emily catches the phrase and almost smiles despite herself. She and Anna have apparently been demoted. Her dad catches her eye across the table and gives her a look that says he's noticed too. She loves that look. She will miss it when it's gone — and it will be gone tonight, because she's about to change everything again, for all of them, and it won't be Stephen who's to blame this time. This time it will be her.

Dinner is long and lively. Keagan talks about the Falklands — properly, for the first time with the family, in a way he can control. He keeps it away from the worst of it, but he doesn't water it down either. He's at ease. Her dad leans forward across the table, her mum refills wine glasses without noticing she's doing it, and Anna barely touches her food. They haven't taken their eyes off him all evening.

Emily eats and says little.

She thinks about Wales. The first night they'd been nervous — both of them, neither saying as much. They'd just held each other in the dark, all night. She'd felt completely safe. By the last night something had shifted and she'd wanted him, and she'd asked for it because she wanted one last time to know what it felt like to be loved by him without fear or shadow in the room.

He didn't know it was a last time. He knows nothing. He still thinks they're heading somewhere together.

She should have told him sooner. She should have said it in Wales, or before Wales, or weeks ago. But she hadn't, and now she has to say it here, at her family's dinner table, with toad-in-the-hole going cold on the plates.

'If it's all right, George,' Keagan says, 'there's something I wanted to ask you. I know everyone's here, but I don't mind if nobody else does.'

Emily sees her father's expression shift — pleased, curious, already half-guessing.

'Keagan,' she says quietly, 'maybe we could do this later — '

'That's all right, Emily,' her dad says. 'Let the man speak.' He's enjoying this.

'Yes, go on,' Anna says.

Keagan straightens. 'Right. It's two things, really. First, I've been offered a job. It's a brilliant opportunity — running a department for an investment company, good money, real scope for me to do something. But it's in Pittsburgh, in America.'

Silence around the table. Forks put down.

'And second,' he says, 'I wouldn't want to go there without Emily. I love her and I'd want her to have a new life with me.' He looks at George. 'So I'm asking your permission to marry her.'

Smiles begin to break across the table — her father, Anna, the warmth in the room going up immediately. Only Valerie pauses. She looks at Emily — really looks at her — and something in what she sees makes her say, gently, that perhaps the two of them should have a moment to themselves first.

'It's a huge thing,' Valerie says, 'for you both. Perhaps you should talk to each other before anything else. We'd be thrilled, of course we would, but — Emily?'

'Yes,' Emily says. 'Yes, let's clear the table and — let's give us a few minutes.'

The family move quietly to the kitchen, carrying plates, keeping the noise low. Keagan and Emily are left alone at the dining table with the candles still burning.

'What's the matter?' he says. 'I thought you'd be pleased, Em's. It's your family, they're happy for us — '

'It's not that.' She keeps her voice steady. 'I didn't know about Pittsburgh. Or the job. You'd accepted before we talked about any of it, and — I need you to listen to me now. I have something to say first.'

'Go on then, I'm listening.'

'It's not simple.' She looks at him. 'I love you. I need you to know that before I say any of this, because it's the reason I'm saying it. I want you to have a good life. And I don't think I can give you that now. Not after everything.'

'That's rubbish,' he says, 'we've already started working through it. Wales — '

'Wales was wonderful. It was. But Keagan, there's something else. Something you don't know yet, and when I tell you, you'll understand why I'm saying what I'm saying.'

He waits.

'I'm pregnant.'

The word lands and the room goes quiet. Not quiet the way rooms go quiet when they're empty — the other kind, the dense kind, where something enormous is taking up all the space.

'His?' Keagan says.

'Yes.' She doesn't look away from him. 'There's no doubt. You were away for months and I'd stopped taking the pill because — it doesn't matter why. There's no doubt.'

'You're going to keep it.'

'Yes.' Her voice holds. 'I've thought about it and I know what I think. It's not a choice I'm making lightly. But this baby didn't choose its father, and I won't punish it for that.'

'And you don't want me around.'

'I'm not saying I don't want you. I'm saying I can't ask you to stay. Not for this.' She leans forward slightly. 'You would try, I know that. For a while you'd manage. But there would come a day — a day when that child does something, or looks a certain way, or you're tired, or frightened — and you wouldn't be able to help it. I know you, Keagan. I know how much you love me and I know what this would cost you. It would cost us both everything, eventually. And I won't do that to either of us. And I won't do it to this child.'

'So that's it,' he says. 'I come here tonight with all of this — a job, a future, all of it — and this is where we are.'

'I'm sorry.'

'You're sorry.' He stands up. 'I don't understand. I genuinely don't understand why you want this baby so much that everything else — us, the job, America, everything — just goes. WHY? JUST TELL ME WHY YOU WANT THIS.'

He crosses to the wall and punches it, open-handed, hard enough to make a sound.

Emily flinches.

The door opens. George puts his head in, reading the room in a second.

'Everything all right?'

'Yes, Dad. Keagan's upset. It's all right.'

'Upset.' Keagan turns. 'Yeah. Upset. Are you happy about this, George? About the baby?'

George goes very still. 'What?'

'Dad, it's all right. Keagan's leaving. I'll explain everything in a minute.' Her voice is controlled. Just about.

'Go on then,' Keagan says. 'Good luck with that.' He looks at George, then at Emily. He breathes in. 'Three months I was away. Fighting a war. My closest friend died in front of me, and I spent that night trying to hold him together in a ditch in the dark. I came home and found out what happened to you. I've been there for every minute of it. I've been careful about everything I've said, everything I've done, thinking about you every step of the way. And all this time, you've known about this baby and you've said nothing.' His voice breaks slightly at the edges before he brings it back. 'Now you tell me to go. Because you've decided. No conversation, no — nothing. Just: go. Well fine, Emily. If that's all you think of me, then you're right. I should go.'

He moves past George in the doorway and out through the hall. The front door opens and shuts.

Emily sits at the table and does not move for a moment.

Then she breaks — quietly, without drama, the way people break when they've been holding something too tightly for too long. The tears come and she doesn't stop them. Her father crosses the room and puts his arms around her. Her mother and Anna come in from the kitchen without being called, the way families do, drawn by something they couldn't hear but felt anyway.

They go through to the living room. Her mum sits on one side of her, Anna on the other. Neither of them speaks. They wait.

'I'm sorry,' Emily says, when she can. 'I'm sorry. I've made a mess of everything again.'

'You haven't made a mess of anything,' Valerie says.

'Don't say that.' Emily wipes her face. 'You don't know everything yet.'

So she tells them. She does it carefully and without drama, because she has been carrying it long enough that the words are worn smooth now. The pregnancy. The decision to keep the baby. Her reasons for ending it with Keagan — not because she has stopped loving him, but because she doesn't want to watch love turn into resentment over twenty years, and she doesn't want her child to grow up in the middle of that, and she doesn't want Keagan to feel obligated to be something he cannot be.

She tells them she will leave NatWest. She wants to stay at home while the baby is small. She will manage. She will be all right.

When she finishes they look at her, and she sees on their faces what she expected to see: devastation, softened by love.

Nobody fills the silence with the wrong thing. That is, she thinks, one of the things she loves best about her family.

'I need to phone Jenny,' she says. 'I promised.'

She goes out to the hallway.

~

Peter has been sitting on the sofa, barely moving, for the past half hour.

He hears Jenny's voice in the kitchen — low, steady, the kind of tone she uses when she's working hard at holding herself together.

'I'll come over tomorrow. We love you, Em's. It's going to be all right. Goodnight.'

She comes back into the room. She sits down beside him and puts her arms around him without saying a word. Her shoulders move. He holds her and looks straight ahead at the wall.

Keagan walks alone through the overgrown path that runs behind the estate, his hands in his pockets, the night air cold against his face. In his jacket pocket is a small ring box. He hadn't even had the chance to take it out.

He walks for a long time.

CHAPTER

NINETEEN

JOY AND PAIN, JULY 1982

He double-checks the lock as he steps out onto the street.

It's been a better couple of weeks than he'd expected. The previous morning at the police station had been almost anticlimactic — a brief conversation, a few forms, and then he was back out on the pavement in the mild morning air, free and clear. No charges. No prosecution. Exactly as he'd known it would be, because there was nothing to prosecute.

He'd called his brother straight afterwards and they'd spent the evening doing the circuit of the local pubs, celebrating. His brother was a fireman with the London Fire Brigade — wouldn't be up until midday, shift not starting until evening — and a man of many sidelines, some of which Stephen had long suspected weren't entirely above board. He didn't ask questions about those. He never had.

He turns up his collar against the cool morning air and walks. The same thoughts circle back to him on the walk to the station, as they always do.

She wanted it. He'd been over and over it a hundred times and the

160

answer was always the same. Coming to his flat like that, making herself at home, lying down on his bed. All right, she'd had a bit too much to drink, and perhaps she'd felt guilty afterwards — embarrassed about what she'd done, in the cold light of morning — and so she'd reached for a word that made her feel better about herself. That's what it was. Because rape was what perverts did to strangers in parks and alleyways. Not two adults who'd fancied each other from the first week she started and had finally got round to doing something about it. She'd said no, certainly — they always said no, it was practically reflexive — but that wasn't the same thing. It was not the same thing at all.

The sheer bloody cheek of it. Going to the police with a story like that, dragging him in, putting him through a morning he should never have had to endure. And then that boyfriend of hers turning up at her workplace, all broad shoulders and cold eyes, playing the outraged soldier. Stephen had thought about that more than once. The army type — violent, probably, under the surface. Half of them were. She needed a reason, a story she could tell him so she wouldn't have to admit what she'd actually done. He was convenient. That's all he was. Well, she'd picked the wrong man for a scapegoat.

He'd heard she hadn't come back to work yet. Being transferred to another department, apparently — his contacts in HR had confirmed as much. Fine. He was already looking forward, as he always did. Patricia, for instance, was patient work, but he had time. He always had been good at waiting.

The station entrance comes into view and he picks up his pace slightly.

The platform is busier than usual. He checks the board: the 7:05 cancelled. Two trainloads of commuters standing in one space, shuffling and sighing and clutching their newspapers. He takes in the situation quickly, then begins to move through the crowd — slowly, deliberately, with the practised, slightly aggressive confidence of a man who does this every morning and intends to reach the front before anyone notices quite what he's doing.

He gets there. Centre of the third carriage doors — his spot, the same spot every day for years, chosen because the doors always stop exactly there and from there you can be first on, first seated, away from the standing crush. It's not comfortable, the pressing crowd behind him, the heat of other people's coats and coffee cups, but he has his ground and he won't be moved from it.

The man beside him is not one of the regulars. He's carrying one of those big pilot cases, the kind that businessmen carry as though the size of the case corresponds to the importance of the meeting, and he sets it down on the platform in front of him. Not quite in front of himself, though. Half of it extends across into the space in front of Stephen's feet — the exact ground he needs clear for when the doors open.

'Excuse me,' Stephen says, tapping the man on the shoulder. 'Would you mind moving that?'

The man turns briefly, then turns back and carries on his conversation, laughing at something the person on his other side has said.

Stephen looks at the man's profile for a moment. Then he slides his foot under the handle of the pilot case and nudges it firmly to the right, back to where it belongs.

He looks along the platform for the train. The crowd shuffles around him, two hundred people and the breath of them, the combined heat of impatience. He can feel the case again at his feet. The man has pushed it back without even looking round.

The track gives off the faint hum that precedes the train's arrival. Thirty seconds, perhaps. The crowd leans slightly forward as one. Stephen glances along the platform and sees the lights of the train at the far end, coming in fast, beginning to brake.

He bends down to push the case away one final time — shoulders forward, weight shifting — and in that exact moment he feels a firm, deliberate push against his back.

His balance goes completely.

His leg connects with the pilot case and there is nothing to grab, nothing to catch himself on, and he spins as he falls and sees — just for a second, just a flash — the back of a man moving quickly through the crowd, already gone, already absorbed into the mass of coats and shoulders, and then the edge of the platform is beneath his feet and then not beneath his feet at all, and the grey morning sky tilts sideways.

The train is there.

The last thing he feels is fear. Absolute and total. A terror that fills every part of him in the single second he has left — the only honest thing he has felt in a very long time. He doesn't think about Patricia. He doesn't think about the police station or the pubs or the friends he called to celebrate. He doesn't think about that bloody woman, or the boyfriend, or anything at all that has occupied the last months of his life.

He is simply afraid.

And then he is not anything at all.

~

JENNY HAS BEEN with Emily all morning.

Neither of them had slept much. She'd told Peter that on the doorstep when he dropped her off, though there wasn't much more she could say in thirty seconds with her coat on. He'd understood. He always did. He'd squeezed her hand, and she'd gone inside.

She'd found Emily already up, already on her second cup of tea at the kitchen table with the expression of someone who had been sitting in the dark for some time before deciding to put a light on. They'd talked — properly, just the two of them — until Valerie came downstairs and took over the tea-making and moved them through to the living room with the quiet authority of a woman who needs to feel she is doing something useful.

'You're going to be all right,' Jenny says. 'I'll be here. We all will.'

'I know.' Emily has both hands around her mug. 'I just keep going over it, Jen. Asking myself if I've done the right thing. I love him so much and I still did it, and I can't quite — I don't know what to do with that.'

'I can't tell you whether it was right. But you did what you believed was right for both of you, and that's all any of us can do, in the end. I'll always back you on that.'

'It's not just me, though. It's all of them.' Emily glances towards the door. 'Mum, Dad, Anna. I look at their faces and I can see it, even when they don't say anything. They loved him. He was part of this family and now he isn't and this time it's not anybody else's fault. It's me.'

'Don't do that.'

'Anna's devastated. She called him her big brother, you know. She's lost that now and I don't — '

'Come in, you two,' Valerie says from the doorway. 'Come and sit down properly. We'll have some tea and talk about how we're going to get through this.'

The living room is bright with pale summer sun. George is in his armchair, mug in hand, wearing the particular expression Emily associates with him having already made a decision about something and working up to announcing it. He'd taken another day off work. He has the look of a man with a plan, which is both a comfort and mildly exhausting when what Emily actually wants is to sit quietly and not think about anything for a few hours.

Jenny sits at one end of the sofa. Emily takes the other.

The radio is on in the kitchen. Jimmy Ruffin's 'Farewell is a Lonely Sound' drifts through, quiet and warm and absolutely impossible under the circumstances. Jenny gets up, goes to the kitchen, switches it off, and comes straight back without saying a word about it.

Valerie stands at the centre of the room and begins. She and George have clearly been planning since before six. The large bedroom will be moved around for the baby. She isn't working full time so she can be there through the day. George will pick up additional hours at work if they need it. Emily should leave her job as soon as possible — the stress will be too much and there's no point putting herself through it. They can manage. They'll do this together.

Everything Valerie says is built around the family, around closing ranks, around making it work. It's what Emily needs to hear. She knows that. She listens and nods and is genuinely, deeply grateful for every word.

And underneath all of it, part of her mind keeps drifting somewhere else.

The Isle of Wight. A window open on a summer morning, the smell of the sea. The way Keagan always turned back at the door before he left — always, without fail, as though he couldn't quite bring himself to simply walk away. The night she'd been frightened and he'd held her without speaking because he understood, somehow, that speaking wasn't the point.

She will get through this. She knows herself well enough to know that — she will make a good life for herself and for this baby, and she will not be defined by what happened to her, and she will not let her child feel the shadow of it. But this is not what she wanted. It was never what she wanted. That's the thing she has to sit with now, alongside everything else.

The doorbell rings.

George goes to it. A moment later Peter's voice comes from the hall and then he appears in the doorway, asking how everyone's doing, how Emily is, with the directness of someone who doesn't need a detailed answer but wants you to know he's asking genuinely.

Jenny looks at him and her worry sharpens. He's pale. Not dramatically — he wouldn't allow that — but she knows his face better than she knows her own by now, and he's pale and there's a tightness around his jaw that means he's been managing something on his own this morning. His hands are cold, colder than the morning justified.

'Let me get you a cup of tea,' she says, taking him by the arm towards the kitchen.

Once they're through the door she looks at him properly. 'Did you go round to Keagan's mum's?'

'Yeah.' He leans against the worktop. 'He's not there. His mum thinks he's gone back to the barracks — left early this morning with his kit and said he'd ring her later. I called the barracks but he hasn't arrived yet. I'll try again this afternoon.'

'Did he tell her about Emily?'

'Yeah. She's worried about him.' Peter pauses, choosing his words. 'She asked me to pass on her love to Emily. Said she'll always be part of the family, no matter what, and if she needs anything — anything at all — she just has to ask.' He's quiet for a moment. 'She was holding herself together, his mum. Just about.'

Jenny fills the kettle. 'I hope he doesn't do anything stupid.'

'He needs time. He won't talk to anyone right now, not even me. He needs to get his head around it first.' Peter sets his hands flat on the worktop. 'And we can't lose sight of the fact he's just got back from a bloody war. Six months away, everything that happened out there,

Danny. And then he comes home to all of this. He must be going through absolute hell.'

'That's exactly what worries me,' Jenny says. 'He won't be thinking straight.'

'Probably not.' He leaves it at that. She wonders sometimes, with Peter, how much he leaves unsaid for her benefit. 'Let's just give it a day or two. He'll surface.'

She turns and looks at him. 'Are you all right? You look pale.'

'I'm fine, just tired. Didn't sleep much.'

'Peter — '

'I mean it.' He says it in the tone she recognises as the one that closes the subject. 'Early night and I'll be right. I promise.'

She holds his gaze for a moment. Then she reaches up and kisses him.

'I love you,' she says.

'I love you too. Now come on, before your Valerie starts assigning us tasks.'

Jenny follows him back into the living room, where Valerie is still at the centre of things, and Peter is folded into a chair and drawn into conversation about the market — how it works, what he sells, how the days go — and for a few minutes the room has the texture of something almost normal.

Then the phone rings in the hall.

George gets up. He's gone a minute, and when he comes back to the doorway he looks at Emily.

'It's for you, love. Patricia, from work.'

The room settles. Not Keagan. Emily gets up and goes out to the hall.

She's only gone a minute or two. When she comes back into the room the colour has gone from her face.

'Em?' Valerie says.

Emily stands in the middle of the room. She looks at her mother, her father, at Jenny, at Peter.

'Stephen's dead,' she says. 'This morning. At the station. He fell in front of a train.'

Silence.

'Fell?' George says.

The word sits in the room. Nobody adds to it. The space around it is enormous.

'They don't know,' Emily says. 'Patricia heard from Debbie in personnel — they had a call from the police this morning. They're looking into it.'

She stands there with her arms loose at her sides. Nobody moves. Nobody quite knows what the right thing to say would be, and nobody tries.

CHAPTER

TWENTY

GOING UNDERGROUND, JULY 1982

The Horns Tavern is quieter than usual for a Friday night. Keagan sits at the bar with Danny, who is halfway through a story about last weekend that seems to involve a woman, a minicab and the car park of a Tesco somewhere near Romford. Nothing changes. Keagan drinks his pint and lets it wash over him.

He'd been at the barracks all week. He'd needed the structure of it — the routines, the faces, the particular kind of noise that requires nothing from you beyond being present. He'd promised Peter he'd come home this weekend. They'd decided against the house: Keagan had said he didn't feel up to Jenny at the moment, which wasn't about Jenny really, and Peter had understood that without needing it explained. The pub was easier. Neutral ground.

He'd dropped his washing at his mum's before coming over, stayed long enough to drink a cup of tea and assure her he was all right. She'd looked at him the way she always did when she knew he wasn't, said nothing more than she needed to, and let him go.

During the week the police had come to see him. Two of them, plain clothes, sitting across from him in a bare room at the barracks with

168

their notebooks open and their expressions carefully arranged into something that was not quite friendliness and not quite accusation. They wanted to know his whereabouts on the morning Stephen died. He'd told them: he'd been driving back to the barracks. Alone. He'd left his mum's early, before six, before she was up, so there was no one at that end to confirm the time. He'd arrived just after midday, which they clearly found interesting given the distance, but he'd told them about the service stations he'd stopped at — twice, he thought, maybe three times. He'd been tired. He hadn't been in a hurry. They'd written it all down and told him to remain contactable, that the circumstances of the death were still under investigation, that the cause was not yet confirmed.

He'd driven home from that particular conversation and sat in the car park for a few minutes before going inside.

'Peter's here,' Danny says, nodding towards the door.

Peter comes in, spots them at the bar, and raises a hand. He looks all right. A little pale, perhaps, but Peter always looked a little pale this time of year, and he moves with his usual unhurried ease, exchanging a word with someone he recognises near the door before making his way over.

'Danny,' he says.

'Mate, where've you been hiding?' Danny says. 'Domesticity suits you, I can see it. You've got that look.'

'What look?'

'The look of a man who knows where his socks are at all times.'

Peter smiles. 'That's deeply accurate, actually.'

Keagan orders a round. When it comes, Peter tilts his head slightly towards the corner of the room, away from the bar and Danny's orbit. Keagan catches the look, nods, and tells Danny they'll be back shortly. Danny, already surveying the room for more interesting prospects, doesn't seem troubled.

They settle at the corner table with their pints between them.

'How are you doing?' Peter says.

'Yeah, I'm good.'

Peter waits.

'I'm fine, mate.'

'Keagan.'

'I said I'm fine.' He drinks. 'Look, I know you've come to talk about it, so go on then. Get it over with.'

'I'm just asking how you are.'

'And I've told you. Now, we going to do this properly or are you going to sit there with that face all night?'

Peter's expression doesn't change. 'What face?'

'The one where you're waiting for me to say something worth responding to.'

'Fair enough.' Peter picks up his pint. 'How are you, then. Really.'

'She made her choice,' Keagan says, his voice flat. 'She can get on with it. So can I.'

'You don't mean that.'

'Don't I?'

'You don't stop loving someone overnight. Not like this. So stop with the shit, it's me you're talking to.'

'Yeah, well.' Keagan turns his glass on the table. 'Being taken for a mug has a way of clarifying things.'

'She hasn't taken you for a mug. She's been through something terrible and she's trying to deal with it the only way she knows how. Put yourself in her position for five minutes — '

'I've been doing nothing else for a week.'

'And?'

'And I've come to the conclusion it's pointless. She made her decision without me. Didn't ask, didn't give me a chance, just decided. All right. That's her right. I'll respect it and I'll move on.' He looks up. 'I've handed in my papers. I'll be gone to the States as soon as it can be arranged. Pittsburgh. The company's been on to me about it for months. I'll go.'

Peter is quiet for a moment.

'Let me talk to her,' he says.

'No.'

'Keagan — '

'I said no. I don't want you in the middle of it and I don't want her talked into anything. What would be the point? She'd be doing it for the wrong reasons and I'd know that and then where would we be?' He shakes his head. 'There's nothing to fix, Pete. She decided she'd rather deal with this on her own than deal with it with me, and maybe she's right. Maybe I would have made a mess of it. I'll never know now, will I, because she didn't see fit to find out.'

'She's frightened.'

'I know she's frightened. I was there. I came back from a bloody war and she couldn't even — ' He stops. Presses his mouth together. 'It doesn't matter. None of it matters. I'm going.'

'Don't do that to yourself.'

'What am I doing to myself? I'm starting over. New city, decent money, something I'm actually good at. Sounds like a plan to me.'

'Running away sounds like a plan.'

'Maybe it is. Maybe that's exactly what it is.' Keagan holds his gaze. 'And maybe I'm entitled to it, after the year I've had.'

Peter looks down at his pint. When he looks up again there's something careful in his expression, something he's deciding how to say.

'Look,' Keagan says, dropping his voice. 'I know she's your family now. I know Jenny's her sister and I know where that puts you and I'm not asking you to be on my side. I'm just asking you to let this go. Don't make it a thing between you and me, because I don't want that.'

'I'm not making it a thing.'

'Good. Then drop it.'

'I won't, though,' Peter says quietly. 'Not entirely. Because you're my brother and you matter more to me than any of this, and if I think you're making a mistake I'll tell you so. That's what I'm here for. You can tell me to mind my own business and I'll shut up for the evening, but I won't pretend I don't think it.'

Keagan stares at him for a long moment.

'You're a pain in the arse,' he says.

'Yep.'

'I know you mean well.'

'I do.'

'It doesn't change anything.'

'I know it doesn't.' Peter turns his glass slowly. 'But I wanted you to know I mean well, even so.'

Keagan is quiet for a moment. When he speaks again some of the flatness has gone from his voice.

'I don't mean it, what I said about not wanting the bother of other people. I don't mean you. I never mean you. You know that, don't you?'

'Course I do.'

'You're my brother. That doesn't change. Nothing changes that. We can row about this every time we see each other for the rest of our lives and it won't change that.' He pauses. 'I'm just angry. I'm angry and I don't quite know what to do with it yet.'

'Yeah,' Peter says. 'I know.'

They sit with that for a moment, both drinking.

'The police came to see me,' Keagan says then, and tells Peter about it: the two men in plain clothes, the questions about the morning, his alibi that wasn't really one, the service stations he'd named on the drive back that he hoped to God were on camera.

Peter listens without interrupting. His face gives very little away.

'They said suspicious circumstances,' Keagan says. 'They haven't confirmed anything yet.'

'Right,' Peter says.

A silence.

'I didn't do it, Peter.'

Peter looks up.

'I know.'

'Do you?'

'Yes.' Peter's voice is quiet. 'I know.'

Keagan studies him for a moment, then looks back at his pint. 'Wish the police did.'

'They will.'

'You sound very sure.'

Peter takes a drink before answering. 'I know you.'

Something passes between them that neither of them will say aloud. Keagan picks up his pint. Peter does the same.

'Tell me about Pittsburgh,' Peter says.

'Right.' Keagan leans back slightly. 'Roger's operation is expanding over there. Training and management development, mostly. Taking men who've come out of the forces, or lads with the right kind of discipline, and teaching companies how to use them properly. Leadership, organisation, pressure, all that.'

'Sounds very grand.'

'It probably is, once Roger says it. When I say it, it sounds like shouting at businessmen until they learn to stand in a straight line.'

Peter smiles. 'You might be good at that.'

'That's what worries me.' Keagan turns his glass on the table. 'It's proper work, though. Proper money. A department of my own eventually, if I don't make a mess of it. Roger thinks I can do it. Dai thought I could do it, which is harder to ignore.'

'And you want it?'

Keagan looks away towards the bar. 'I want something that isn't here.'

Peter lets that sit.

'You'd come and visit,' Keagan says.

'Wild horses,' Peter says.

'First chance you get.'

'I'll visit as soon as I'm able. I promise you that.'

Keagan looks at him properly for the first time since they sat down. He doesn't say anything. He doesn't need to.

After another drink they head back to the bar, where Danny is deep in conversation with a woman who looks mildly alarmed by the intensity of his interest. They fold back into the evening, the noise, the warmth of it, the familiar rhythms of this particular Friday night in this particular pub in this part of the world. Later, Danny will collect on Keagan's earlier promise and they'll move on to the Epping Forest Country Club with a handful of others, and the night will unfold the way Danny's nights always unfold, loud and slightly chaotic and not entirely without incident.

Peter leaves before that. They say goodbye outside in the car park, brief and easy, the way they always have.

'Take care of yourself,' Peter says.

'You too.' Keagan pauses. 'I mean it, Peter. Take care of yourself.'

Peter gives him a look he can't quite read, and then he's in the car and away, and Keagan stands for a moment watching the headlights disappear before going back inside.

∼

THE CORONER'S court is half empty on the second morning of the inquest. The public seats hold a handful of interested parties and a bored-looking young man with a notebook who may be from the local press. Stephen's family sits to one side — his parents side by side, his older brother with his arms folded and his jaw set.

His parents have not questioned the circumstances for a single moment. An accident. A terrible, random accident, the sort of thing that happens on crowded platforms, the sort of thing the newspapers write about in the winter and everyone reads with a chill and then tries to forget. They had a boy, and now they don't. The how of it doesn't change that.

Stephen's brother knows exactly how it happened. He has known since the day it was reported back to him, the details filtering through by phone — the briefcase, the platform, the overcrowded state of it, the train coming in — and he has been making calls ever since. The police. A private detective whose offices were above a dry cleaner's in Romford and whose competence he has come to seriously doubt. He has written letters and knocked on doors and been told repeatedly that investigations are ongoing, that there is no evidence, that these things are sometimes exactly what they appear to be.

He knows better.

The coroner resumes his position. His voice is measured and unhurried, the voice of a man accustomed to bearing difficult news in careful language. He details the findings methodically: the platform overcrowding caused by the delayed earlier train, the additional volume of passengers compressed into the space, the evidence of a minor confrontation between the deceased and a fellow commuter concerning a piece of luggage placed in the thoroughfare.

He pauses to consult his notes.

A witness statement from a fellow traveller describes seeing an exchange of words, describes the deceased bending down, describes the forward movement of the crowd as the train entered the station. The coroner observes that the combination of these factors — the heightened density of people on the platform, the physical distraction of the confrontation, the sudden collective movement as the train approached

— created conditions in which a loss of balance was plausible without any deliberate act.

He records the verdict: accidental death.

Stephen's parents receive this in silence. His mother closes her eyes briefly. His father reaches for her hand. The relief is real, whatever the shape of it — not that their son is not dead, not that anything is restored, but that there is no further horror to carry. It was an accident. Nothing they could have done, nothing they missed or failed to prevent. They can hold that, just barely, and it will have to be enough.

Stephen's brother does not look relieved. He sits with his arms still folded, watching the coroner gather his papers, watching the room begin to shift and murmur as it does when a verdict has been delivered and people start to remember they have other places to be. He had not expected anything different. He'd known the likely outcome for days; the private detective had made that much clear before he'd stopped returning calls.

But he is not finished with this.

He waits until his parents are ready to leave and walks them out into the corridor, one hand briefly on his mother's arm, then steps outside alone into the grey morning and stands on the pavement with his hands in his pockets.

He had a name. He'd had one for a while now — the soldier, the boyfriend, the one Emily had been seeing before Stephen — and the police had asked their questions and apparently found their answers wanting. That was their job. He had a different one.

He'd give it time. He was good at waiting. But he would not forget, and he would not stop, and sooner or later something would give.

He'd see to that.

CHAPTER

TWENTY-ONE

ST. ELMO'S FIRE, JULY 1984

The shop is still three days from opening when Anna struggles through the door with a large pot plant.

'Put it over there,' Emily says to her sister, 'It'll look good in that corner.'

Emily steps back and looks at the room. Three days until opening. The sign outside still needs the electrics connecting, the stock arrives tomorrow, and the cash register is proving more trouble than it's worth, but even like this — half-finished, half-stocked — it already looks like something. Her something. Savon, set right in the middle of Barkingside High Street, everything she has been working towards for the past twelve months.

She'd spent a long time planning this. Researching suppliers, testing products, reading everything she could about the cosmetics industry and what the big companies were and weren't doing. She'd built her range around ethical sourcing — soaps, perfumes, skincare, all of it cruelty-free and not tested on animals. It limited what she could offer, but she'd sourced over thirty products she believed in, and that felt like enough to start with.

Her father had helped her raise the finance, using his contacts at the bank. Peter and Jenny had put in capital of their own, refusing her repayment plan and taking an equity stake instead. They'd insisted. She'd been moved by that, and still is.

Rose is eighteen months old now. Adored, busy, currently giving Emily's mother a hard time somewhere across town. Aside from her daughter, this is what gets Emily out of bed in the morning.

'This is looking beautiful,' Anna says, standing in the middle of the shop floor with her hands on her hips. 'When does the stock arrive?'

'Tomorrow morning,' Emily says, still wrestling with the cash register. 'I need to ring and confirm the time. I want those natural soaps near the front door — the smell will draw people in straight away. I've got baskets for those, and then everything else goes along the shelves.'

'What about banners for the opening?'

'All coming tomorrow as well. The shop-fitters are finishing the sign outside, it just needs the electrics connected.'

The door opens and Peter puts his head round it.

'Hello, workers.' He looks around the shop, taking it in properly. 'This is looking great, Emily.'

'Thanks. I've got to make sure it pulls people in — I've got shareholders to keep happy.'

'Only ten per cent,' he says. 'I should have held out for more.'

'I owe you both. Big time.'

'It's an investment. As Rose's godfather, I need to make sure her mum provides for her.'

Anna looks up from unpacking a box. 'Where's Jenny?'

'She'll be along later. She's just at the doctor's this morning.'

'Doctor?' Anna's face shifts.

'Nothing serious. Just a check-up.'

'Don't do that to me, please.'

What Anna doesn't know — what most people don't know — is that Jenny is at a fertility clinic. It's a long shot. CF had left Peter with almost no viable sperm, but they'd managed to harvest what they could, and now Jenny is having her eggs collected. The chances are no better than twenty per cent and they both know it. They've told no one except their parents and Emily. They didn't want excitement around something that might come to nothing.

Peter has been the more reluctant one. Not because he doesn't want a child, but because he knows what comes after. He knows he won't be there for most of it — and that's the thing that keeps him awake, not his own death but the thought of leaving Jenny alone with a small child. Jenny has made her choice. She wants something of Peter she can hold onto. She'd been screened to confirm she doesn't carry the CF gene, so if it works, the baby will be healthy.

If it works.

'Right,' Peter says, clapping his hands together. 'What do you need?'

'The storeroom needs organising before tomorrow. Shelving, mainly.'

'I'm on it. Anna — coffee first, I think. I'll need the energy.'

'Oh, I see,' Anna says, already on her way to the staff area. 'I'm the junior, am I. Coffee and sweeping.'

'You're very perceptive,' Peter says.

'And how's my Rose?' he asks Emily, moving across to help with the cash register.

'Giving my mum grief, apparently.'

'She's not. Your mum's in her element — she's got her all to herself this morning and she won't admit it for a second.' He fiddles with the back of the register. 'I'll pop in on my way home. I haven't seen her for a few days.'

'You're so good to her, Peter. To both of us.'

'Don't be soft about it. It's my pleasure. She's brilliant and I love being around her.' He looks up. 'And don't you dare let her take those first steps without me there, all right?'

'I'll try. But if this place is as busy as I'm hoping, Mum'll see most of the firsts this year.'

'Think of what you're building though. For both of you.' He gives her shoulder a brief squeeze. 'It's going to be a great success. I know it.'

Emily is quiet for a moment.

'I know,' she says. 'I'm excited. I just wish things had been different. You know what I mean.'

'Yeah.'

'I miss him.' She says it quietly, almost to herself.

Peter puts his arm around her and she leans in.

'I know you do. I miss him too.' A pause. 'Maybe one day.'

She nods, and they stand there a moment without saying anything more.

'I hope it works,' she says eventually. 'For you and Jenny. It would be wonderful. And Peter — whatever happens, keep an eye on her. She's pinning a lot on this.'

'I know. It worries me too, if I'm honest. But whatever the outcome, I'll make sure she's all right.'

'Seeing you with Rose tells us all we need to know.'

He smiles but says nothing.

'So what happens next?' Emily asks. 'After today?'

'They try to make an embryo from what they've collected. If it takes, they'll implant it at the end of the month. The early weeks are the most critical — the risk of miscarriage is high. But if she gets through those, it's just like any normal pregnancy.' He pauses. 'Sounds straightforward when you say it like that.'

'You've made it sound easy.'

'I know.' He straightens up and turns back to the register. 'Right. Let's see if I can sort this thing out.'

'Coffee's ready,' Anna calls from the back. 'Best Bourbon biscuits as well. Only the best at Savon.'

KEAGAN SITS ALONE at the bar of a downtown strip club, nursing a bottle of Rolling Rock and looking at the nearly empty room. A few men at separate tables, not talking to anyone, not catching anyone's eye. He fits right in. That's why he comes here. Get a British accent into any ordinary American bar and within five minutes someone's over wanting to know where you're from, have you met the Queen, do you know their cousin's friend who moved to somewhere in Surrey in 1973. Here, nobody cares who you are or where you're from. It suits him.

He's been in Pittsburgh nearly two years now. On the surface, life is good. His department is expanding, new business coming in almost constantly, and his bonus has been at the top of the scale two years running. He's travelled a fair bit with it, got to know the different cities, how they work, how they think. Roger Marks comes over every quarter to review, and Keagan has given him very little to be unhappy about.

He'd brought his mum and dad over last year, and Maureen. Spent the whole week taking them round everything the city had to offer. His mum had spent most of it looking mildly suspicious of her surroundings, which was exactly as expected, but she'd enjoyed herself. Maureen had loved the nightlife and was already planning a return visit. He'd promised Peter he'd come home at Christmas, and when it came down to it he'd found a reason not to. A work crisis that had been real enough on paper, but hadn't actually required him to stay. He knew it. He hadn't gone.

The apartment is good. Central, comfortable. Grand piano in the living room, like he'd said he'd have. He spends most evenings at it, which is the one thing that still does reliably what he needs it to do.

What he doesn't say to anyone — not even Peter, who rings every week and has noted his newfound maturity with some approval — is that he feels nothing. Not pain exactly, not the raw anger of the first year. Just an absence where his enthusiasm used to be. He's become very good at performing the version of himself that has it together. At work they see the drive and the focus and take it at face value. At home, alone, the dreams come. He still sleeps in four-hour stretches. He wakes in the dark and lies there until the images arrive — Marks in the ditch, the noise of it, or Emily somewhere he can't reach, calling out, and he can't get to her — and he stays awake until it's light enough to justify getting up.

He tells himself it will pass. That it's just the natural consequence of what he's been through, and one day the dreams will stop and he'll feel like himself again.

He orders another beer.

'You don't look like the usual class of punter we get in here early evening.'

He turns. A young woman has settled onto the stool beside him. She's taken her coat off, draped it over her bag on the counter, and ordered herself a Coke. The barman is casual and easy with her in the way he only is with people he knows well.

Keagan looks at her for a moment.

'Hello to you too. You don't look like the usual class of person I run into in here either.'

She gives him a measured look, then extends her hand.

'Beverly, Beverly Deleon. And for what it's worth, I'm not a hooker.'

'Keagan, Keagan Devlin. And I didn't say you were.'

'Your face said it.' She smiles. 'I'm joking. Mostly.'

'You've had a long day.'

'The longest. I've spent most of it dealing with people with no brains and enormous attitude, and my tolerance for sarcasm is currently at zero.' She picks up her Coke. 'You're British.'

'From London. You?'

'New York originally. I'm here by circumstances I'd rather not go into in detail.' She glances towards the stage. 'I take my top off and dance. I don't sleep with anyone for money. And honestly, right now I'm beginning to question the whole concept of sex on principle. Over-rated. Causes nothing but problems.'

Keagan laughs — properly, which surprises him.

'That's quite an opening.'

'I've learned to be efficient.' She tilts her head at him. 'You think I'm hard work.'

'I think you're interesting. There's a difference.'

'Most men can't tell them apart.'

'Tell me something about yourself that isn't this place.'

'Why?'

'Because I suspect there's more to you than what's on the stage.'

She considers him. Then: 'Single. Twenty-three. Singer — that's what I actually do, or what I'm trying to do. I've been working here long enough to save up for a move to Detroit. That's where the real circuit is, that's where the scouting happens. I have a daughter, she's three, she's brilliant, and she's the reason I do any of this. And I've recently concluded that men, while theoretically appealing, are in practice mostly a disappointment.' She raises an eyebrow. 'Your turn.'

'I work here in Pittsburgh. Corporate. Been here nearly two years. Ex-army before that.' He pauses. 'Single. No children.'

'You've told me almost nothing.'

'I know.'

Beverly smiles and sets down her Coke. 'I've got a shift starting. But you've made me laugh, which doesn't usually happen in here, so.' She stands. 'When I'm on, I'll need a proper tip. That's the deal if you want to carry on talking after.'

'How proper?'

'Don't embarrass yourself.'

'And I have to — '

'Tuck it in, yes. That's generally how it works.' She picks up her coat. 'Don't look so horrified. It's part of the job.'

She disappears behind the silver curtain at the back of the stage.

Keagan moves from the bar to a table closer to the front. Not right at the edge — he's not that man — but close enough. He's made a deal.

The previous act comes off, collecting the folded notes from the stage with practised efficiency. The music changes. Beverly appears in pink lace, and within about thirty seconds it's obvious she is entirely in control of every person in the room. She catches his eye as she moves to the pole and holds his gaze just long enough to make the point.

He steps up to the stage, meets her eye, and tucks a ten-dollar bill into the side of her underwear.

'Beers on you,' he says.

'You're going to regret that,' she says, not missing a beat, not breaking her rhythm.

He goes back to his table and sits down.

'WHERE ARE YOU TAKING ME?' Beverly says as they come out into the night air. 'And ten dollars — seriously? I had you down for a twenty, minimum.'

'Call it a deposit.'

'For what, exactly?'

'Still working that out.'

'I've told you — '

'I know what you've told me.' He looks up the street. 'Do you fancy O'Brien's? There's usually a céilí band on midweek. It'll either be brilliant or terrible, no middle ground with céilí bands.'

'I don't usually do Irish.'

'I'm half Irish.'

'Then I definitely won't be doing you.' She laughs as they walk, and there it is again — that laugh — and he wants to hear more of it.

The bar is lively for a Wednesday evening, a decent crowd in but plenty of tables. Keagan picks the quieter corner away from the band so they can actually hear each other. They order beers and he talks about Pittsburgh — what he thinks of it, how it compares to what he expected — and she asks him about the job, which he finds himself talking about with more enthusiasm than he'd realised he still had.

'So you clearly love the work,' she says. 'What about everything else?'

He talks about London. About growing up in East London, school, the army, the Falklands. He talks about Peter — explains the CF, how he's managed it all these years, the life he's built with Jenny. Beverly listens properly, the way some people don't. The Falklands had been in the American press, she says, but she'd never really understood what it was.

He doesn't talk about Emily.

'Right,' he says, after a while. 'Your turn. This singing career — what have you had so far?'

'Cover slots, mainly. Whenever a regular performer drops out. Nothing long-term. Once a band gets a residency they hold onto it — can't blame them.' She turns her glass. 'That's why Detroit matters. Bigger circuit, more venues, more turnover, and people are still being scouted there. It'll happen. I just need to get us there.'

'Do you have musicians you work with?'

'A few friends who pull together when I get a slot. It works well enough.' She looks at him. 'Why?'

'I know the manager at Chauncy's in Station Square. He's always looking for acts at the weekends. I could have a word, if you want. No promises.'

Beverly raises an eyebrow. 'And your percentage would be?'

'Nothing.'

'Everyone wants something.'

'Dinner,' he says. 'That's it. You pick the place.' He holds out his hand. 'Deal?'

She looks at his hand, then at him.

'Deal.' She shakes it. 'But this better not be your version of management.'

'It's a phone call, Beverly.'

'I know.' She pauses. 'Thank you. Actually.'

Before he can reply, a man materialises at the edge of their table, collection box extended.

'Donation for Noraid?'

Keagan looks up at him.

'No, thank you.'

'Just collecting for the Irish communities — '

'No,' Keagan says, his voice level. 'You're collecting for the Provisional IRA, and I'd rather you didn't do it at this table. So if you wouldn't mind.'

'Come on now, it's for the children — '

'It's for buying weapons, and we both know it.' Something in his expression has closed off entirely. 'I've been there. I've seen what that money pays for. So I'll ask you once more, politely — go away, please.'

The man looks at Beverly, then back at Keagan, then takes his collection box elsewhere without another word.

Beverly is quiet for a moment.

'Sorry,' Keagan says. 'I shouldn't have done that.'

'No, it's — I get it.' She watches him. 'You all right?'

'Fine. It's just — ' He exhales. 'My father was Irish. I've got an Irish passport sitting in a drawer somewhere. And I spent years in the army during a decade when the IRA were blowing up pubs and hotels and people in their beds. So when someone stands there with a collection tin and calls it charity — ' He stops himself. 'I know it's complicated. I know the history. But those bombs don't fall on the powerful. They fall on ordinary people who just want to get on with their lives, and those ordinary people don't want any of it.' He glances at her. 'Rant over. Sorry.'

Beverly is watching him with an expression he can't quite read.

'You're a lot more than you looked like at the bar,' she says.

'Is that good or bad?'

'Still undecided. But interesting.' She picks up her drink. 'So. Not exactly the best first date on record.'

'Is this a first date?'

'I don't know yet. Is it?'

'I'd like it to be,' he says. 'And I'd like there to be a second one. A proper one — dinner, somewhere that isn't an Irish bar, and nobody shaking a collection tin.'

Beverly looks at him for a long moment, then nods, just slightly.

'Saturday,' she says. 'You pick the place this time. And Keagan?'

'Yeah?'

'Next time, bring a twenty.'

He laughs, and the sound of it surprises him too.

TWENTY-TWO

WALKING ON SUNSHINE, APRIL 1985

Peter can't contain himself. The moment Jenny says the words he releases her and jumps straight up, clipping the light fitting on the way down. It swings wildly from side to side.

'Calm down,' she says, laughing despite herself. 'We don't want to have to repair the whole house.'

They've just hung up from the clinic. The call they've been waiting weeks for. She's pregnant. He comes back to her and pulls her into a long, tight hug, her face against his shoulder, and for a moment neither of them says anything. After the disappointment of the first attempt the previous summer, neither of them had dared believe this round would be different.

'I love you,' he says quietly.

'I love you too.' She pulls back and looks at him. 'But listen to me now. You know what they said. The first couple of months are critical. The risk of miscarriage is much higher than in a normal pregnancy, so we take it steady. Yes?'

'Yes. I know.' He's beaming. 'I know all of that, and I know it, but it's the best news, Jen. It's the best news I've ever had.' He cups her face in his hands. 'Everything's going to be all right.'

'You don't know that.'

'No. But I believe it.' He kisses her forehead. 'Right. Your mum first, then mine, then Emily. That's the order, isn't it.'

'Yes, and then I suppose you'll be ringing Keagan before I even get off the phone to my mother.'

'Obviously.'

She shakes her head, still smiling, and picks up the receiver.

Peter leans in the doorway while she makes the call, watching her. The moment Jenny tells her mum, her voice shifts — goes up half an octave and then cracks slightly — and she puts one hand over her eyes like she's trying to hold herself together. He looks away to give her the moment.

When she's done, she hands the phone to him and he rings his mother. Vera Chubb answers on the second ring and within thirty seconds she's crying, which sets Peter off, which he will deny to his dying day.

'All right, Mum. Yes, I know. Yes. All right. We'll come over soon. Love you.'

He hangs up and clears his throat briskly.

'Right,' he says.

'Your eyes are red,' Jenny says.

'Dust.'

'Right.' She hands him a tissue.

He presses it briefly to his eyes, then straightens up. 'I'll get you a drink. The doctor said you've to take it easy, so you sit down. And I just want to say now, for the record, before we ring Emily and Keagan and half of Essex — that I meant what I said. Everything is going to be all right.'

Jenny looks at him for a moment, then nods.

'And the other thing the doctor said,' she adds, sitting down and folding her hands in her lap with an expression of absolute serenity, 'was no sex for at least three months. So whatever's going through your head right now, you can get it out again.'

Peter stares at her. 'Three months.'

'Minimum. His words.'

'Right.' He considers this. 'I might go and stay with Keagan in Pittsburgh for a bit. I'm sure he could sort me out with an American — '

'Don't you dare finish that sentence,' she says, already reaching for the phone.

~

PETER WAITS until that evening to ring Keagan. With the time difference, early evening in England puts him at lunchtime in Pittsburgh, which is usually a reasonable window.

Keagan answers on the third ring, which means he's at his desk.

'Yes mate, it's confirmed,' Peter says. 'She's pregnant. Yeah. I know. Thanks.'

He can hear Keagan's reaction even at this distance — genuine, unguarded delight, the kind that doesn't require performance. Peter feels a rush of warmth for him.

'No, I don't know yet — I'd have to check with Jenny and then with the doctor, I'm not sure what flying does in early pregnancy — ' He pauses, listening. 'That's — mate, that's too much. You don't have to do that.'

Jenny looks up from the sofa. She can hear enough to know what's being offered.

'Let me put her on,' Peter says, and stretches the phone across to Jenny. 'He needs to speak to you.'

'Hello, Keagan,' she says. 'How are you?' She listens, then laughs softly. 'Yes, it's very early days, but we're hopeful.' A pause. Her expression shifts. 'Keagan, stop. It was never your fault, none of it was, and we love you. We both do. It's a tragedy what happened, but that part of it — no. Don't carry that.'

Peter watches her face and says nothing.

'Well, let me talk to Peter and we'll ask the doctor at the next appointment. But yes — one way or another, we will see you soon.' She listens again. 'I will. And you take care of yourself. Someone's got to, seeing as I'm not there.' A pause, and she smiles. 'Yes. Love to you too. Bye, Keagan.'

She hands the phone back to Peter.

'He wants to pay for us to fly out,' Peter says, hanging up.

'I know. I heard.'

'He got a first-year bonus, apparently. Over thirty thousand dollars.'

'That's brilliant for him.' She sounds like she means it. 'I'd love to go. But I want to ask the doctor first. If he says it's fine to fly in a couple of months, then yes. Absolutely yes.'

'Yeah.' Peter sits down beside her. 'He mentioned someone called Beverly, by the way. Earlier in the week.'

Jenny turns to look at him. 'He mentioned a woman by name?'

'He did.'

'Well. That's something.'

'It is.' Peter pauses. 'He still hasn't got over Emily, that's the truth. He puts a good face on it, but when I try to get him to talk about it, he moves on pretty quickly. I worry about him sometimes.'

'He'll get there,' Jenny says. 'He just needs time.'

'It's been two years.'

'I know.' She's quiet for a moment. 'If this Beverly makes him laugh, that's a good start. He's had precious little to laugh about.'

Peter nods. He looks at Jenny sitting there in the lamplight, still with the faint brightness in her face from the phone call with the clinic, and thinks — not for the first time — that he is stupidly, unfairly lucky.

'Jen,' he says.

'What.'

'Should we get married?'

She looks at him. 'That is the least romantic sentence I have ever heard in my life.'

'I know, but — '

'You don't even have a ring. You haven't taken me anywhere nice. You've just dropped it in, casually, at the end of a sentence, like you were asking what's for tea.'

'Yes, but — '

'Peter.'

He gets down on one knee. Not gracefully — he misjudges the distance slightly and has to shuffle closer — but he gets there.

'Jennifer Callison,' he says. 'Would you do me the great honour of being my wife? Of sharing the rest of your life with me and letting me love you every single day of it?'

Jenny looks at him for a long moment.

'That was better,' she says. 'That was genuinely better.' She reaches out and touches his face. 'But you still haven't got a ring.'

'I'll get you a ring.'

'Yes, you will.' She takes his hands and helps him up. 'Peter — we always said we didn't want to waste the time we have together on organising a big wedding. We said that years ago and I still mean it. I love you more than I ever have done and we're happy. I'm not sure we need it.'

'I was thinking about the baby,' he says. 'I know we've said we don't need the big occasion, and we don't. But I think it would be nice — for a son or daughter to have married parents. And if anything happened to me early on, you and the baby would share the same name through marriage. That matters to me.'

Jenny is quiet.

'You want our child to be a Chubb,' she says.

'I didn't say it like that.'

'No.' She's quiet for a moment longer. 'I want that too, actually. A Chubb. It'd be a reminder of their father, wouldn't it. A wonderful man.' She meets his eyes. 'All right. Let's do it. Small, quick, no fuss. Registry office, close family, that's it. But — ' She holds up a finger.

'Emily,' he says.

'Emily has to be there. She's the only person I could have as bridesmaid.'

'I wouldn't have it any other way.'

They both know what comes next.

'Do we invite Keagan?' Jenny says.

'I can't have any other best man,' Peter says simply. 'That's just a fact.'

Jenny gets up and moves to the window. Outside it's a quiet evening, the street nearly empty. She's thinking it through properly, he can tell. She doesn't say things lightly.

'I don't doubt for a second that either of them would create any atmosphere,' she says. 'They're not like that. What worries me is whether it would hurt them. Being back in the same room together. With everything that's happened.'

'They're going to have to be in the same room at some stage,' Peter says. 'Working on the basis that they'll both be the baby's godparents, which I can't imagine any other way — they'll have to meet eventually.'

'Yes.'

'And they love each other, Jen. Whether either of them says it out loud or not. Two years and neither of them has had anything serious. There's a reason for that.'

Jenny turns back from the window. 'We said we'd stay out of it.'

'We're not setting anything up. We're getting married. We want the people we love there. It happens to be them.' He spreads his hands. 'That's it.'

'And Rose will be there.'

Peter smiles. 'Have you seen that child? She's the image of her mother. I wouldn't be surprised if Keagan takes one look at her and — '

'Peter.'

'I'm just saying.'

'I know what you're saying.' Jenny sits back down. 'And you're probably right. But we say nothing. We make no suggestions, we create no moments, we do not engineer anything. We invite them both because they are our best friends and we love them, and then we let them be. Agreed?'

'Agreed.'

'And if either of them decides it's too much, they can say so. We accept that too.'

'Of course.'

'What about Stephen?' she says quietly.

Peter is still for a moment. 'What about him?'

'Does anyone mention it? To Keagan?'

'Nobody would be that stupid,' Peter says. 'And Emily wouldn't open that up even if she wanted to. She knows Keagan well enough to know it would serve nobody.'

'She still thinks he killed him, you know.'

Peter looks down at his hands. 'I know.'

'Does that worry you?'

'Of course it worries me.' His voice is level. 'But Stephen is dead. Whatever anyone believes, nothing good comes from dragging him into our wedding.'

Jenny nods slowly. 'Are we just pulling everything open again, though? Everyone's steady now. Emily's got the shop. You and I have the baby. Keagan's — getting there. Do we risk all of that?'

'We're getting married,' Peter says. 'We're doing it for us, and for this baby. And the people we want there are Keagan and Emily. Not as a setup, not as an experiment. Because they're family, Jen. Same as you and me are family. So we invite them, and we trust them, and the rest is theirs to decide.'

Jenny looks at him for a long moment.

'Two months,' she says finally. 'Before I'm showing too much.'

'Right. We can arrange a small registry office in two months, no trouble.'

'And you need a ring before next week or I'm calling it off.'

'I'll get one tomorrow.'

'Today would be better.'

'Most of the shops are shut.'

'Hmm.' She narrows her eyes at him. 'And another thing. You have to be nice to me for the entire next nine months. Doctor's orders.'

'Absolutely,' Peter says, without hesitation. Then: 'Does that rule out — '

'Yes.'

'Worth asking.' He pats her knee. 'Right, should we go over to the shop? See how Emily's getting on? See how it all looks?'

'You want to see Rose,' Jenny says.

'I want to see Emily's new business and support her as a shareholder and a friend.' He stands up. 'Also yes, I want to see Rose.'

'You're hopeless.'

'She's brilliant.' He gets their coats from the hook. 'Come on. And while we're walking, you can start thinking about what you want the place to look like. Registry office, a few flowers, bit of food after — it can be lovely without being a production. Our son deserves a proper start.'

Jenny looks up sharply.

'Our son?'

'I can't keep calling it it.'

'It's a girl,' she says, taking her coat from him. 'I can feel it.'

'Noted,' Peter says, opening the door. 'Our daughter, then. Come on.'

CHAPTER

TWENTY-THREE

FORGET ME NOTS, JULY 1985

Keagan and Beverly board the British Airways flight to London just after midday. Business class — a luxury Keagan still finds faintly absurd — and he makes sure she's settled before kicking off his shoes and reaching for the menu card. In his brief years with the Paras he never once felt nerves climbing into a Hercules, but the thought of crossing the Atlantic in this 747 is something else entirely. Probably the lack of a parachute, he decides.

Beverly tucks her feet beneath her and looks at him. 'How long's the flight?'

'We stop at Philadelphia, then on to London. Ten hours in all, give or take.'

She leans across and takes his arm. 'Thank you, Keagan.'

He looks at her and smiles, and for a moment that's enough.

He is genuinely excited for Peter and Jenny. They deserve this — the wedding, the baby, all of it — and the joy he feels for his best friend is real and uncomplicated. His own situation is rather less straightforward, he thinks, and laughs quietly to himself. A bloody mess, if he's honest. Two years in Pittsburgh: working, drinking, finding his way through the

194

city's bars and clubs and, for a while, not much else. A few women. Nothing that counted. He had accepted Emily's position — not agreed with it, never quite that — but grown to respect the fact that it was fixed. He knows her. She wouldn't change her mind, and maybe she was right not to. Whatever had happened between them, Emily had built a life. She had Rose now. And Rose was the daughter of the man who had destroyed everything, a man who no longer existed, which was the only thought Keagan allows himself about him. None of that makes the healing easier. But Beverly makes him smile, genuinely, and that matters more than he'd expected.

He looks across at her. She is, he thinks for what is probably the hundredth time, a beauty. He is a very lucky man.

The flight is uneventful. They sleep for most of it, helped along by the free-flowing red wine, and use the lounge at Heathrow to freshen up before they emerge into the arrivals hall. The terminal is crowded with passengers off the morning transatlantic wave, but Peter's sign is hard to miss. He's holding it above his head: a large piece of card with PADDY written on it in black marker pen.

Keagan shakes his head and walks towards him.

Peter pulls him into an embrace that goes on long enough to become slightly ridiculous.

'All right, all right,' Keagan says. 'Ease up.'

Peter releases him, grinning. Keagan turns and introduces Beverly, then immediately looks at Jenny's stomach.

'I'm looking for evidence,' he says.

'There's nothing to see yet,' Jenny says, tolerating his scrutiny with dignity. 'And hello to you too.'

'You look brilliant.' He kisses her cheek. 'Both of you.'

They load into Peter's car, Jenny opting to sit in the back with Beverly, which Keagan is quietly relieved about. As Peter pulls away and navigates towards the city, he decides to take the scenic route through London rather than the motorway, and Beverly leans forward between the seats to watch the skyline open up as they come in through the west. Jenny is already deep in conversation with her about the wedding plans, and Keagan listens to them with one ear and watches the city out of the windscreen with the other.

'Stag night tonight,' he says to Peter.

Peter keeps his eyes on the road. 'What have you got planned?'

'I'll manage it. You've nothing to worry about.'

'That's exactly when I do worry,' Peter says.

'You look after him, Keagan,' Jenny calls from the back. 'I mean it. No whisky, and no trouble. I am not collecting either of you from Ilford police station the night before my wedding.'

'It's a Thursday, Jen. What are we going to do?'

'With you? Anything. That's the problem.'

'Beverly,' Keagan says, 'will you tell her I'm a perfectly respectable businessman?'

'I knew you had a dark side,' Beverly says pleasantly. 'I'm not covering for you.'

'She hasn't heard all the stories yet,' Jenny says.

'She will by tonight,' Peter says.

'Oh, God save me,' Keagan says.

'Stop calling on Him, He won't help you. Now — do I start with the hospital disco, or work up to it?'

Keagan looks at Peter. 'You told her about that?'

'Everything,' Peter says. 'Every last detail.'

'Right.' Keagan settles back in his seat. 'I'm absolutely done for.'

IT IS A GLORIOUSLY sunny Friday morning, the sky a clean, cloudless blue, as if the weather has made a special effort.

Jenny and her father leave the family home for the short journey to the Registry Office in Barkingside. The white Rolls-Royce waits at the kerb, the doors already open, the car dressed in yellow and blue flowers — Jenny's colours. Her father kisses her before he helps her in, and she takes one last look at the house before the car moves away.

PETER STANDS in the lobby of the Registry Office with the look of a man who slept perhaps four hours. Which is broadly accurate. The stag night had begun at The Horns Tavern — their old local, much as it ever was — and progressed into Ilford to the Room at the Top. Chasers compulsory, Keagan had decided, and there had been rounds of them. But he had been true to his word. No trouble. They had spent the whole evening laughing, most of it at old school stories, at times Keagan had narrowly avoided catastrophe, at things that had long since stopped being painful and become simply funny. The only sombre moment had come early, when the pub was still quiet. Peter had mentioned, almost in passing, a recent hospital stay — nearly ten days, a ventilator involved at one point. Keagan had gone very still. Then he'd given Peter a thorough and comprehensive talking-to about the fact that being five thousand miles away was not a reason to keep something like that from him. Peter had said Jenny hadn't wanted to worry him. Keagan had said that was not Jenny's decision to make, and he would be saying so to her directly.

Now Peter stands in the lobby looking slightly grey, and Keagan stands beside him organising the arriving guests with the calm efficiency of a man who has, at various points in his life, been responsible for considerably more demanding logistics.

He is currently telling the photographer which shots he wants.

The photographer is managing this with impressive restraint.

Beverly is in conversation with Peter's parents nearby, telling them about Pittsburgh, about how she met Keagan. His mother is already devoted to her, Keagan can tell.

'Do you reckon she's had second thoughts?' Keagan says quietly to Peter, nudging him.

Peter glances towards the door. 'If she has, I'm done. Just bury me here.'

'She hasn't,' Keagan says. 'Pull yourself together.'

He gets the last of the guests settled into the small room set aside for the ceremony, then catches sight of the cars arriving. He moves Peter inside and takes his position.

The music starts from a tape player in the corner of the room. Not a church, not a pipe organ — just this room, these people, and a song that means something to them, something by The Commodores.

All eyes go to the door.

Jenny enters on her father's arm, followed by her bridesmaids. She wears an off-white dress that falls to the floor and a small veil that gives her a quality of expectation, of something just about to happen. No visible bump. She is radiant. Peter's face when he sees her is not something Keagan will forget in a hurry.

Keagan looks past the bride.

Emily follows. She walks with a quiet confidence, her posture easy, her chin up. She is wearing a shorter blue dress, styled along similar lines to Jenny's, and she looks — he makes himself keep breathing — she looks extraordinary. His heart conducts itself without his permission. He keeps his expression neutral with considerable effort.

He glances at Beverly. She is watching him. She catches his eye and smiles, and it is a careful smile, one that knows more than it says.

He looks back to the front.

And then he sees her. Holding Emily's hand, clutching a bouquet that is nearly as large as she is, is a small girl with dark hair and green eyes. Rose. Emily's daughter. Those eyes are Emily's exactly — the same shade, the same shape, the same thing behind them. A memory arrives unbidden: the first time he saw Emily at King George Hospital, years ago, the world entirely different. Rose looks up at him and smiles, a full, unguarded smile, the kind only small children manage, and it catches him completely off guard. Something shifts in his chest.

The Registrar begins. Her voice is a welcome structure to hold onto.

He concentrates on her words. He has a job to do — he has the ring in his pocket, he has a cue to listen for. He focuses.

A small tug on his trouser leg.

He looks down. Rose is looking up at him with an expression of frank, uncomplicated interest.

Emily puts a gentle hand on her daughter's arm and mouths the word sorry to Keagan over her head.

He shakes his head and smiles to show it is entirely fine.

Peter taps him on the arm. Keagan reaches for the ring, passes it across, and Peter turns back to Jenny.

Keagan watches his best friend place the ring on Jenny Callison's finger, in a Registry Office in Barkingside on a sunny Friday morning in July, and feels something that is mostly happiness and only a little grief.

AFTERWARDS, the guests assemble outside for photographs and cigarettes and the catching-up of people who have not seen each other in some time. The wedding party is steered from landmark to landmark by the photographer, who has evidently recovered his composure and taken back control of proceedings.

Keagan stands with Beverly. It is warm. He lights a cigarette.

'Nice service,' she says.

'Short, unlike a Catholic wedding. Did you get much sleep?'

'Enough. Unlike you.'

'I'm fine.'

'You say that.' She looks at him sidelong. 'Are you?'

Before he can answer, he spots the Callisons making their way across — Emily with her parents and Rose walking alongside them.

'Hello, Keagan.' Emily stops in front of him. 'It's lovely to see you. And I'm sorry about Rose in there — she's a bit forward sometimes.'

'Don't be sorry,' he says. 'She's lovely. She's the image of you.' He collects himself. 'Beverly, this is Emily. Emily, Beverly.'

Beverly offers her hand. 'It's wonderful to meet you. And you look stunning, if you don't mind me saying.'

'That's very kind,' Emily says, 'thank you. You look beautiful too. I'm really glad you could both be here — Jenny and Peter are so pleased you made it.'

Keagan registers the phrasing. Jenny and Peter. He lets it go.

Valerie Callison steps forward and embraces him warmly. 'It's lovely to see you, Keagan. We miss you, you know. With you being so far away.'

'I miss you all,' he says, and means it. He glances at her. 'You look too young to be a grandmother, Valerie, I have to say.'

She laughs. George shakes his head.

Rose is watching him from behind her grandfather's leg, her eyes very bright.

'Hello again, Rosie,' Keagan says, crouching slightly. 'Very nice to meet you properly.'

'Hello,' she says. She does not move from behind George's leg but she does not stop looking at him either.

They talk for a while — easy, ordinary talk about the ceremony, the weather, the reception. Then Peter and Jenny appear, newly released from the photographer, and the whole group begins moving towards the cars.

~

'HERE WE ARE and here we go—'

Status Quo crash into the afternoon and Wembley Stadium erupts.

Keagan is on his feet before the chord has finished, along with approximately seventy thousand other people. Peter, beside him, looks like a man who has been given something he thought he'd lost. Beverly and Jenny are already singing. They have good seats — low down, just to the side of the stage, a few rows up from the pitch — and Keagan had insisted on this. He had been worried about the crush on the floor, specifically about Jenny.

'See?' he shouts to Peter, gesturing at the seething mass of people pressed against the stage barriers. 'That's why. Jenny would have been flattened.'

'Yes, yes, you were right,' Peter says, with the slight reluctance of a man conceding a genuinely solid point.

'What's happened to him?' Jenny says to Beverly. 'This sensible version — where's it come from?'

'Don't look at me,' Beverly says. 'He was like this when I met him.'

'I'm standing right here,' Keagan says.

'We know,' Jenny says.

The afternoon moves through its acts in waves of noise and heat and brilliant light. They are on their feet for most of it, singing things they know and standing through things they don't. The sun stays out. The drinks are expensive and warm. None of them particularly cares.

'Drinks run,' Keagan says, as Spandau Ballet finish their set. He nods at Peter. 'Come on.'

'What was the song?' Beverly asks.

'"True",' Jenny says. 'It's their biggest.'

'Oh, I know that one.' Beverly starts to hum it.

Jenny and Beverly settle back into their seats as the stage crew begin to set up for the next act, and Keagan and Peter join the lengthy queue working its way towards the concessions.

'Beverly's lovely,' Peter says. He means it simply, without agenda.

'Yeah, she is.' Keagan looks at the queue ahead of them. 'She makes me laugh. I hadn't done much of that for a while.'

'How were you yesterday? Really?'

'Lovely wedding.' Keagan pauses. 'Hard day.'

Peter says nothing. Lets him go on.

'I didn't know what I'd feel, seeing Emily again. I thought maybe I'd be angry, or sad, or over it, or — I didn't know. Two years, and not a week goes by I don't think about getting on a plane and coming back.' He shifts forward in the queue. 'But she has Rosie. She wanted it this way, and I respect that, I do. It was difficult. Seeing her, and then seeing Rosie—' He stops. 'But Beverly's my future now. She is. Yesterday was a stumble. I'm all right.'

Peter looks at him steadily.

'You will be,' he says.

'I know.'

'And for what it's worth — Beverly's a stunner. I'm jealous.'

Keagan glances at him. 'Don't give me that. Since the day you met Jenny you've never looked at another woman in your life.'

'I never said anything, though, did I.' Peter smiles. 'Very restrained.'

'You were worse than my mother. Both of you on my back constantly.'

'You needed it.'

'Maybe.' Keagan reaches the front of the queue and leans on the counter. 'But you could have cut me a bit of slack once in a while. I couldn't help being a flirt. It's the Irish blood.'

'That's what I always said,' Peter tells him. 'It's gratifying to hear you admit it.'

'I admit nothing.' He orders the drinks. 'I love you, mate. You know that.'

'I love you too.' Peter takes his cup. 'Brothers.'

'Brothers,' Keagan says.

They stand there for a moment in the roar of seventy thousand people on a summer afternoon, and then they pick up the drinks and head back.

~

Back in their seats, Beverly and Jenny are deep in conversation, which is, Keagan thinks, one of the more surprising and pleasant things about the day.

During the sets that follow — acts they know, acts they half-know, acts they've never heard of but will remember — Beverly struggles occasionally with songs that haven't crossed the Atlantic yet. But when she knows one, she sings, and when Beverly sings, the others tend to stop.

Jenny notices it during the fourth or fifth time it happens. 'You should record,' she says. 'Genuinely. You could do something with that.'

'I'd love to,' Beverly says. 'Maybe Detroit one day. There's more opportunity there for what I want to do.'

Then the stage clears, and the crowd settles into the anticipatory hum of people who know something good is coming. Two comedians appear — familiar faces from television — and the introduction goes up like a flare.

The crowd goes berserk.

Peter and Keagan are on their feet before Freddie Mercury has crossed the stage. Keagan is already singing, loudly and without particular accuracy, as the opening bars of 'Bohemian Rhapsody' fill the stadium and seventy thousand voices join him. Jenny and Peter exchange a look. Beverly watches Keagan with an expression of genuine affection.

Queen take Wembley apart piece by piece. It is the best thing they have seen all day and everyone knows it as it's happening, which is rare. Song after song, the noise climbing, the afternoon gold and warm around them. When Freddie starts his call-and-response with the crowd — the pure, extraordinary, acrobatic voice lifting and turning above them all — the stadium becomes something else. Not just a concert. Something you know you'll spend twenty years trying to explain to people who weren't there.

Keagan sings every word at the top of his lungs.

'Someone tell him to leave the singing to Beverly,' Peter says, just loudly enough.

Jenny points at him. 'That's exactly what I was thinking.'

Keagan turns and scowls at both of them with complete lack of conviction, then turns back to the stage and carries on.

CHAPTER

TWENTY-FOUR

I AM... I SAID, JULY 1985

Keagan sits at a window table in Le Mont, high up on Mount Washington, and looks out across the city. The rivers catch the last of the evening light below, and The Point is spread out before him, the Three Rivers Stadium blazing against the dark. It is, by any measure, a beautiful view.

He barely sees it.

He and Beverly have only seen each other twice since they got back from England. The trip had been good — after the wedding they'd travelled the length of the country and crossed to Paris, and those weeks had felt easy and right. But something shifted on the way home and neither of them has quite managed to name it. Tonight was meant to be a chance to find their way back to each other. He'd booked the table two weeks ago.

His concern for Peter surfaces again, as it has kept surfacing. He had seen the deterioration clearly, all the more starkly for the time apart. It had shocked him. He had not let Peter see that.

Beverly arrives in a red dress he has never seen before. Red is her colour — he has always thought so — and she walks through the restaurant as though she has always known it. He stands and pulls her chair out for her.

'Good evening, my love,' he says, kissing her cheek. 'You look fabulous.'

'Good evening?' She settles into her seat and raises an eyebrow. 'Are you turning English gentleman on me?'

'Just the restaurant. And you look glamorous. I thought I'd make an effort.'

She smiles, and it almost reaches her eyes.

The barrier is still there. He feels it through two courses — Beverly's salad and lobster, his Caesar and steak, the conversation easy on the surface and careful underneath. It is a very good dinner. That makes it worse somehow.

'Dessert?' he asks as the waiter clears the plates.

'Only if we share. I've got to watch my waistline.'

'If you don't mind, I'll keep watching it as well.'

'You're a bad man, Keagan Devlin.'

He orders the cheesecake and a bottle of house champagne. When it arrives, Beverly looks at the bottle.

'Champagne?'

'I wanted tonight to be special.' He watches her face. 'Beverly. What is it?'

She sighs. 'Oh, Keagan.'

'Is that "oh, Keagan, I love you dearly, take me to bed"? Or is that "Keagan, there's a problem"?' He keeps his voice light. 'I'm suspecting the latter.'

She looks down at her glass, then back at him. 'Since our first night together, I was convinced we'd spend the rest of our lives together. But the trip changed that. And I can't get the pieces to fit anymore.'

'We had a good time.'

'We did. We also met your past.' She holds his gaze. 'We met Emily. And I finally understood why you've never told me what happened between you two.'

He says nothing.

'You're still in love with her, Keagan. Probably always will be. I didn't expect it to hit me the way it did, but it has. It's not your fault.

You've been nothing but loving to me, and I know you love me. I know that whatever you feel for her, you'd bury it. You'd bury it so deep that you'd convince yourself it wasn't there.' She pauses. 'But it is. And I've had to face the fact that it always will be.'

Her tears start, quietly, without drama.

'Beverly.' He leans forward. 'I have never done anything to make you feel second best. I've loved you from the beginning. Yes, I have feelings for Emily — we were together a long time and a great deal happened. It will always be part of who I am. But it's the past. You're my future.'

'I know you believe that,' she says. 'I love you for it. But I've already made a decision.' She takes a breath. 'I've had an offer. Someone from Detroit approached me at the club last week about recording. A real offer, not just talk. I wasn't sure about it at first, but the more I thought about us, the clearer it became.'

He waits.

'What we have is wonderful. Three months ago it was everything I wanted. But seeing you back in England — with Peter and Jenny, with all of them — I saw something in you that I don't see here. There was a life in you. An energy. And I realised I can't give you what you actually need. I've thought about putting you on the spot, demanding your full heart, but that's not fair. Because if you said yes, you'd be lying. We'd both know it eventually.' She reaches into her bag for a handkerchief. 'So I'm going to do us both a kindness. I'm going to Detroit. And I think you should think about going home.'

The terrible thing, the thing he cannot say, is that he knows she is right.

He will never stop loving Emily. That is simply a fact, the same way his height is a fact or his name is a fact. It doesn't cancel what he feels for Beverly. He loves her — genuinely, differently, completely in its own way. But how do you explain that to a person? How do you say: there is another, and what I feel for her is not the same thing as what I feel for you, but it exists alongside it and it always will? You cannot say that. And because you cannot say it, she is right.

'Keagan.' She sets her handkerchief down. 'I want to ask you one thing, and I trust you to be honest with me. Do you still love Emily?'

There it is. The question he has avoided for two years — not just with Beverly, with everyone. His Achilles heel, laid out on the table between the champagne and the cheesecake.

'Yes,' he says. 'I do.'

She nods, as though he has confirmed something she already knew. 'Then I'll go to Detroit. And I'll carry what we had with real gratitude, Keagan. You gave me more than you know. You believed in me when I wasn't sure I believed in myself. This chance is happening partly because of you.' She presses her eyes with the handkerchief. 'Will you walk me to the club? It's a nice evening. I'd like to walk with you one last time.'

'Of course,' he says.

It is all he has.

~

THEY LEAVE Le Mont arm in arm and walk down the gentle slope towards the Duquesne Incline. Neither of them speaks. At the front of the car, they stand together and look out over the city as it drops away below them — the rivers, the bridges, the grid of lights reaching east and west.

He looks at her profile. She is looking straight ahead.

He wants to hold her. He wants to say something that would change this. He can feel neither impulse producing any action.

At the staff entrance to the club, Beverly turns and asks him to hold her. He takes her into his arms and holds on, and she presses her face against his shoulder, and for a long moment neither of them moves. There is nothing left to say. Everything has already been said.

She pulls back. Looks at him.

'Don't stay,' she says. 'I'll get a lift home with the band.'

She goes in through the staff entrance, and at the last moment she turns, and then she's gone.

~

HE GOES ROUND the corner and through the main doors.

He knows he should walk away. He cannot make himself do it. He finds a stool at the bar to the side of the stage and orders a Rolling Rock and sits in the noise and the warmth of the crowd. The waiting staff say hello as they pass — he knows all of them. He has spent a lot of evenings in this room. Some of the best evenings he's had in Pittsburgh have ended in here long after closing time, doors locked, just the staff and Beverly and the band playing whatever they felt like playing.

He has a feeling he will not sit here again.

The lights dim. John Miles's 'Music' builds in the background, and then the curtains pull back to reveal the band, and Beverly at the front.

She checks the microphone and looks out across the room.

'I'd like to start with a very special song,' she says, 'for a very special person. For a man who has helped me in more ways than I can count. I wouldn't be here without him, and I wouldn't have such wonderful memories. Wherever life leads me, I'll always treasure our time together.'

The music starts.

He sits there and watches her sing.

She is performing as he has never seen her perform. Her voice is full of something he recognises as grief, controlled but barely, and even from this distance he can see the tears on her face. Every note costs her something. He grips his beer glass and stares at the stage and does not move.

Every instinct tells him to go up there. To end this now, because they love each other, don't they, so what is any of this for? But the discipline holds. She is right. He knows she is right. You love her, his mind says, but she is not the only woman you love. You go up there now and you wreck both your lives. Do what she says. Go and sort yourself out first.

The last bar plays.

He asks for his check, leaves a twenty on the bar, and walks out into the chill of the evening.

~

HE DOESN'T TAKE the taxi.

He walks. Down past Station Square, out across the Smithfield Street Bridge over the Monongahela, and somewhere in the middle he stops.

He stands at the barrier and looks down at the water. The river is fast tonight. He watches it move against the bridge supports, dark and indifferent, carrying whatever the city puts in it downstream and away.

He tries to locate what he is feeling.

Hurt? Anger? He can't quite get to either. There is something worse than anger, something duller. A numbness that has been settling on him for a long time now, since the Falklands if he's honest, since before that maybe. He used to feel everything — love, rage, joy, pain — and he would react, not always wisely but always vividly. Now the feelings arrive and flatten out before he can reach them.

He thinks about Peter. You tried to protect him. You could batter any bully who looked sideways at him, but you can't protect him from the thing that's actually killing him. What did that ever amount to? Did it save him? Did it do anything except make you feel like you were doing something?

He thinks about Emily. You told her you would always be there. Then you joined the army and left her. She was raped while you were half a world away convincing yourself you were something special, and when you came back you couldn't hold it together long enough to give her the stability she needed. You left again. That's what you do.

He thinks about Marks. He followed you because you had to charge a defended position. You had to be the one going forward. And now he's in the Falklands and you're standing on a bridge in Pittsburgh and it doesn't balance, it will never balance.

Beverly saw you clearly and she left. Peter has Jenny and a baby on the way and he doesn't need you. Emily has Rosie and her business and a life she has built without you. Beverly will go to Detroit and she will get the record deal she deserves. All of them, he thinks, all of them are better for your absence than your presence.

The thought arrives with a strange stillness. That's the word for it. Stillness. As though something has been settled.

He looks along the river. He looks at the drop.

The people he loved didn't need a selfish man. They had all said so in their different ways, and they were all right.

He lifts himself up and sits on the barrier. His legs hang over the edge. The water below is a long way down and moving fast. He leans forward slightly to watch the current push against the ironwork.

He thinks: would it hurt? And then: does it hurt more than the last three years?

His mind becomes very clear suddenly. Particular moments arrive not as memories but as something closer to presence — he can see them and feel them and taste them the way you can only do in dreams. The lido at Valentines Park. Peter laughing so hard he couldn't breathe. Emily's green eyes the first time he saw her, in the hospital corridor, the whole world rearranging itself around that moment. His mother at the kitchen table. The look on Peter's face when Jenny walked into the Registry Office.

He says his goodbyes.

An elderly woman's voice comes from beside him.

'Are you all right, son?'

He turns. She has stopped on the pavement, a small woman in a pale coat, her bag held in both hands, looking at him with an expression of calm and direct concern.

'Yes,' he says, with the smile he has been practising for years. 'Thank you.'

She holds his gaze for a moment. Then she nods, slowly, and moves on, and he watches her go, and she turns once, a little further along the bridge, to look back at him.

He turns back to the water.

He thinks: you couldn't even be honest with a stranger.

And then he sits there, on the barrier, legs over the edge, the river moving below him in the dark.

CHAPTER

TWENTY-FIVE

IF I COULD TURN
BACK TIME, JULY 1985

Emily sits with Peter and Jenny around the small table in the back office of her Barkingside shop.

'I may open another shop in Ilford,' Emily is explaining, 'I've been offered a unit right on the High Street — opposite Harrison Gibson's, which is the busiest part of the whole road. The way this shop is going, I think it could be a real flagship.'

'I'm so pleased for you, Em's,' Peter says. 'You've worked hard at this. It deserves to go well.'

'And thank you both for your support. I wouldn't have managed any of it without my shareholders.' She smiles at them both.

She means it. When she first opened, she had no idea whether she was capable of running a business. She had the eye for it, the instinct, but instinct doesn't pay the rent or keep the stock moving. Peter and Jenny had believed in her before she fully believed in herself, and the shop had rewarded that faith. She has three full-time staff now, and her sister Anna has come in to help with the management side. The plan is to leave Anna in charge here while Emily concentrates on getting the

Ilford shop up and running. It is exciting. More than exciting — it feels like something she has built from nothing, something that is genuinely hers.

At this particular moment in time, everything she touches in her business life seems to turn to gold. The rest of her life is rather more complicated.

'So Keagan flew back all right?' she asks, reaching for her tea, the question landing just slightly too casually.

'Yes,' Peter says. 'We took them to Heathrow and had a coffee before they went through. Flight was on time.'

There is a small pause. Emily turns her mug in her hands.

'What did you think of Beverly?'

Both Peter and Jenny feel the question, which is precisely why Emily asked it that way. They both knew it would land like that. Keagan is Peter's best friend and always will be, and they had all had a genuinely good time at the wedding. They had both liked Beverly. They ought not to feel awkward about that, but they do.

'I think she's lovely,' Jenny says carefully. 'I think it must have been a bit of an unusual situation for her, all of it, but she was friendly and warm. And she spoke very highly of you, actually.'

'Did she?' Emily says.

'She did. She wasn't strange about it at all. I thought she was great.'

'Yeah.' Emily nods slowly. 'I only met her properly at the wedding, but she seemed polite. She took a lot of interest in Rose, which I noticed.'

'Talking of whom,' Peter says, clearly grateful for the route out, 'where is my little angel?'

'She's out the back with Anna. Go and say hello — she'll be beside herself.'

'Good idea. I'll leave you two to it.' He is already on his feet and heading through the doorway before the sentence is finished.

Jenny waits until she hears Peter's voice through the wall, and the shriek of delight from Rose that follows it, and then she turns back to Emily.

'Are you all right?'

'Yes, of course. It's busy, but that's a good thing.' Emily looks at the desk for a moment. 'I just worry sometimes that I'm not doing enough for Rose. She spends a lot of time with Anna and Mum, and I know that's fine, but once the Ilford shop is settled I can slow down a bit. Spend more time with her.' She looks up. 'Anyway. How are you? Have you got over the morning sickness?'

'I think so, yes. And now the wedding's out of the way I feel more relaxed, which probably helps.'

'It was a beautiful day, Jen. Rose loved the evening — the dancing especially. She was absolutely in her element.'

'She was.' Jenny smiles properly, and then the smile gentles. 'Were you all right though? I know it couldn't have been easy for you. All of it.'

'What, with Keagan?' Emily straightens slightly. 'No, it was fine. If anything, it probably helped that he brought Beverly. It reminded me that we'd both moved on. Which we have.' She pauses. 'He was wonderful with Rose though. Wasn't he?'

'He was,' Jenny agrees.

'He's always been good with children, to be fair.' Emily is quiet for a moment. 'He's got a way with them.'

'Yes.' Jenny watches her.

'What?'

'Nothing. I just—'

'What?'

'I always thought he would be,' Jenny says. 'Good with kids. Good with Rose.'

Emily sets her mug down. 'What are you saying?'

'I'm not saying anything. I was talking about the wedding. Though maybe you're wondering about what might have been.'

'I'm not wondering anything of the sort,' Emily says. 'I know I did the right thing. It's one thing to be civil to someone for an afternoon. That's very different from inviting them to be part of Rose's life permanently. You know that, Jen.'

'I do know that, Em's. I supported you, remember? I'm not questioning it.'

'Good.'

'I'm just saying you don't have to convince me.'

'I'm not convincing anyone,' Emily says, and there is an edge to it now. 'I'm just stating facts.'

Jenny doesn't push it. She knows Emily. She knows when to leave a gap.

It's Emily who fills it.

'It wasn't quite as easy as I thought it would be,' she admits, more quietly. 'Seeing him there. With everyone. The way he was with Rose.' She looks down. 'Mum was delighted to see him. She's always adored him and I know she never really believed me about Stephen.'

Jenny goes very still.

'She still thinks the world of him. And she never believed, and will never believe, that he had anything to do with what happened on that platform.'

'Em—'

'I know what the court said. Accidental death on a crowded platform, witnesses couldn't be certain, all the rest of it.' Emily's voice is measured but firm. 'I know Keagan. He would never have let it go. Not after what Stephen did to me. Not after losing me. I don't know how he managed it, and to be honest I'm not even sure I'm sorry — Stephen was a vile excuse for a human being and the world is a better place without him in it. But Keagan was involved. I will believe that to the day I die.'

Jenny is quiet for a moment. 'Emily,' she says carefully, 'if you genuinely believe Keagan is capable of killing someone in cold blood, then you're right. You made the right decision. Whatever he is or isn't, if that's what you believe, then I agree — it was for the best.'

'Are you defending him?'

'I didn't know he needed defending. I'm just listening to you.' Jenny looks at her directly. 'What's actually going on with you, Em's?'

'Nothing.' Emily pushes back her chair. 'I'm fine. Come on, let's go out back and get some proper tea and see what Peter and Rose are up to.' She is already moving towards the doorway. 'Anna made a cake yesterday.'

Jenny follows her, but she keeps her thoughts to herself.

~

'Sir.'

The voice cuts straight through. Keagan turns his head.

A police officer is standing beside him on the pavement. A step back, a little to the left, the stance deliberate and unhurried — calm enough not to startle, close enough to act. And standing just behind him, her pale coat unmistakeable, the elderly woman from the bridge.

'Sir, would you mind stepping back over this side of the barrier?'

Keagan looks at him. Then at the woman. She holds his gaze steadily, without apology.

'Sir, I'll ask you one more time. Please get back on this side.'

'Er — yes. Officer.' Keagan makes no move.

'Are you all right, sir? Can I offer some assistance?'

'I'm fine,' Keagan says. 'Just — give me a minute. Please.'

But even as he says it, something is shifting. The strange warm euphoria he had been inside — that wide, peaceful feeling, that settled clarity — is dissolving. In its place comes the shaking. His hands first, then his whole body, adrenaline pouring through him like cold water. He recognises the sensation. He felt it after Goose Green, coming out the other side of the first contact, when the world returned to normal size. The body making sense of something the mind has not yet fully processed.

What he doesn't know yet is what there was to process.

Was he going to jump?

He genuinely does not know. He sat there, looking down at the water, and said his goodbyes, and then there had been a voice, and now there is an officer standing four feet away from him on a bridge in Pittsburgh at half past ten at night. He cannot quite account for the space between those two things.

He climbs back over the barrier. His legs feel strange.

The elderly woman steps forward and speaks quietly to the officer. She thinks perhaps Keagan should be taken to hospital. The officer nods and looks at Keagan.

'I think that might be sensible, sir. Just to be safe.'

'I'm all right,' Keagan says.

'I'd strongly suggest—'

'Listen.' Keagan makes himself stand straight, makes his voice reasonable. 'I appreciate it, I do. And I appreciate her fetching you.' He nods towards the woman, who receives this with a small, serious dip of her head. 'But I was in a world of my own. I wasn't concentrating. I know it was stupid, and I know it looked bad, but there's not a lot a hospital can do for someone who's been careless, is there?'

The officer doesn't smile at that.

'I have the authority to insist, sir. You do know that.'

'I know you do. But I'm fine, and it would be a waste of everyone's time, mine included. I live five minutes from here. I just need a hot bath and some sleep — it's been a long day. You'd be saving yourself a lot of paperwork.'

He means the paperwork comment to land lightly, and it almost does. The officer glances again at the woman, who studies Keagan for a long moment and then nods, slowly.

'I'll walk with you,' the officer says. 'To your building.'

'Fair enough.' Keagan turns to the woman. 'Thank you,' he says. 'For going to get him.'

She holds his eyes. 'You take care of yourself,' she says.

It is the simplest thing anyone has said to him in a very long time.

THE OFFICER'S name is Mitchell. He was a sergeant with the 82nd Airborne before he joined Pittsburgh PD, and once Keagan mentions the Paras they have plenty to talk about. Mitchell does most of the talking — questions mainly, about the Falklands, the terrain, the advance on Goose Green — and Keagan answers honestly where he can, and doesn't where he can't, and the walk home takes twenty minutes instead of five and he is glad of it.

The cold air and the conversation clear something in his head. The shaking has stopped by the time they reach the door of his building. He and Mitchell shake hands, and Mitchell tells him to get some sleep, and Keagan says he will, and watches the officer cross the street and disappear in the direction of the bridge.

Then he goes upstairs and runs a bath.

He has adapted to coffee since arriving in Pittsburgh — tea never quite tasted right here, the water or the milk or something — and he makes a cup and takes it to the bathroom and sits in the hot water with the cup balanced on the edge of the tub. The steam rises. The apartment is quiet.

He thinks about Beverly.

She was right. He knew she was right sitting opposite her in Le Mont, and he knows it now. That doesn't make it less painful. He will miss her — genuinely, seriously miss her. Her voice. The way she carried a room. The way she saw straight through him and chose to stay anyway, for as long as she did. She deserved better than half of him.

He thinks about the bridge.

He thinks about the old woman in the pale coat turning back on the pavement to look at him.

He thinks about Peter. Jenny. The baby on the way, due in the winter, a child who will arrive into a world Peter might not see enough of. The thought of not being there for that, of not being there for any of it, arrives in him with a force he wasn't expecting. He grips the edge of the bath.

He was close tonight. He doesn't know exactly how close, but he was close.

He thinks about Marks. About the way Marks followed him forward without being asked. About the promise he made to use whatever Marks had given him with his death and make something of it.

He has not been doing that. He has been surviving, which is different.

Roger approached him last month about a directorship in the London office. At the time he had not taken it seriously. He was twenty-three years old and the idea of going back to London had felt like failure, like retreat, like admitting he had run out of road here. He had told Roger he would think about it and then put it to the back of his mind.

He takes it out now and looks at it differently.

He could go home. He could be there for Peter and Jenny, for the baby. He could be in the same city as people who know him — really know him, all of it, the worst of it and the best of it. He could be twenty-three years old and a director of a large international company, which is something almost nobody could say at his age. He could do what Marks's death bought him the right to do.

He could also find someone to talk to about the dreams, and the panic that comes with them, and the way he sometimes cannot feel things properly. He resists the thought for a moment, then lets it sit. There is no shame in it. There might even be some sense.

He will call Roger in the morning. He will accept the transfer.

He finishes the coffee. The water has gone lukewarm around him. He lies back and looks at the ceiling and for the first time in a long while the thoughts that arrive are not entirely dark.

Thank you, Marks, he thinks. I owe you one, mate. I'm not done yet.

TWENTY-SIX

HEAVEN CAN WAIT, NOVEMBER 1985

The taxi pulls away before Keagan has properly straightened up. He stands for a moment on the hospital forecourt, the morning sun breaking through a thin layer of cloud, casting pale shadows across the concrete. He breathes once, and then he runs.

The woman on reception gives him directions to Ford Ward — second floor, follow the signs for the lifts — but Keagan is already moving before she finishes, cutting left towards the stairwell. The lifts can take as long as they like. He runs up two flights at a time, the rubber soles of his shoes squeaking on the linoleum, the stairwell smelling of paint and bleach and something else he can't name and doesn't want to.

He had been back from Manchester less than an hour when he picked up Jenny's message. Her voice on the machine had been frightened and controlled in the particular way people control themselves when they are frightened, and he had been in a cab before the message had finished playing.

He finds Jenny in the corridor outside Ford Ward, sitting on a wooden bench with her hands in her lap. The pregnancy has rounded her, changed the way she sits and moves. She looks up as she hears him and is on her feet before he reaches her, and then her arms are around him, her head against his shoulder, and he holds her as steadily as he knows how.

'Keagan.' The word is barely there.

'I'm here, Jen. I'm here.' He holds the back of her head gently. 'Tell me what they've said.'

She pulls back enough to look at him. Her eyes are raw.

'They can't treat the pneumonia anymore. His lungs can't get enough oxygen. His heart rate is—' She stops. 'He's still with us, but — Keagan, I don't think it'll be long. I don't think it'll be long at all.'

Keagan looks at her. He has known this was coming for months. They both have. It does not make standing in this corridor any easier.

'You've been so brave,' he says. 'Through all of it.'

'I don't feel brave.'

'No. You never do.' He takes her arm. 'Can I see him?'

'His mum and dad are in there. But he'll want to see you.'

THEY PUSH through the double doors into the ward. It is flooded with natural light from the tall windows along one side, which feels wrong somehow — Peter has always deserved better than bright light on a day like this. Jenny leads him to the private room at the far end. She opens the door and Keagan follows her in.

The room is small and dense with equipment. Monitors, drip stands, tubes running in several directions at once. Peter is propped up against a bank of pillows, his head tipped slightly back, a mask over his face. He looks smaller than Keagan remembers. Thinner across the shoulders. Pale in a way that has nothing to do with the winter.

Mrs Chubb is on the near side of the bed. She sees Keagan before her husband does and she is up from her chair and crossing the room in three steps, and then she has her arms around him with a strength that surprises him, the way it always does, the way it has done since he was fifteen years old in a different corridor of this same hospital. He holds her back and neither of them says a word because there is nothing to say, and the silence is enough, and the silence says everything.

'We'll step out and give you a moment,' Mr Chubb says quietly. He touches Keagan's arm as he passes. Mrs Chubb releases him, composes herself in that quick, practical way she has always had, and follows her husband to the door.

'Take my chair, love,' she says.

Then the door closes, and it is just the three of them.

Keagan pulls the chair to the edge of the bed and sits down. Jenny is already on the other side, her fingers finding Peter's hand. Peter has lifted his mask, which costs him something — Keagan can see the effort — and is looking at him with the specific expression he has always reserved for when Keagan walks into a room after too long away. A kind of dry, affectionate exasperation, like a man who has been waiting at a bus stop for slightly longer than was reasonable.

'You look like shit,' Keagan says.

Peter's mouth moves into something that is almost a smile. 'Thanks, mate. I'm taking my last breath over here and you come out with the smartarse remarks.'

'You know me.'

'I do.' He pauses to breathe, the mask resting below his chin. 'I really do.'

'Sorry,' Keagan says.

'What for?'

'Not being around more. These last few months. I should have—'

'Don't,' Peter says. The word is quiet but firm. 'Don't apologise. You've been around my whole life. Don't go ruining your record at the end.'

He replaces the mask for a moment, his chest rising and falling with visible effort, the breath audible and irregular. Keagan watches him and does not look away.

When Peter pulls the mask down again, Keagan looks over at Jenny. Something passes between them. She knows what it is.

'I'll get some fresh water,' she says, picking up the plastic jug from the bedside table, and slips out of the room.

Keagan leans forward, elbows on his knees, close enough to be heard without being heard outside the room.

'Mate,' he says carefully. 'Would you let me get the priest in? I know it's not your thing. But it would do me good, knowing you'd had — just let me do that. For me, if not for you.'

Peter is quiet for a moment. He is looking at the ceiling.

'You know, don't you,' he says.

It is not a question.

Keagan holds his eyes. 'Yeah,' he says. 'I know.'

'How long?'

'A while. I worked it out eventually.' He pauses. 'There's no other explanation. Not one that makes sense. Not the kind of accident that lands a man in exactly the right place at exactly the right time on a crowded platform.' He keeps his voice level. 'You knew what I was going to do. And you decided to save me from myself.'

Peter doesn't answer. His hand moves slightly on the blanket.

'Jenny doesn't know,' Keagan says. 'Does she.'

'No.' The word costs him something. 'I could never — no. She doesn't know.'

'She won't. Nobody will. I promise you that.'

Peter closes his eyes for a second. When he opens them again there is something different in them — something released, a weight he has been carrying for years that he is allowed, now, at the very end, to put down.

'Thank you,' he says.

Keagan has to look away for a moment. He looks at the window, at the pale winter sky outside, and breathes once through his nose and gets himself back.

'I want to say something to you,' he says. 'Before Jenny comes back and before I go and fetch that priest, whether you like it or not.' His voice is not entirely steady, but he pushes through it. 'I know you always said it was me who looked out for you. But you've got that backwards, mate, you always have had. You've been the one looking out for me. From the very beginning. More times than I can count.' He stops, starts again. 'This illness has been throwing at you everything it's got since you were a kid, and you've beaten it every single time. They told your mum you'd never see your twenties. Then they said you'd never be a father. Well. Here you are.' He has to pause again. 'You are the bravest person I have ever known, Peter Chubb, and I have known some brave people.

What you did — not just what you did for me, but the way you've lived — I will carry that with me every day for the rest of my life.'

Peter's eyes are wet. He doesn't try to hide it.

'I love you, mate,' Keagan says. 'And I will be there for Jenny, and for your son. Whatever they need. I promise you that too.'

He leans forward and presses his lips briefly to Peter's forehead. When he straightens up, Peter's eyes find his, and they are as clear and as steady as they have always been.

'Now,' Keagan says, pulling back and rubbing his face with both hands in one rough motion. 'I'm going to find that priest, and you're not going to argue about it. And then I'm sending Jenny in, and I'll be right outside. All right?'

Peter gives him the faintest nod. His eyes are closing.

Keagan squeezes his hand once, and goes.

THE HOURS PASS the way they do in hospitals — slowly, and all at once.

Keagan sits with Peter's parents in the corridor outside the room, the three of them exchanging words occasionally, or sitting in silence, which is its own form of conversation. The priest comes and goes, a quiet man who asks nothing difficult of anyone. Keagan stands in the corridor while he is in the room and looks at the window at the far end and does not try to think about anything in particular.

A doctor comes out of the room mid-afternoon, draws them aside, and speaks gently. He says the words that need to be said: that Peter is comfortable, that they are managing his pain well, that it would be a good time now for anyone who wishes to be with him to go in.

They go in.

Jenny is in the chair beside the bed, where she has been for most of the day, holding Peter's hand and talking to him in a low voice. She doesn't stop when they come in. She just keeps talking, steady and calm, telling him that everything will be all right, that their son will grow up knowing exactly who his father was. Peter cannot answer now — but his eyes move, and his fingers respond to her touch, and he can hear her. Keagan is certain of that.

His breathing has changed. There is a visible effort to it, the chest rising and falling in long, irregular movements, each breath harder won than the last. His skin has taken on a greyish, waxy quality, and a nurse is moving quietly around the far side of the bed, wetting his lips with a damp cloth. He looks, Keagan thinks, as though he is being asked to do something extremely difficult by someone who has asked too much of him already.

Mr Chubb goes to the bed, takes his son's free hand, and holds it.

'Let it go now, son,' he says. His voice does not break, though it costs him everything not to let it. 'You've done all you can, my brave boy. You've done more than enough. Have some peace now.'

Mrs Chubb presses her husband's arm. She is not crying. She is too focused on Peter for that, watching him with all of herself, the way she has always watched him since he was born — with a particular quality of attention that only mothers who have been told to prepare themselves ever fully develop.

Keagan stands at the foot of the bed. He stays where Peter can see him if he needs to look.

For a few minutes, nothing changes. The machines monitor and beep. Jenny keeps talking. The nurse works quietly. Outside in the corridor, someone walks past, their footsteps fading.

Then Peter's eyes search the room. They move past his mother, past his father, and settle on Keagan.

Keagan does not move. He holds Peter's gaze steadily, the way Peter has always held his — through everything, through every stupid thing Keagan ever did, every crisis, every moment when someone needed to look at him and not flinch.

'Goodbye, my friend,' Keagan says. Just above a whisper.

Peter's eyes close.

The movement from his chest gradually stills. The nurse looks up at the monitor and then at the doctor in the doorway, and the doctor nods once. Jenny is still holding his hand. She presses it to her lips and does not let it go.

The room is quiet.

Outside the hospital, the afternoon is carrying on as afternoons do, indifferent and unhurried, the way the world always carries on when someone has just left it. Inside the room, none of them move for a long time. There is nothing to do. There is nowhere to be. Peter Chubb is gone, and the world is smaller for it, and everything that comes next will be faced without him.

Keagan stands at the foot of the bed and does not try to speak and does not look away.

CHAPTER

TWENTY-SEVEN

HE AIN'T HEAVY, HE'S MY BROTHER, NOVEMBER 1985

The morning is grey and still, the kind of November cold that gets into the bones and stays there. Keagan arrives at the crematorium early. He parks the car and sits in it for a moment, looking through the windscreen at the bare trees along the path, their branches black against a white sky. Then he gets out.

The chapel at Barkingside is small — smaller than he remembers from the last time he came here for someone else's funeral, years ago, somebody's grandmother he'd barely known. It won't hold everyone. He can already see that. A dozen people are standing in the car park talking quietly, stamping their feet against the cold, and more are arriving. Peter Chubb, it turns out, was known to more people than he ever gave himself credit for.

Keagan buttons his coat and goes inside.

The chapel smells of cut flowers and wood polish and something older underneath, something that belongs specifically to places where the dead are brought. Someone has arranged white lilies at the front. They are too formal for Peter, Keagan thinks, but then perhaps that isn't the sort of thought you're supposed to have. The coffin is already there, on the low platform at the front, the curtains open on either side. He makes himself look at it. Dark wood, brass handles, a small spray of flowers along the top. He looks at it for three seconds and then he looks away.

Mrs Chubb sees him from across the aisle and comes straight over. She is in black, composed in the way she has been composed throughout all of this, the way women of her generation and temperament are composed in public regardless of what is happening inside. She takes both of his hands in hers.

'You all right, love?' she says.

'I'm fine. How are you?'

'Getting through it.' She squeezes his hands. 'Thank you for agreeing to speak. He would have wanted you. You know that.'

'I know.'

She gives him a look that says everything and nothing and then goes back to her husband, who is standing near the door greeting people as they come in, the way a man hosts his own home even when he can barely stand.

Keagan finds his seat in the second row. Around him, the chapel fills. He watches the doors, watches the faces arriving — people from Peter's work, neighbours he recognises from the Chubbs' street in Goodmayes, a few faces from school he hasn't seen in fifteen years who look at him and nod the way people do when the only thing that's brought them back together is this. He knows everyone here. He grew up with most of them.

Jenny comes in with Emily on one side and her mother on the other. She is a few weeks from her due date and she walks carefully, deliberately, her chin up. She is wearing a dark navy coat and she looks, Keagan thinks, extraordinary — not despite everything but somehow because of it. The grief is in her face but so is something else, something steady. Emily keeps a hand on her arm the whole way to the front row. They take their seats across the aisle from Peter's family.

Emily glances back once and finds Keagan. She holds his gaze for a moment. He gives her a small nod. She turns back to Jenny.

The vicar is efficient and kind. He keeps the prayers brief and the readings well-chosen, and he is clearly a man who has done this enough times to understand the difference between a service that comforts and one that merely fills time. Keagan barely hears any of it. He is looking at the coffin and thinking about nothing in particular, which is what he does when he is actually thinking about everything.

When the vicar nods to him, Keagan stands.

He walks to the front and takes his place at the lectern. He looks out at the chapel, which is so full that the doors at the back have been wedged open and people are standing along the wall and out into the porch. He looks at Jenny, at Mrs Chubb, at Mr Chubb who has not been able to fully straighten his back since the night Peter died and perhaps never will. He looks at the coffin.

Then he begins.

'Good morning, everyone. I've been asked by Peter's family to say a few words.' He pauses. 'Like all of you, I sincerely wish I wasn't here today. I wish this wasn't happening. But it is, and so I want to do justice to it, because Peter would have expected nothing less.'

He looks down at his notes, then puts them in his jacket pocket. He won't use them.

'As a Catholic, I was taught that a funeral should be a celebration of a life. I've always found that difficult to actually believe until you're standing somewhere like here, looking at the faces of the people who loved somebody. And then you understand what it means. Not a celebration of death. A celebration of everything that person brought into the world while they were in it. And Peter Chubb brought quite a lot.'

A ripple of feeling moves through the chapel. He gives it a moment.

'I've known Peter since we were eleven years old. We were put next to each other in form room on the first day of secondary school because the teacher went alphabetically and Chubb comes before Devlin. I thought he was quiet. He thought I was an idiot. We were both right.' He hears a small laugh from somewhere, and the tightness in the room eases by a fraction. 'We were best friends by the end of that first week, and we stayed best friends for the rest of his life. I want you to know what that meant to me. I also want you to know some of what that actually looked like in practice.'

He leans slightly forward on the lectern.

'There was a summer — I think we were about thirteen — when Peter and I decided that the best use of our school holidays was to scrump apples and cherries from people's gardens along the back lane behind his road. We had a system. Peter was the lookout, I was the one who went over the fence. The operation ran beautifully for about three days. On the fourth day, I got into the tree, got to the highest branch where the best cherries were, and fell.' He waits a beat. 'I broke my arm. Peter, to his credit, did not panic. He also did not catch me, which I took exception to at the time. I told him quite firmly that he'd let me down.' Another laugh, broader this time. 'I apologised to him for that about six months later. I pointed out, in my defence, that in all our years of friendship I had somehow never mentioned to him that I was relying on him to catch me if I fell. He said that seemed like important information to have withheld.'

He turns slightly towards Mrs Chubb.

'Which brings me to something I have to confess to in public, because Vera Chubb is in this room and she deserves to know the truth.' He faces Mrs Chubb directly. 'Many years ago, you came to my mother — and I can only assume you had been driven to a point of absolute desperation — and you asked her, very kindly, not to encourage me to calm down. You told her that Peter benefited from my more energetic approach to life.' He pauses. 'Mum, every piece of trouble I have ever been in — every single one — was not my fault. I was helping.' He turns towards the coffin. 'Sorry, mate. Slight amount of poetic licence there. I did warn you I'd be difficult to stop once I got going.'

The laughter is genuine now, and warm, and it does exactly what it is supposed to do. He feels the room breathing.

He pauses. He lets the laughter settle. When he speaks again, the register has shifted, and the chapel knows it.

'The thing about Peter — the thing you had to understand about him, if you knew him — was that he was never supposed to have any of this. Not the adulthood, not the friendships, not the life.' He speaks plainly. 'From a very young age, Peter knew that his illness would shorten his life. He didn't talk about it much, and he wasn't looking for anyone's pity. But he knew. And knowing that — carrying that — he still managed to be the most generous, the most patient, the most genuinely good person I have ever met in my life. While the rest of us were moaning about the weather and complaining about nothing, Peter was just getting on with it. Living it. All of it. As fully as he could.'

He looks at Jenny.

'Sitting in the front row is Jenny, who Peter chose to share his adult life with. I have watched the two of them together and I have rarely seen two people so naturally fitted to one another. His love for her was absolute. And as you can all see — as Peter knew, and as he was prouder of than he ever quite let on — that love is to be blessed with a child.' He stops for a moment. 'The fact that Peter won't be here to hold his son is the hardest part of today. I won't pretend otherwise. But I want you to know what Peter himself said when he found out they were having a boy. He wasn't sad about it. He was grateful. He was glad that there would be a child to survive him, that something of him would carry forward. That was Peter. Not wallowing. Just grateful. And I think we owe it to him to try to do the same.'

He reaches into his jacket pocket and takes out his notes, then puts them back without looking at them.

'I want to finish with a promise. And I want to make it here, in front of everyone, so that there can be no going back on it.' He turns to face the coffin. He speaks to it directly, without embarrassment, because there is nobody in this chapel who thinks it strange.

'Peter. I have told some stories this morning. Some of them were true.' A breath of laughter from the congregation. 'But here is a thing that is entirely true, and that I want to say out loud. Your mum thanked me once, years ago, for being your friend. She had it backwards. It was you who saved me. More than once, more than you ever took credit for. Without you, my life would have been a great deal shorter and considerably less worth living. I will never be able to repay that. But I am going to try.'

He holds himself steady.

'In a few weeks, Jenny will give birth to your son. I am making you a promise, in front of everyone who loved you, that I will be there for her and for him. I will be the best I know how to be. Your son will grow up knowing who his father was and what his father was worth. That is my word to you. And you know I keep my word.'

He reaches into his jacket pocket again. This time what he removes is small and flat and round, suspended on a ribbon — the deep red, white and blue of a campaign medal. He holds it for a moment. Then he steps forward to the coffin and lays it carefully on the wood.

'Your bravery,' he says quietly, 'was worth a great deal more than this. But it's all I've got that's worthy of you.'

He stands there for just a moment with his hand on the coffin. Then he straightens, turns, and walks back to his seat.

The chapel is absolutely still. In the porch, a woman he doesn't recognise presses her hand to her mouth. Mrs Chubb has her eyes closed. Mr Chubb is staring at the ceiling in the specific way men of his age and type stare at ceilings when they will not allow themselves to break down in public.

Jenny and Emily are in each other's arms, Jenny's face pressed against Emily's shoulder, Emily's hand holding the back of her head with a fierce, steady tenderness.

Keagan sits and stares straight ahead.

AFTERWARDS, outside, the cold hits everyone at once. People stand in small groups on the path and in the car park, talking quietly, hands wrapped around cups of tea that someone has conjured from somewhere. The crematorium has a small room off the side where tea and sandwiches have been laid out, and people drift in and out of it. The sky has gone from white to a flat, pale grey, and the bare trees are perfectly still.

Keagan stands near the chapel door, receiving condolences in the way you do at these things — nodding, shaking hands, accepting the words people offer because they mean well and they are the only words available. He thanks people for coming. He says yes, it was a good service. He says yes, Peter would have liked that story. He says yes, I'll pass that on to Jenny.

Mrs Chubb finds him when the crowd has thinned a little. She takes his arm.

'The medal,' she says. 'You didn't have to do that.'

'I know.'

She looks up at him. 'He would have argued with you about it.'

'I know that as well.'

She pats his arm once and says nothing else. She doesn't need to.

Emily is near the gate, talking to Jenny's mother. She has her coat pulled tight against the cold and her hair is down. When Jenny's mother moves away to speak to someone else, Emily stands alone for a moment, looking out at the road. Keagan crosses the car park towards her.

She hears him coming and turns.

'You did well in there,' she says.

'I wasn't sure I was going to get through it.'

'I could tell.' She says it without cruelty. 'You did, though.'

They stand side by side, looking at nothing in particular. Around them, the slow movement of people leaving, the sound of car doors and muffled conversation. A cold wind moves through the car park and lifts the edge of Emily's scarf.

'How's she doing?' Keagan asks.

'She's managing. She's incredibly strong. She won't let herself fall apart until the baby's here and safe, and then I don't know.' Emily pauses. 'She needs people around her. She's going to need people around her for a while.'

'She'll have them.'

Emily glances at him. He looks back.

'I meant what I said,' he tells her.

'I know you did.' She turns to look at the gate again. 'Peter knew you did as well. That's why he wasn't worried. About Jenny, about the baby. He wasn't worried, because he knew you'd be there.'

Keagan doesn't answer. He isn't sure there is anything to answer.

'He talked about you a lot,' Emily says. 'At the end. He wanted you to be all right.' She turns back to him and the look on her face is direct and unguarded in the way Emily only ever is when she has decided to be, when she has chosen to stop protecting herself for a moment. 'He wanted all of us to be all right.'

A car starts somewhere behind them. Jenny's mother calls Emily's name from across the car park, and Emily raises her hand in acknowledgement.

'I have to go,' she says. She pulls her coat tighter. 'Keagan—'

'You don't have to say anything.'

'I wasn't going to say anything complicated.' The smallest suggestion of a smile. 'I was just going to say he was lucky to have you. And so was anyone else who ever had you in their corner.'

She holds his gaze for one moment longer. Then she goes, walking across the car park towards Jenny and the waiting cars, her heels careful on the tarmac, her head up against the cold.

Keagan watches her go.

Around him, the car park is emptying. The chapel doors are closed now. Through the low hedge at the far end, he can just make out the chimney of the crematorium against the pale winter sky. He stays where he is for a while, his hands in his coat pockets, the cold settling around him like something patient.

Then he walks to his car, gets in, and sits quietly for a moment before he starts the engine.

He drives.

CHAPTER
TWENTY-EIGHT

DRIVE, MARCH 1986

Jenny sits across from them at the staff-room table, little Peter asleep nearby.

'I've asked you both here because I have something important to say.'

Jenny sits across the table in the staff room at the back of Emily's shop in Ilford. It's a warm, cluttered space that smells of coffee and new fabric, a world Emily has built entirely on her own. 'I'm sorry to drag you both together like this — I know it's not easy — but Peter and I had one wish before he died. I think you'll probably have guessed it already.' She looks from one to the other. 'We want you to be godparents to little Peter.'

'Of course, Jen,' Emily says. 'You didn't even need to ask.'

'We understand completely,' Keagan says. He glances across at Emily, then back to Jenny. 'We're adults. We know what matters here. You can rely on us both for whatever you need, and our personal feelings don't come into it.'

'Absolutely,' Emily says. 'You can call on us any time. Either of us. That's not going to change.'

234

Jenny nods, visibly relieved. 'Thank you. Keagan — he'll be baptised at the Church of England church in Barkingside. I hope that's all right?'

'The other man's church.' He grins. 'It's fine, as long as you're not asking me to change sides. My dad would kill me.'

'I think you're safe.'

She goes through the rest of the details — who she'd like to do what, how she'd like the day to run — and as she talks, Keagan and Emily both notice how carefully she has arranged things to keep their involvement separate. Neither of them mentions it. This is Jenny's day, and little Peter's, and if a little careful choreography helps everyone get through it with dignity, then that's what they'll do.

Jenny talks, and Keagan nods, and Emily makes a small note on the pad she's brought from the counter. And all the while Jenny is watching them from behind the warmth and the practicality of the conversation, watching the way they both sit a precise and careful distance from one another, the way Keagan addresses his answers to Jenny rather than to Emily and Emily does the same, the way they are both — and this is what she cannot stand — so perfectly bloody polite.

Peter used to notice it too. He'd said more than once that the Keagan he knew had never been polite to anybody he actually liked. He'd been opinionated and sarcastic and loud, and if he said something cutting, it was because he was comfortable. This careful, measured, considerate version of Keagan was not the natural one. It was the version that kept people at a safe distance.

She had promised Peter she wouldn't interfere. He'd been absolutely firm on that point. Get involved in their business, he'd said, and you'll lose them both, and you can't afford that. So she had kept her word. But God, she thinks, watching the two of them nod sensibly at each other across her arrangements for their Godson's baptism, it is harder than he ever gave her credit for.

'Can I get everyone a coffee?' Emily asks, rising. 'I've proper filter on if you want it.'

'That would be lovely, thank you,' Keagan says.

Oh, that's it. That is exactly it. Jenny stands as well, making for the kitchen before she says something she can't take back.

While the coffee brews, Keagan asks if he can have a look around the shop. He's curious about the setup, he says — his firm has an investment arm and if she were ever thinking about expanding more aggressively, it might be worth a conversation. Emily explains a little about her suppliers and how the trade has developed, then leaves him to it and comes back to join Jenny in the kitchen.

'A business partner,' Jenny says, giving her a look. 'Now there's a thought.'

'I don't need a partner.' Emily measures out the coffee. 'I'm doing perfectly well on my own.'

'I know, I know, I'm just saying—'

'Jen.'

'All right.' Jenny holds up both hands. 'I'm not saying anything.'

'Good.'

A pause. Jenny stirs the cups.

'I just think,' she says, 'that maybe it's not completely impossible that you and he—'

'Jen.'

'Being friendly doesn't have to mean anything. It could just mean being friendly. That's allowed.'

'He doesn't want to be friendly.' Emily puts the lid back on the coffee tin. 'I know you don't want to hear that but it's the truth. The Keagan we both know — the one who was Peter's best friend — was never polite. He was irritating and sarcastic and he said exactly what he thought regardless of whether it caused offence, and he got away with it because we all knew underneath it that he was completely on our side. This politeness, Jen — this is how he behaves with people he doesn't particularly want to be around. It tells me more than he probably realises.' She picks up the tray. 'I'm not upset about it. It's what I expected. But let's leave it where it is, please.'

'Fine,' Jenny says.

She says it in the tone that means nothing of the sort. Emily knows that tone very well.

'And when you're proved wrong,' Jenny adds, following her out, 'I will expect a full and proper grovel.'

❧

BACK IN THE STAFF ROOM, Keagan is already in his chair, looking settled and at home in a way that no one who is truly an outsider ever quite manages. He talks about what he has seen in the shop with genuine curiosity, asks a few questions about footfall and turnover, and Emily answers them, and for ten minutes it is almost easy. Almost the way things used to be.

'You've done a brilliant job in here,' he says as they finish their coffee. 'Seriously. The way it's laid out, the smell when you walk in through those doors — you'd have to work hard not to go in.'

'That's the idea,' Emily says. 'We keep the main doors wide open all day. Brings people off the street.'

'Smart.' He means it.

Jenny looks at them both. Just for a moment, the politeness has slipped fractionally on both sides, and something warmer and more natural has come through. She says nothing. She files it away.

IT IS a Saturday afternoon several weeks later, and the sun has come out properly for the first time since the start of the year, bringing a kind of unexpected April warmth that makes the whole of Essex feel like a different place. Keagan had arrived at Jenny's in the morning as usual, spent time with little Peter — the bath, the feed, the patient negotiation with wind — and now, at Jenny's suggestion, they are in her parents' pool in the back garden, having spent the last half-hour at what passed for volleyball with a beach ball and no real net.

Jenny climbs out first, reaching for her towel.

'Beer?'

'Go on then.' Keagan pulls himself up onto the side. 'If you've got one.'

'Grab the deckchairs out of the shed, would you? I'll bring the drinks. Are you hungry?'

'Nah, I'm all right. Mum did me a fry-up this morning.'

'Your mum is too good to you,' Jenny says, towelling her hair. 'Is she still doing your washing as well?'

'She loves it. What else is she going to do on a Saturday morning?' He grins and heads for the shed, and Jenny throws her wet towel at the back of his head and goes inside.

She comes back out with a cold Foster's for him and a Coke for herself and finds him already settled in a deckchair with the second one angled beside it and a small table between them. She sets the drinks down and drops into her chair with a long exhale.

'Right. I've got about thirty minutes before he wakes up.' She tilts her face towards the sun. 'Maybe if I close my eyes and look pitiful enough, you'll do the next feed.'

'I told Peter I'd be here for little Peter. I didn't say anything about being your unpaid domestic.'

'So it's all right for your mother to run around after you, but God forbid a woman who hasn't slept since February asks for a hand.'

'Fair point. One feed, then I'm off to the football. I'm not letting my season ticket go to waste.' He picks up his beer. 'And just so you know, I'm putting in for a second ticket for the little man when he turns five. I want to get him started early, before you or any of your family get any ideas.'

Jenny opens one eye. 'Peter and I would both have been thrown out of his parents' house if we'd let a child of ours become a West Ham fan. You're going to have to compromise, Keagan.'

'I don't compromise.'

'No,' she agrees. 'But you might, for your Godson.'

He considers this with enormous gravity. 'I'll think on it.' A pause. 'No. Sorry. Can't. It would be a betrayal of everything Peter stood for. He'd be appalled.'

'Oh, touché.' She laughs.

The garden is quiet. Little Peter is asleep upstairs, the monitor propped on the table between their drinks. The afternoon settles around them, warm and still. After a minute Jenny closes her eyes again and Keagan drinks his beer and looks at the garden — the flower beds Jenny's mother tends, the apple tree at the back that has been there since before any of them were born, the fence with the loose slat they never quite get around to mending.

'Thank you for this,' Jenny says, without opening her eyes. 'For all of it. Every Saturday.'

'Don't thank me. I'm not doing it as a favour.' He looks at the garden. 'It keeps him here, a bit. Does that make sense? Coming here, being with the little man. It's like — I don't know. He's still around, just stepped out for a bit.'

Jenny is quiet for a moment.

'I know exactly what you mean,' she says. 'And that's why I hate it when people avoid talking about him. My family do it, Emily does it — they're trying to be kind, I know that, but it feels like they're trying to make him disappear tidily. As if that would help.' She opens her eyes and looks at the apple tree. 'I want to talk about him. I want to laugh about him. I want him to still be here, in the conversation, even if he can't be anywhere else.'

'Then we'll keep him there,' Keagan says. 'That's not going to stop.'

Jenny nods. And then, quite suddenly, the tears come.

She doesn't make a sound at first. Her face just changes, the careful composure of the last few months giving way all at once, and then she is crying in the full, helpless way that grief eventually demands, the way she has not quite allowed herself to in all these weeks of managing and organising and keeping everything going.

Keagan puts his beer down and gets out of his chair. He sits on the edge of hers and pulls her into him, and she goes without resistance, her head against his neck, her shoulders shaking.

'It's all right,' he says. 'Let it out. I'm here.'

He holds her and she cries, and he rubs her back slowly, the way you do when there is nothing useful left to say, and the garden stays quiet around them.

After a while, Jenny lifts her head. They are close, face to face, and she is still crying but the worst of it has passed, and she is looking at him with an expression he can't quite read — not quite grief and not quite anything else. Just an openness, a rawness, the way a person looks when they have stopped pretending.

He is not certain, afterwards, who moves first. It is probably her. Their lips touch, and for a moment it is tender and confused and nothing is decided, and then it becomes something slightly more than that, and then Jenny pulls back.

They look at each other.

'I'm sorry,' Keagan says. 'That was — I'm sorry.'

'No.' Jenny shakes her head. 'It was me. I don't know why I did that. I'm so sorry.'

Neither of them says anything else for a second. And then the deckchair, which has been bearing Keagan's weight at an increasingly precarious angle throughout all of this, makes a decisive structural decision and collapses completely. They go over together in a tangle of canvas and aluminium, both landing on the patio and lying there looking at the sky, and it is so thoroughly ridiculous that they both start laughing, properly laughing, the kind that gets hold of you and won't let go.

He kisses her once on the top of the head, gets to his feet, and helps her up.

ON THE TRAIN FROM CHIGWELL, Emily has given up on the crossword and is staring out at the back gardens sliding past, thinking about things she had decided not to think about.

She had been certain, since the meeting at the shop, that Keagan simply didn't want to be around her. His politeness had confirmed it: he was perfectly capable of being warm and present with people he actually cared for, and with her he had been careful and correct and generous in a way that was entirely unlike the person she had known. She had told Jenny as much and she had meant it, and she still thinks she is probably right.

And yet.

He had looked at the shop with real curiosity. He had asked questions that showed he had actually listened to what she'd told him. And once or twice, for just a moment, something had come through the careful distance — something dry and quick and familiar that had made her want to laugh, or cry, or both.

She thinks about Rose.

Rose is the priority. That is not negotiable and has never been. Whatever she does or doesn't do has to be considered first through that lens, and the idea of bringing any kind of complication into her daughter's life — any uncertainty, any risk of another upheaval — is one she is not prepared to entertain lightly.

But maybe, she thinks, as the train slows for her stop, maybe friendship is not the same as complication. Maybe it is the opposite of it. And she does miss him — not in the way she used to, not with that particular ache, but she misses having someone around who knew her before all the things that happened happened. Who knew her when she was seventeen and sure of nothing and convinced she was about to discover everything.

She gets off the train, crosses the bridge, and starts walking. It's a nice afternoon for it. She quickens her pace.

~

SHE TURNS the corner into Jenny's road, comes through the side gate, lifts the latch — and stops.

Jenny and Keagan are in the middle of the patio, Jenny's face slightly flushed, both of them conspicuously upright in the way people are upright when they have just become very aware of being looked at.

'Don't mind me,' Emily says.

'Hi, Ems,' Jenny says. Her cheeks are pink. 'We just had a bit of an accident with the deckchair.'

'Hello, Emily.' Keagan reaches for his beer with the ease of a man who has decided the best response is to behave as if absolutely nothing has occurred. 'Perfect timing, actually. You can do the next feed, which means I can go to the football with a clear conscience.'

'How convenient,' Emily says.

She pulls over a chair that Keagan fetches from the shed and Jenny disappears to get her a cold drink, and the three of them sit in the afternoon sun and talk about little Peter. The conversation is careful and warm and slightly strained, the way conversations always are when two out of three people in them are working something out.

After twenty minutes, Keagan makes his apologies, says his good-byes, goes inside to change, and leaves for the football.

Emily waits until she hears the front door close.

'Deckchair,' she says.

'Yes,' Jenny says, looking at the garden.

'Right,' Emily says, and picks up her drink.

CHAPTER

TWENTY-NINE

NEVER TOO MUCH, APRIL 1986

There is a typical April chill in the air as the guests assemble outside the Holy Trinity Church in Barkingside for the baptism of little Peter. Jenny and her parents stand at the front of the church, welcoming people as they arrive, while Emily holds Peter, who is sleeping peacefully through his own big day.

'All right, Ems.' Keagan appears at her side. 'Where's little Rosie?'

'Her name's Rose. If I'd wanted her called Rosie, I'd have christened her Rosie.' She points across the entrance. 'She's with my parents over there.'

'Right then, I'll go and say hello to Rose,' he says, turning away, 'since I'm clearly not welcome here.'

She watches him cross the churchyard. He crouches down to Rose's level and says something that makes her laugh, and her parents are beaming at him the way they always have. He lifts Rose onto his shoulders and she shrieks with delight, and Emily can see his hand behind her back, keeping her steady, making sure she won't fall. She looks down at the sleeping baby in her arms.

She and Keagan should have been holding a baby like this together.

243

Years ago that was the plan, the future she had pictured without ever saying it out loud. Stop it, she thinks. Stop dwelling.

She watches him carry Rose across the churchyard and tells herself she is not angry. She's not sure she believes it.

~

THE SERVICE IS warm and simple. The vicar makes a special mention of Peter — the boy's father — and says that little Peter will be the living embodiment of his spirit. Keagan and Emily stand together at the font and make their promises, and somehow they manage to do it without difficulty, without so much as a sideways glance, their voices steady and clear in the quiet church.

Afterwards, Jenny has laid on a buffet in the church hall next door — tea, sandwiches, plates of cake. Rose finds a group of children close to her age within about thirty seconds of arriving and proceeds to career around the hall with them to Emily's mounting anxiety.

Keagan finds Jenny near the sandwiches, a few family friends gathered around her.

'Good service,' he says. 'Nice what the priest said about Peter.'

'He's a vicar,' Jenny says. 'We're not with your lot in here.'

'My mistake.'

They stand for a moment, comfortable in the way they have become comfortable, and Jenny watches him across the room as he tracks Rose's progress through the other children. He has his eye on her without being obvious about it.

'I've set up a savings account,' he says. 'Nationwide Building Society. Five hundred to start, then a regular amount each month. It's his when he's eighteen — university fund, hopefully.'

'That's really kind of you, Keagan. My parents have done the same. He'll be well looked after.'

He nods, keeps his eyes on the room for a moment. 'Has Emily said anything to you? She's been a bit distant with me lately and I don't know if it's about — last time. What she walked into.'

'She hasn't said anything, but she hasn't called as much either, which isn't like her. Do you want me to—'

'No, it's fine. I'll talk to her. We probably need to clear the air anyway, we've not said anything real to each other since I got back and it'd be better for everyone if we could manage a bit less awkwardness.' He pauses. 'For little Peter's sake. For Rosie's too.'

'Be careful, though. I wouldn't go digging up the past.'

'That's the last thing I want. It's the future I want to talk about. We're going to be around each other for years — both of them — and I'd rather we found a way to be all right.' He glances across to where Emily is standing, watching Rose with her arms folded. 'Who knows, we might even manage being friends.'

'Do you still love her, Keagan?' Jenny says. Direct as ever.

He is quiet for a moment.

'I thought I'd got past it. When I was in America I told myself it was done and I could move on. There was no hate, the anger had mostly gone, I was getting on with things. But the wedding.' He shakes his head. 'Being back here. I suppose I can't lie to myself about it anymore.'

'Oh, Keagan.'

'I'm not expecting anything. I know she doesn't want me as part of her life, hers or Rosie's — Rose's. I can live with that. But that doesn't mean we can't find some way to — I don't know.' He looks down at his drink. 'I've met Rose now, and I keep thinking how wrong I was. She's nothing but a child. None of this is her fault. Maybe I could have been a father to her. Maybe I still could, in some way. Or maybe that's stupid.'

Jenny smiles. Peter always said exactly this. He was so certain of it, even when she had her doubts.

'Peter always believed you'd feel this way,' she says. 'He knew from the start you would be nothing but loving to Rose. He never once changed his view on it. In those early days I thought he was just defending you out of habit, but I came to understand he was right. He used to say you had two sides — the one you showed the world and the one that cared too much for your own good.' She pauses. 'He was right about that too.'

Keagan looks away. The mention of Peter always costs him something.

'Stop beating yourself up,' Jenny says. 'Peter always said you'd never believe you were a good person because you'd hurt people. But the people you hurt were the ones who'd hurt the ones you loved first. I've never agreed with it, but it shows you care. The sooner you accept that, the sooner you can get on and enjoy your life.' She glances across the room. 'Emily's standing on her own over there. No time like the present.'

He kisses her on the cheek. 'I love you. As a sister, before you say anything.'

'I know,' she says. 'I love you too — brother. Now go on.'

~

HE WALKS across to where Emily stands watching Rose with the other children.

'Emily. Can we talk?'

She looks slightly startled. She turns, instinctively checking on Rose, who is still running around with the other children. Rose spots her mother standing with Keagan and comes racing over.

'Hello, Rosie.' He says it before he can stop himself. 'Sorry — Rose.'

Rose laughs, apparently finding this extremely funny.

'Rose, go with Grandma for a bit,' Emily says. 'I just need to go outside for a minute.'

Rose is already sprinting back across the room towards her grand-parents. Emily looks at Keagan and tilts her head towards the door.

~

OUTSIDE, the churchyard is quiet. There is a bench by the main church, and no one else about. They sit at either end of it, a proper churchyard distance between them.

'First of all,' Keagan says, 'you've been different with me this past week and if it's about me and Jenny, then I want to be clear about what that is. She is like a sister to me. I don't have Peter anymore, and my promise to him is that I'll look after little Peter and his mum. That's all it is. What you walked in on — two minutes before that she was in bits, crying for Peter. I was trying to be there for her. That's what you didn't see.'

'Thank you for explaining it,' Emily says. 'I hoped one of you would eventually.'

'What does that mean? You saw two friends being there for each other.'

'I didn't say anything else.'

'You implied it.'

'And now you're being defensive when I haven't actually accused you of anything.'

'I'm not being defensive — are you deliberately looking for an argument?'

'I don't need to argue with you, Keagan. If I had an argument, it'd be with Jenny, and I don't, because she's my family.'

'Right.' He looks straight at her. 'And I'm not.'

'That's fairly obvious, I'd have thought.'

'You didn't need to spell it out, no. You made that clear three years ago. Whether I wanted it was irrelevant.'

'I didn't say I didn't want you. I said it was for the best.'

'You decided.'

'What's wrong with that?'

'What's wrong with it is that you decided, on your own, without discussion, that I couldn't handle it. That I wasn't capable. No conversation, no let's talk about this. Just — I'm pregnant, you can't cope with that, please leave.'

'You didn't handle it. You proved me right.'

'Because I didn't get the chance. You'd already made up your mind before I had a chance to say anything.'

'You went and killed Stephen within twenty-four hours. Don't give me the accident rubbish, Keagan. I'm not stupid. It was too much of a coincidence.'

'Judgemental, maybe, but not stupid. If you're so certain I killed him, where's your evidence? You made the same decision you made about the baby — you didn't ask, you just decided. Judge and jury, Emily.'

'We always had honesty between us. Don't take that away now.'

'The court ruled it an accidental death. If they reached that conclusion from the evidence, that should be good enough for you. Unless it's easier to paint me as a killer — makes the choice you made simpler to live with.'

'That's not fair.'

'Isn't it?'

'We made our decision and we both accepted it. Why are you bringing all this up now, three years later?'

'Because we never actually talked about it.' He pauses. 'I wanted to talk about the future. Not the past. But maybe you've made it clear enough that there isn't any future, so there's nothing to discuss.'

'So now you don't want to talk.'

'What's the point? You've told me what you think of me. I don't see the point in talking about anything if that's where we are.' He stands. 'Maybe having Rose was the easiest way to end things. Maybe you'd already wanted out and this gave you the reason.'

She is on her feet.

'How dare you. Are you saying I wanted to be raped?'

'That is not what I'm saying and you know it.'

'Then what are you saying?'

'I'm saying maybe you wanted me gone and it gave you the reason.'

'Fuck off, Keagan.'

'Done.'

She turns and walks back into the church hall. Keagan stands in the empty churchyard for a moment, then turns away and walks along Mossford Green to where he parked the car.

'YOU'RE BACK EARLY,' Lizzie says as he comes in through the kitchen door.

'It's only a christening. They don't last long.'

'Everything all right?'

'Yeah. Just tired. I'll grab my washing and head home, early night.'

'How was it? Jenny and little Peter?'

'He slept through the lot of it. Except the water on the head — that woke him up sharpish.' He sits down at the kitchen table. 'Kettle on?'

'Yes. Why — are you making me one?'

'You don't like my tea.'

'I wouldn't know. It's been so long.'

'Sorry.'

'For what? I'm winding you up, you eegit. What's happened?'

'I'm fine.'

'Emily?'

He laughs despite himself. 'You're unbelievable, d'you know that? Have you got spies everywhere or is this some skill you've been hiding?'

'I know you, son. I don't need to be a clairvoyant.'

'Everyone seems to know me except me.'

'No. You know exactly what you want. You just spend too much time convincing yourself you don't deserve it. That's always been your problem.'

'Thanks for that.'

'Don't thank me, I'm telling you the truth.' She sits down across from him. 'You love Emily. She loves you. And for some bloody stupid reason the pair of you won't see through all the rubbish and work out how to get back to where you were. I've had this conversation with Emily's parents — lovely people, by the way — and we all think the same thing. But nobody wants to tell you, because we all know you'll do the exact opposite.' She looks at him over the table. 'Do you want my advice or not?'

'Go on then.'

'You are two lovely people — well, one and my son.' She smiles at her own joke. 'You should be together. I thought Beverly was lovely, and in other circumstances she'd be right for you. But you never stopped loving Emily, so something needs to be done about it.'

'I think that ship's sailed. She made it fairly clear today she doesn't want me around.'

'Did she say that?'

'Not in so many words, but along those lines.'

'So you've decided, based on what you think she means, instead of listening to what she's actually saying.'

'Harsh.'

'True. You've always done it. Peter tried to help you, didn't he? And you'd react first and wreck a perfectly fixable problem before you sat down and thought about it properly.' She gets up and pours the tea, brings both cups to the table. 'Keagan. Think about what you want. If it's Emily — if you want to be her husband and a father to Rose — then you need to plan how you get there. You can't keep assuming you know what Emily wants. You need to listen to her. If what she wants is also what you want, then you've got a chance.'

'Yeah.' He wraps both hands around the mug. 'Yeah, I know. Thanks, Mum.'

'Don't thank me. Drink your tea.'

$$\sim$$

'YOU TOLD HIM TO WHAT?' Jenny says.

She and Emily are in the kitchen, little Peter asleep in his pram beside them, the church hall cleared and everyone gone home.

'I've never heard you use that word,' Jenny adds. 'What did he do?'

'He walked off. As he always does.'

'I expect he did, yes. Considering he'd just gone over there to tell you he still loves you and would like to be a father to Rose.' There is just enough edge in Jenny's voice.

'He should have tried saying that, instead of implying I'm a whore who deserved what happened to her.'

'He said that?'

'Not exactly. But it's what he thinks. It always has been.'

'Oh, for Christ's sake.'

'What's that supposed to mean?'

'It means you're as bad as each other. You both think you know what the other one's thinking. And you're both wrong.'

'You've become very close with him,' Emily says carefully, 'so I'm glad you feel you know him better than I do.'

'And there it is.' Jenny looks at her steadily. 'You still think something's going on.'

'You were on the floor together, Jen.'

'We were friends being there for each other. I told you — I need him now the same way he needed Peter. He's little Peter's godfather and he shows up every single Saturday and does everything he can, and he does it because he misses his friend more than he will ever say out loud. If you think it's anything more than that, you're not only wrong, you're being very unfair to me.'

Emily is quiet. She knows she has gone too far.

'I'm sorry,' she says. 'I don't really think anything is going on. But when I walked in and saw you both — I felt something I wasn't expecting. Honestly, Jen, since the wedding I haven't been right. I was so pleased I'd see him again, and then he turned up with Beverly and it knocked me sideways. I suppose I'd hoped that being at the wedding would make us both realise — I don't know. But he brought her. And now he's come home and ended things with her and he's close with everyone except me. Even Rose — you can see how much he loves her already and that was the thing that finished us. It tells me I got it all wrong, doesn't it? I made the wrong decision and I've had to live with it.'

'You can't know that, Em. You made the best decision you could at the time. Rose could have been a boy, the image of Stephen. Nobody could have known what she'd be like.' Jenny reaches across and touches her arm. 'But listen. Maybe you two can work this out. You're both angry and confused and you've got enough history between you to fill a library, but if you still love each other it can be done. He's never stopped, you know.'

'Not after today.'

'I think you'd be surprised. Being told to clear off isn't exactly new for Keagan.' Jenny pauses. 'Although — is that what's really stopping you?'

Emily looks at the table.

'I told him I know he killed Stephen,' she says. 'I'm not saying I wanted Stephen to live, but what Keagan did — it frightens me, Jen. He killed in the Falklands and I've always been able to separate that, he was a soldier and it was war. But Stephen was different. That was cold and deliberate and it makes him someone I'm not sure I can—'

'Keagan didn't kill Stephen.'

'He didn't deny it.'

'Keagan didn't kill Stephen,' Jenny says again. 'I know that for a fact.'

Emily looks up. 'You can't know that.'

'I can. And I do.' Jenny is quiet for a moment, looking down at the pram where little Peter sleeps. She has carried this for a long time. She makes her decision. 'What I am about to tell you does not leave this room. It doesn't go to anyone. Not ever. I've never said it to a single person, not even Keagan. I'm only saying it now because you both deserve the chance to fix things and I would never say this if I didn't believe, with everything in me, that Peter would have wanted me to.'

She waits, making sure Emily is listening properly.

'It was Peter.'

Emily stares at her.

'He told you?' she says, barely above a whisper.

'He never told me. Not in so many words. He used to talk in his sleep, and I started to piece things together. And when I found out he hadn't actually been at the market that morning — it came up months later in conversation — I knew. I knew because of all of it together.' She takes a breath. 'And I knew why. He did it to save Keagan. He knew exactly what Keagan would have done if he'd got there first, and it would not have been a quick push onto a railway line. Keagan would have wanted Stephen to suffer. He would have wanted him to feel every bit of the pain he put you through. Peter knew that. He told me once, when he was trying to convince me it couldn't have been Keagan — he said, if it was Keagan it would never have been as clean as an accident. He was right. And he was far too calm on that morning when the news came through. Everyone else in that room went through the same thoughts — oh God, what has Keagan done. Everyone except Peter. Because he already knew.'

The church hall had always been cold and it is cold now. Emily sits very still.

'When Peter was near the end,' Jenny continues, 'Keagan asked to speak to him alone and then he asked for the priest to come in and give Peter absolution. I didn't go in. I've never asked Keagan about it and I never will. But Keagan knows, I think. He's always known. And he has never once said a word about it to protect Peter's name. He will take it to his grave.' She looks at Emily directly. 'That's the man you think is a murderer.'

Emily's eyes are wet.

'I never knew the trouble I caused you both,' she says quietly. 'Peter putting himself at risk like that — because of me, because of my stupidity—'

'Stop it. It wasn't your fault. None of it was your fault. And Keagan never thought otherwise. He blamed himself for not being there to protect you. Never once thought badly of you for any of it.' Jenny leans forward. 'What you cannot do is go on accusing him of something he didn't do. You can love him or hate him or decide you never want to see him again — that's your choice and I'll respect it. But it can't be because you think he killed Stephen. He didn't.' She sits back. 'And this conversation never happened. As far as Keagan knows, Peter took this secret to the grave. I want it to stay that way.'

Emily nods. She cannot quite find words yet.

Outside, the afternoon has gone quiet. Little Peter stirs slightly in his pram, makes a small sound, then settles back into sleep. Jenny reaches in and adjusts the blanket around him.

'He'd have known what to say to you both,' she says. 'He always did.'

CHAPTER

THIRTY

ONE MORE TRY, APRIL 1986

Keagan sits at his piano, working his way through 'Clair de Lune'. He is in the middle section, the piece gathering pace and intensity, driven by everything he cannot quite bring himself to think about directly. It has been the most difficult of weeks. As the lead on the latest acquisition, the negotiations had been long and brutal, sleep barely happening as he ploughed through reports and valuation papers until the small hours. Two hours ago the talks concluded and with the contracts ready for signature on Monday, it should be over. He should be able to relax.

He can't.

All week, in the gaps between one meeting and the next, his mind has drifted to Emily. He'd kept it boxed away, the way he always does — compartments, one thing at a time, deal with the work in front of you — and it had held. But the work is done now. It's Friday night. He's alone in his flat and there's nothing left to hide behind.

The discussion with his mum had hit home. He needed to decide. But deciding meant knowing what he actually wanted, and that wasn't as simple as it used to be.

He loved Emily. He knew that. But what did she feel? The last few times they'd been in the same room she'd been sharp with him, guarded, angry in ways he hadn't always understood. He thinks about it properly now, gives it the attention he has been refusing it all week. He'd turned up at the wedding with Beverly — that must have stung. Then she'd walked in on him and Jenny, and whatever it had looked like, he hadn't exactly rushed to explain himself. He'd tried being friendly and she hadn't wanted it. He'd tried with Rose and that had gone all right, but it hadn't broken anything open between the two of them.

Everyone keeps saying they know him better than he knows himself. Maybe they're right. In his youth he'd made stupid mistakes, but he was a different man now. He'd always been able to hold his own when the threat was physical — that had never been the problem. But the emotional threats? He'd always been better with his fists than his words. So the question was whether he was genuinely different now or just telling himself that, the same way he always had.

Too many questions. What he needs is answers.

He stops playing, gets up, grabs his jacket and his keys, and goes out for a pint. Tomorrow, one way or another, he will put this to bed.

It is a busy Saturday morning in the Ilford shop. Trade has been building week on week and with four full-time staff it is hectic from the moment the doors open. Emily is restocking shelves while the staff deal with the queue at the counter, and her mind is only half on the task. The revelation from Jenny has been sitting inside her all week like something she can't digest. It had undermined one of the foundations of the decision she'd made three years ago, and without it, she wasn't sure she had as firm a footing as she'd always believed. She had been comfortable with her life — hers and Rose's — and she'd found a kind of peace in it. Then he came back and unsettled everything, and she wasn't sure whether to be furious with him for it or with herself for allowing it.

She is thinking about this, a box of soap bars in her arms, when she looks up and sees Anna coming through the door. She should be at the Barkingside shop this morning. Something must be wrong.

Emily sets the box down and walks towards her, already forming the question — then she sees him. Keagan, waiting at the shop door. He has a smile on his face. Anna is smiling too.

'Get your coat,' Anna says, with a firmness Emily has almost never heard from her. 'I'll look after the shop. You've got someone waiting for you and, big sister, you are not saying no.'

Emily opens her mouth. Closes it. Goes through to the staff room and gets her coat.

'We need to restock all the soap lines,' she calls back through the door, 'and the promotion signs for next week need to go up, and—'

'Go,' Anna says. 'And be nice to him.'

Emily raises her eyebrows and walks out through the shop.

Keagan is still smiling when she reaches him. She's not sure how she feels about that.

'Hello,' he says. 'I'm sorry about all this. But it's time we talked.'

'All right,' she says.

'Come on then.'

'Where are we going?'

'You'll see.'

He offers his hand. She looks at it for a moment, then takes it. He waits for a gap in the traffic and leads her across the High Road. They walk fifty yards or so before he stops. Emily looks around, slightly baffled — there's no café nearby, no obvious destination, just the shops and the pavement and the Town Hall.

The Town Hall.

Of course.

'Come on,' he says. 'Let's go in.'

She smiles despite herself. He leads her inside and asks her to wait by the door while he crosses to the security guard at the desk. There is a brief conversation she can't hear, and it looks very much like some money changes hands. Then Keagan comes back, takes her hand again, and leads her through the curtained glass double doors into the main hall.

It is empty. The stage where Froggy used to set up his decks, the drinks station along one wall, still laid out for serving teas. The dance-floor where she was fifteen years old and didn't know any of this was coming. Keagan leads her up to the stage and lifts her onto it, so she is sitting above him.

'Right,' he says. 'If you look behind you, there's a small box.'

She turns. There it is.

'I'm going to give you a choice,' he says, 'and I want you to know it's a final one, because this back and forth is doing neither of us any good and I'm not prepared to let it carry on. Option one — we agree that whatever we had is in the past and we both move on from it properly. We can be friends, there's no reason we can't, but I'll move away again because for me that's easier. Yes, I know that's running away, I'm aware of the irony. But I'd leave you in peace to build the life you want, without me getting in the way.' He pauses. 'That's option one.'

He meets her eyes.

'Option two is what we should've done three years ago. And it involves the box behind you. In that box is the ring I brought to your door that night. I understand now why you said no, and I'll admit I probably accepted it too easily. I was angry, Emily, and it hurt me. But I was also wrong to walk away without fighting for us. You made the right decision about Rose — I know that now — you just made the wrong one in sending me away before I had the chance to decide what I was capable of. We both made mistakes and we have both lived with that for three years. Now we have the chance to end it. One way or the other.'

He is quiet for a moment.

'I asked your father — three years ago, I'll grant you, but I don't think we agreed a time limit. So I'm asking you again.' He takes a breath. 'Emily Callison, will you marry me? I love you. More now than I did then, which I didn't think was possible. I don't want to spend another day not knowing the answer to this. I want to be your husband and I want to be a father to Rosie.'

He grins slightly, waiting for the correction. She doesn't give him one.

'She deserves a life with parents who love her,' he says. 'You were planning to give her that on your own and you'd have done it brilliantly. But I want to share it with you. I'd like us to have more children, but I want to say this clearly — I would never for one minute give them more than I give her. She'll be the big sister to all of them.'

He reaches into his jacket pocket and pulls out a folded piece of paper.

'I looked at a house this morning. It's in Chigwell, near Jenny, so we'd be close for her and little Peter. Good schools. Near enough for you to run the shops.' He seems to register he is talking too much. 'I'll even stop calling her Rosie if that helps.' He pauses. 'Right. I'll shut up. Marry me, Emily.'

'Be quiet, Keagan,' she says. 'Or I might change my mind.'

He stares at her.

'Change your mind?'

'Keagan Devlin.' She looks down at him from the stage. 'You are one of the kindest people I have ever known. You are always thinking about other people, sometimes so much you forget to think about yourself. I've seen you with Rose and I know you're not pretending — you feel something real for her. And that makes me very happy.' She steadies herself. 'I want to be honest with you. I've been jealous. About Beverly, and even about Jenny, even though I knew it was wrong — I just didn't want anyone else to have your love. I want all of it for myself and I'm sorry for that. I've been unkind to you and it wasn't fair. Keagan, I'm sorry for everything. For letting you down. For not trusting you when you deserved better.'

'But?' he says quietly.

She reaches behind her and picks up the box.

'But I'm sorry to tell you,' she says, opening it, 'that you will have to put up with me and Rose for the rest of your life.' She looks up at him, her eyes bright. 'And if you think I'm hard work, wait until you've spent real time with her.' She smiles. 'I love you, Keagan. I always have. Nothing would make me happier than being your wife. Yes. I will marry you. And I'm sorry you've had to wait so long.'

He lifts her down from the stage and pulls her into him. Her body does what it always does when he holds her, this warmth spreading through her from somewhere central, and she thinks, this is the safest place in the world. He has always been the safest place, and she nearly lost it, and she won't again. He pulls back and looks at her, and then he kisses her, and the years collapse together and it is like coming home.

He lets her go. Takes the ring from the box and slides it onto her finger. She looks at it — the ring she first saw when she turned him away at the door, the ring she has thought about more times than she would ever tell him.

'That's lucky,' he says. 'I thought you might have put on a few pounds. I was half expecting it wouldn't fit.'

She gives him a light smack on the arm and kisses him again.

'Come on,' she says. 'Let's go back and tell Anna. You know she'll be the happiest person out of all of us. She's missed you.'

'I've missed you all,' he says. And he takes her hand, and they walk back out into the High Road.

THE ALGARVE,
THREE YEARS LATER

'Daddy! Daddy, come and look at this!'

Rose calls from across the beach, where she has been digging with single-minded determination for the better part of an hour, looking for shells. Keagan shades his eyes with his hand.

'One minute, sweetheart.'

He looks back at Emily, who is cradling their daughter Elsie against her chest — a name Emily chose deliberately with the softened ending, to make it harder for him to do what he had done with Rose. He looks at the two of them and something in him settles that he can't quite find the words for.

'You wanted this,' Emily reminds him, smiling. 'I did warn you. I said you'd never sit down again.'

'I thought you were joking,' he says, and goes to see what Rose has found.

'Little Peter will be awake in a minute,' Jenny calls from her sunbed. She has her sunglasses pushed up and is watching the scene with obvious satisfaction. 'Then uncle Keagan will have two of them at him.'

'It's fine,' Keagan says. 'All that military training came in useful for something.'

It is more than three years since Keagan and Emily married, and life has moved on quickly. Keagan is now a shareholding director at the company, his reputation in the investment arm solid enough that the deals keep getting larger and the long weeks keep coming. He grumbles about the hours but he is good at it, and he knows it, and the life it has given them all — including the villa in the Algarve, which had seen a great deal of use since they bought it last year — is not something he takes lightly.

The City had changed quickly after deregulation, and Keagan's business had changed with it. There was a cost — the drain of pressure and long hours — but there were rewards, and Keagan was clear-eyed enough about both to know which side of the scale he was on.

Emily's business had grown beyond anything she had originally imagined. The company had taken on serious outside investment — Keagan's investment arm had helped structure it — and now operated more than forty shops. Anna had moved into the general manager role and Emily had been able to give a little more of herself to family life. Keagan wanted more children still. Emily suspected he was quietly hoping for a son, though he had never said so, and she wasn't sure whether to find it funny or tell him off.

Jenny is a regular at the villa. She has not started a new relationship — a couple of casual things, nothing serious, and in her own words she is happy as she is. She has little Peter and her work, and she doesn't seem to feel the absence of anything else. Emily believes her, mostly. She watches her sometimes, though, when she doesn't know she's being watched.

A familiar song starts on the radio. Emily sees Keagan pause — just for a second, barely anything — before turning back to Rose. It is Beverly's new single, Beverly Deleon, the one that has been all over the radio for the past month. She had finally secured the recording contract she had always wanted — Motown, no less — and her career had taken off spectacularly on both sides of the Atlantic. There were stories coming out of the American press — rumours of various entanglements, of excess — but that was the industry, and Emily had decided long ago not to think too much about it. She sees the flicker of something on Keagan's face when the stories surface, and she understands it. He had cared for Beverly. That was real, and she does not begrudge him that.

What she knows, more certainly than she has ever known anything, is that his love for her is total, and nothing is going to alter it.

Little Peter stirs in his buggy. He blinks himself awake and immediately locates Keagan across the sand.

'Uncle Keagan!'

'I told you,' Jenny says, delighted.

'Come on then, little man.' Keagan holds out a hand. 'Rosie's found something brilliant. Let's see if we can find something better.'

Little Peter scrambles out of the buggy and sprints across the sand. Keagan scoops him up briefly, spinning him around before setting him down beside Rose, who shows him the shells with proprietary pride. Emily watches them from behind her sunglasses.

'Peter would be so proud of that boy,' she says.

'Yes.' Jenny's voice is quiet and steady. 'He's the best part of him I have left. That sounds terrible, I know.'

'It doesn't. It sounds true.'

'I miss him every day,' Jenny says. 'But I'm not the only one who does, am I.' It is not quite a question.

'Keagan goes every Friday morning,' Emily says. 'To the cemetery. Rain, work, whatever — he goes. It's become a thing for him and I don't think it'll ever stop.' She glances across the beach at him, crouching down now with both children, examining something in the sand with complete seriousness. 'I think it settles him. Talking to Peter. He goes when things are difficult at work or something is weighing on him, and he comes back a bit lighter.' She pauses. 'In some ways it's as if Peter never quite went away. He's still giving him advice. And sometimes, these days, Keagan even takes it.'

She says it with a smile, and Jenny laughs — properly laughs — and for a moment the two of them sit in the Portuguese sun with the sound of the children and the sea, and the day is as good as a day can be.

The End